THE LOST SHRINE

By Nicola Ford

The Hidden Bones
The Lost Shrine

THE LOST SHRINE

Nicola Ford

Allison & Busby Limited
11 Wardour Mews
London W1F 8AN
allisonandbusby.com

First published in Great Britain by Allison & Busby in 2019.

A CIP catalogue record for this book is available from
the British Library.

First Edition

HB ISBN 978-0-7490-2392-8
TPB ISBN 978-0-7490-2485-7

Typeset in 11/16 pt Adobe Garamond Pro by
Allison & Busby Ltd.

The paper used for this Allison & Busby publication
has been produced from trees that have been legally sourced
from well-managed and credibly certified forests.

Printed and bound by
CPI Group (UK) Ltd, Croydon, CR0 4YY

For the Crickley diggers

CHAPTER ONE

The strengthening breeze rippled the newly green foliage of the ancient giants. His breath was coming in gasps as he made his way towards the stand of beeches that crowned the hilltop. He was out of nick, that was for sure.

It was unseasonably warm for the May Day Beltane ceremony. Beneath the full-length white tunic that he'd fashioned from an old cotton sheet, his leather biker's trousers chafed against his skin. He hadn't had time to change. They'd been expecting him and he couldn't afford to be late for the ceremony. Behind him he could hear the murmuring of the small, ramshackle assortment of middle-aged men and women who had followed him from the pub car park in the village far below. He halted, glad of the chance to catch his breath. Then, he raised the gnarled yew branch high above his head and the crowd behind him fell silent.

'Great goddess of the sacred grove, accept our libation.'

He lowered the staff and rammed it into the ground, then turning, beckoned a short woman sporting a faded denim jacket and Indian cotton print dress forward. She approached him carrying a small wooden bowl outstretched in her cupped hands.

As he took the bowl from her, the sticky amber liquid within swished against its roughly hewn surface, releasing the scent of honey into the warm May air. Three times he circled the staff before turning to face the trees. Then, raising the vessel skyward, he tipped it forwards, sending the contents splattering onto the ground in front of him. The crowd erupted into a spontaneous cheer.

Holding his hand aloft to silence them he began to move – this time alone – in the direction of the wood. As he strode uphill towards the small clearing at the centre of the copse he could hear the clamour of shouts accompanied by the insistent beat of a bodhrán, skin stretched tightly across its large wooden frame, rising to a crescendo on the hillside below. Brushing past ribbons and strips of coloured cloth tied to the overhanging branches, the spaces between the great, smooth trunks grew wider. Light filtered through the gently swaying leaves and branches in a hypnotic dance of light and shade.

The intensity of the sunlight cascading through the gap in the woodland canopy as he stepped into the clearing was overwhelming. His vision dazzled, he cast his eyes to the ground. When he raised them again he struggled to comprehend the scene in front of him.

Dark shadows crossed the few remaining leaves from the previous autumn's leaf fall in a confusion of oscillating stripes. He squinted, straining to focus. All around him, swinging from the limbs of the trees that fringed the clearing, were an assortment of crudely carved wooden figures. As his vision grew accustomed to the light he could see that they'd been smeared with a viscous brown liquid. And, hanging between them, he could now make out other figures too. Figures that had until recently lived, and walked, and breathed just as he did now. And whose time had been deliberately cut short. He was surrounded by a macabre menagerie of creatures: crows, magpies, rabbits, even a fox. All dangling from lengths of orange baler twine, congealed blood matting their fur and covering their feathers.

He felt suddenly light-headed. He closed his eyes and hungrily gulped in air. All at once the memory of the sweet, floral aroma of the mead that had filled his nostrils was replaced by the overpowering stench of death. In front of him, in the centre of the clearing, lay the body of a hare, head tipped back. Its throat ripped open. Its blood splattered across the centre of the glade.

A sudden gust of wind caused the grotesque statuary hanging round the fringes of the clearing to jerk violently from side to side like dancing marionettes. One shadow longer than the rest swung pendulum-like, its inky presence casting a shiver-inducing chill across him.

He moved forward, blinking, struggling to cope with the fluctuating light. He was close enough now to see a bluebottle crawl across the head of the figure, moving from the corner of the lipstick-covered cherry-red of her mouth, across the bridge of her aquiline ash-grey nose and finally alighting on her open eyeball. He took in the dark hair falling almost to her waist, and the familiar form of her tall, slim figure. From somewhere a memory surfaced of those lips moulded seductively around a cigarette. He turned aside, retched and threw up.

CHAPTER TWO

'I think I've solved our little problem.' Despite herself Clare couldn't prevent a smile spreading across her lips as she put the phone down.

David looked up from his seat on the other side of Clare's desk and snorted. 'I'd hardly call being forced to close the unit a little problem.'

'Do you want to know what the solution is or not?'

He gestured towards her impatiently.

'I asked Margaret to put some feelers out. See if she had any contacts who knew if there was any work going.'

David looked at her disapprovingly. Professor, now Dame, Margaret Bockford had been a supporter of the Hart Archaeological Research Institute since its foundation. Her support had even survived the university marketing department's decision to give them a trading name of the Hart Unit. In Margaret's view a lamentable development, and one that had proved to be a source of endless mirth among their colleagues. But Clare knew David resented having to ask anyone, and especially Margaret, who'd already done so much to help them, for assistance.

'You can pull all the faces you like, but you've seen the figures. We're in no position to be precious about this. Anyway, there's no point in having friends in high places if they can't do you the odd favour.'

David raised his eyes to the ceiling. 'OK. What did Margaret have to say for herself?'

'She's found us a job.'

'What sort of job?'

'Fieldwork. An evaluation ahead of a housing development.'

He straightened up in his chair. 'Really? I haven't heard of anything going round here.'

'It's not round here.'

'Where, then?'

'The Cotswolds.'

'Where exactly in the Cotswolds?'

Clare hesitated. She knew he wasn't going to like her reply. 'Bailsgrove.'

'Bailsgrove! You're not serious?'

'What's wrong with Bailsgrove?'

'Don't give me that. You know as well as I do. Bailsgrove was Beth Kinsella's dig.'

'And?' She looked at him defiantly, struggling to keep an even tone to her voice. If truth be told she was no keener on this than he was, but if they had to close the unit she'd be out of a job. It was alright for David, he was safe as houses in his lecturing job with the university. But if the unit shut she had nowhere to go.

'And Beth Kinsella was found dangling dead as a dodo amid

12

a collection of assorted rotting bunny carcasses on that site.'

'Since when did you believe everything you read in the papers? Anyway, we can't afford to be picky.'

'Picky! Christ, Clare. The place will be crawling with police. I'd have thought you'd have had enough of that after Hungerbourne. Besides which, Beth Kinsella was a famous nutter. What sort of a state do you think her records will be in? It'll be a nightmare.'

'Did you know her?'

'I knew *of* her – that was enough.'

'Well, maybe you should suspend your judgement until you see the site records.' Clare picked up a sheet of paper from her desk and turned it round so that David could read the figures. She jabbed a finger at the bottom line. 'In any case we don't have a choice.'

He looked down at the page of A4 and exhaled deeply, then mumbled into his chest. 'It'll cost a fortune in fuel.'

'If we turn this job down that will be the least of our worries.'

'To a quiet night in.' David raised his glass, then leant forward and kissed Sally, who was curled up beside him on his living room sofa.

'Amen to that!'

'What shifts are you on next week?'

'God knows. Makes no difference. Until the chief's back from his heart attack – if he comes back – I'm on twenty-four-hour call. So right now I don't even want to think about work. How about you – anything exciting happening in Ivory Towers?'

David took a large glug of his Syrah. 'Looks like we may have avoided bankruptcy, if you can call that exciting.'

'You're joking. The university can't be broke, surely. Not unless someone's been fiddling the books.'

Sally looked genuinely shocked. Even after all this time, David thought, she still suffered from a rose-tinted vision of academia.

He shook his head. 'Not the university. The Hart Unit.'

Sally made no attempt to suppress a smile. 'So Clare's not such a whizz with the finances after all.'

He wished just for once she would at least try to disguise her resentment towards Clare. But he knew that the state of undeclared warfare that existed between the two women wasn't going to end any time soon. He'd learnt to operate on what his grandmother would have called the 'least said soonest mended' principle where the two of them were concerned.

He took another slurp of his Syrah to prevent him from saying something he might regret before he replied, 'She can't magic work out of thin air. The housing game's flatlining.'

'What's that got to do with your lot? I thought you were a research institute.'

'Most of our work is commercial. It comes from the construction industry. That's what finances the research.'

'So, what are you planning to do about it?'

'Margaret's found us a job up in the Cotswolds.' He had no intention of telling her about Clare's involvement. That would only aggravate the situation.

'Whereabouts?'

'Bailsgrove.'

'You're kidding? The Bailsgrove. Where that weirdo hung herself.'

David placed his glass on the coffee table. 'Beth Kinsella was a well-respected archaeologist.'

'That's not what the papers said.'

'I'd have thought you of all people wouldn't believe everything you read in the red tops.'

'Oh, come on, David. Sometimes the facts speak for themselves. She was found strung up alongside a bunch of wooden carvings smeared with rabbit blood.'

'Hare blood,' he corrected her.

'Whatever. It really doesn't matter. It'll be Hungerbourne all over again.'

'Well, that didn't turn out entirely badly now, did it.' He smiled and leant forward in an attempt to kiss her.

She pulled away from him. Evidently she wasn't going to be distracted so easily. 'That's not the point. What the hell were you thinking of?'

That was a question he'd asked himself, though he had absolutely no intention of admitting it to Sally. He stared down into the inky-red dregs in the bottom of his glass. 'We didn't have a choice. It was Bailsgrove or bust.'

Putting down her glass, Sally clasped her hands behind the back of his neck. 'Is the unit really that broke?' He nodded. 'Look, I know a few people from my time in the Gloucestershire force. I could ask around, see what the lie of the land is after the suicide. What was the woman's name again?'

'Kinsella – Dr Beth Kinsella. It's sweet of you, Sal, but I don't see what good it'll do. We've already said we'll do it.'

'Well, at least you'd know what you're in for. And it might help cut through some of the red tape.'

David leant forward and gave her a long, lingering kiss. 'Don't ever let me forget. You're an absolute treasure.'

'Coming from an archaeologist I suppose I should take that as a compliment.'

Clare sat alone in the spare room of her Salisbury flat surrounded by cardboard boxes. It had been more than two years now since Stephen's death and still she found herself enmeshed in what was left of his life.

She'd forced herself to go through all of his personal effects within the first few months after he'd died. There was no denying it had been tough. There were so many memories of their life together. But that's exactly why she'd known she had to get on with it there and then. If she'd left them she knew she'd never be able to bring herself to do it. And there was another reason too. She'd had to sell their house.

Downsizing was a bit of an understatement for the scale of change her life had been subjected to following her husband's death. He'd left her everything. But it had become increasingly clear as time had moved on that everything amounted to almost nothing. The biggest shock came when she'd discovered that Stephen had remortgaged the house without so much as mentioning it to her. Their home, her home. It was in his name so legally he'd had every right to do what he liked with it. But when she'd found out she couldn't help feeling betrayed.

In life he'd provided for her every whim, at least in material terms: a substantial detached house in the home counties, exotic foreign holidays, the best restaurants. But in return she'd given up everything. Including, she now realised, the person that she might have been.

Once her initial anger had subsided she'd come to the realisation that she couldn't put all of the blame on him. When she'd met him, at the May Ball in her second year at university, he'd swept her off her feet. He was stylish, confident and best of all devoted to her. And she'd all too willingly abandoned any dreams she might have had of pursuing a fledgling career in archaeology in order to become his wife.

Their marriage had seemed to her, at least at the time, a happy one. So nothing could have prepared her for the tsunami of emotions that she'd been subjected to when she'd discovered that he'd invested all of their capital – and more – into a property finance scheme in the US that had turned out not to be worth the paper it was written on.

The final straw was being forced to sell her sports car. She'd loved her little Mazda MX5. But it wasn't a very practical mode of transport for an archaeologist and once the precarious state in which Stephen had left their finances became clear she hadn't really had much choice in the matter. And as it turned out she'd rather taken to her little blue Fiesta.

The one untouched part of Stephen's life that she hadn't managed to work her way through was the hotch potch of paperwork and personal memorabilia from his study. In life it had been his space – his retreat – and in death she found his presence there just too overwhelming.

His colleague James had offered to give her a hand. But he'd done so much to help already, she hadn't felt she could impose any further. And, besides, so much of it was personal stuff she wasn't sure she was willing to let anyone else trawl through it, however good a friend he may have been to Stephen. But it must have been obvious to James that despite her protestations she was finding the idea of going through it all too much to bear because he'd suggested just binning the lot.

Eventually she'd acquiesced, but despite it all she couldn't bring herself to do it. By which point she'd run out of time, and when the removals company had arrived she'd just had them box it up. And here it had remained, dumped in a corner of the spare room of her flat where, aside from its accusing presence when her mum or Jo came to stay, she'd been able to ignore it. At least until now.

Clare closed the lid of the box she'd been going through and made her way into the kitchen. She'd had enough for one night. And she had more pressing concerns on her mind at the moment.

Making her way to the fridge, she extracted a half-full bottle of Sauvignon Blanc and poured herself a glass, then set about preparing her supper – a bagged salad accompanied by the finest oven-ready cannelloni the Waitrose reduced shelf had to offer.

Padding back into the living room, she flipped open her laptop and flicked through her emails. Within a couple of minutes she'd found what she was looking for. She clicked the link and it took her thorough to the property web pages. There it was – her house – or at least that's what she was intending it should be. It wasn't anything fancy – a three-bedroom ex-local authority semi. What Stephen would have made of it, heaven only knows. But it had good-sized rooms, a lovely big back garden and best of all it was in her beloved Marlborough Downs.

Despite the traumas she'd undergone while she was digging at Hungerbourne, her time there had reminded her how much she loved the softly undulating hills and wide open skies of the Downs. It was where she'd rediscovered her passion for the past, and where too she'd taken the first steps towards rebuilding her life and embarking on a career in archaeology.

She'd put an offer in on the house a few weeks ago. With the capital she'd scraped together from selling her few remaining assets and her salary from the Hart Unit, she'd worked out that she should just about be able to afford it. She might have to rent a room out but if that's what it took then so be it.

She looked around her at the familiar walls of her rented flat. It had served her well over the last couple of years. And she'd done her best to make it feel welcoming, but somehow it had never really felt like home. She was ready to move on now. Buying her own place felt like a statement of intent. It would be the first home she'd ever bought and paid for herself. She'd gone straight from her mum's council house in Chelmsford to university and then to life with Stephen. But this one would be different; she was finally going to have a home of her own. And finally, too, she felt as if she was in charge of her own destiny – shaping her own life, rather than letting others shape it for her.

But she'd made the offer on the house before she'd discovered quite what a precarious financial situation the Hart Unit was in. If the institute folded, she'd be out of a job and she could kiss goodbye to her dreams of a new home and the next steps in her new life. The vendors had been prevaricating for weeks. It was clear that they wanted more money than she could feasibly offer, but she'd left the offer on the table and it would seem they hadn't had as much interest as they'd hoped. As she'd pointed out to them, the whole place needed gutting. They'd inherited it from their elderly mother, and it was patently obvious that there'd been little or no work done to it since she'd moved in – which, judging from the swirling carpets and avocado bathroom suite, had been some time in the 1970s.

Then finally this morning she'd had a call from the estate agent. The vendors had accepted her offer. So all she needed to do now was to keep the Hart Unit afloat. And she was determined to do just that – whatever it took.

CHAPTER THREE

A deep, musty smell like rotting leaves pervaded the atmosphere in the Portakabin. It had been locked and off limits for over a month. Clare had finally managed to persuade the hire company to hand over the keys, but only on condition that they took over the contract at what seemed to her an exorbitant price. And that certainly wasn't going to help the unit's precarious financial position. But the truth was they were between a rock and a hard place.

She ran her hand across the torn fabric on the back of the swivel chair.

David said, 'Go on, try it for size.'

Clare shook her head. The chair had belonged to Beth Kinsella.

'Surely you're not worried about directing the fieldwork on your own, are you? I'd have taken it on myself if I had the time. But the Runt has been piling on my teaching commitments this year. You're perfectly capable and, besides, you'll have Jo with you a lot of the time. And you know you can always call on Margaret if you need advice.'

Clare knew that the Runt, aka Professor Donald Muir, head of the archaeology department at the University of Salisbury, had, as usual, been doing his very best to make David's life as much of a misery as possible. And she had no desire to add to his woes.

David was right, of course. With Californian human bone specialist Jo Granski at her side, she'd not only be working with one of the best in the business but a friend she'd grown to know and trust over the last couple of years. Jo and Margaret between them had seen her through some tough times since they'd first met at Hungerbourne. But somehow despite all that, now that she was actually here, she really wasn't sure she was comfortable with taking the Bailsgrove job on.

'It's not that.'

David looked exasperated. 'Well, what then?'

She hesitated. 'This is going to sound daft. But it feels like I'm standing in a dead woman's shoes.'

'I can't believe I'm hearing this. You were the one that insisted we take this job. If you were going to get the collywobbles about it, you should have done it before we signed the contract with the developer.'

She didn't need any reminding of the fact. It had seemed the right thing to do at the time. The only thing. And logically she knew that neither she nor the Hart Unit had any choice. But right now, standing here in Beth's site office just a few yards from where her body was found, she wasn't so sure. David, on the other hand, no longer seemed to have any doubts about their decision. But then he wasn't the one who'd actually have to be on-site every day.

Clare raised her hand in a gesture of dismissal. 'Just ignore me, David. Like you say, it's probably just nerves. I'll be fine.'

He plucked a black plastic seed tray from the wooden shelving at the rear of the Portakabin and started rummaging distractedly through an assortment of pottery fragments, before returning them to the place where he'd found them. 'At least we could get in. I was half afraid the police were going to have it all taped off as some sort of crime scene.'

'Mark was very helpful.'

'Mark?'

'DCI Stone.'

David smiled knowingly.

She flashed a warning look at him. 'Don't start.' David didn't have the least interest in her love life. It was a distraction tactic and she knew it. Well, two could play at that game.

'Any luck contacting Beth's excavation team? We'll need to go through all of her records with someone who's worked on the site. We need to be sure everything is here.'

He shook his head. 'I thought I'd leave that to you – you're going to be the one that has to work with them. Maybe you could have a word with Mark to see if he's got any of their contact details.'

'OK. We need to get a move on. I've already had the developer on the phone asking when we're going to be through.'

'Paul Marshall.'

Clare nodded.

'What's he like?'

'Judging by the monotonous regularity of the voicemail messages he's left, impatient.'

'That doesn't bode well,' David said sombrely.

'I know it's not ideal. But you can't blame him. This business with Beth has put him weeks behind schedule. And the way things are at the moment that could be enough to put a developer out of business. He must be pretty desperate. After all, who's going to

23

want to buy a house built on a site that's been splashed all over the red tops as the scene of some bizarre suicide?'

'Well, if he's that desperate for work we're his best bet of recovering his investment. So he'll have to cut us a bit of slack.'

Clare raised her finger to her lips. 'Ssh!'

A low humming sound drifted through the open door.

'What?'

The hum grew louder, rising and falling with a rhythmic insistence. David made his way to the doorway. Clare followed, standing on tiptoe so that she could peer over his shoulder. The noise was coming from a spot about a hundred metres uphill from where their newly acquired office was located. A broadly built man with greying tufts of unruly hair protruding from beneath a battered blue baseball cap was standing with his back to them, facing the stand of beech trees at the top of the hill. Above his head he twirled a length of rope on the end of which was a flat slat of wood about a foot long from which the whirring sound appeared to be emanating.

Clare whispered to David, 'What the . . . ?'

David gave her one of his self-satisfied smiles. 'It's a bullroarer. Indigenous Australians and some Melanesian peoples use them in their ceremonies.'

Clare dug David in the ribs.

'Ow! What was that for?'

Trying to keep an even tone, she whispered, 'I know what it is. But why is there a man in a white sheet waving one about on our site?'

David coughed and flushed uncomfortably. 'Dunno. Let's ask him, shall we?'

Clare caught him by the arm as he was about to step down from the Portakabin. 'We can't just walk up and demand to know what he's doing.'

David turned and looked up at her. 'Why the bloody hell not? It's our excavation. We've got every right to know what he's up to.'

'What if he's performing a ceremony or something. It just seems' – she struggled to find the right word – 'rude.'

But it was too late; David was already marching upslope towards the man. Halfway up the hill he turned and beckoned for her to follow him. 'Don't be soft. Get up here!'

Hearing David's words, the figure in the white sheet turned to face them, bringing the bullroarer slowly to rest in a series of low arcs.

Lowering her head to avoid the possibility of having to meet the stranger's eyes, Clare muttered, 'Give me strength!' and trotted uphill to join David. She caught up with him just as he reached the stranger.

David said, 'Afternoon.'

The man looked the pair of them up and down. Then in a deep baritone said, 'Blessed be!'

For once David seemed lost for words. Clare smiled, stepped forward and offered her hand. 'Hello.'

The stranger, whose hands were fully laden with the bullroarer, lifted it towards her in an apologetic gesture and, inclining his head to one side, gave a slight bow. 'Greetings, my lady.'

David stood beside her, immobile. His broad, fixed smile was quite evidently, to Clare at least, a mask adopted to stop him from laughing. She shot him a warning glance, willing him to succeed.

For some inexplicable reason she found herself offering a small bow in return. 'I'm Clare.'

She dug David in the ribs with her elbow.

'Dr David Barbrook.' She glared at him. 'David.'

The stranger, whom Clare now noticed was sporting black leather biker's trousers beneath his knee-length white tunic, smiled. 'Wayne Crabbs. But most folks call me Crabby.' He nodded in the direction of the open Portakabin door. 'Surprised they've still got you lot raking over Beth's ashes. From what I heard I thought the coppers had long since made their minds up about what happened.'

David hesitated for a moment before shaking his head. 'No, I'm not that sort of doctor. We're archaeologists. We're here to take over the excavation.'

Crabby narrowed his eyes. 'You're going to be carrying on with the dig?'

David was unable to suppress the note of suspicion in his voice. 'That's right.'

'You wanna go careful, then.'

Clare glanced nervously at David.

Crabby nodded in the direction of the copse at the top of the hill. 'It's none too healthy round 'ere for the likes of you.'

Recognising the familiar signs of rising tension in David, Clare decided to step in before he said something he, or at least she, might regret. 'What makes you say that?'

'You'll find out soon enough if you hang around.'

David took a step towards Crabby. 'Is that meant to be some sort of a threat?'

The older man swung the bullroarer in an arc and for a moment Clare thought that he was going to take a swipe at David with it. But instead he deposited it with pinpoint accuracy in a heap a few feet from where they stood. He stepped towards David, placed his hands on David's upper arms and smiled. 'Friend, it's half a lifetime since I threatened a man.' He looked sideways and winked at Clare. 'And I'm not sure I was too convincing even back then.'

David stiffened, and Crabby removed his hands and took a step back.

For a moment the two men just looked.

26

It was Clare that broke the silence. 'You knew Beth.'

Crabby nodded. 'As well as anyone round here. Better than most.'

Clare asked, 'Didn't she mix much with the locals?'

'More a case of most of 'em didn't want to mix with her.'

David seemed to perk up at this information. 'Oh, why was that?'

Crabby sniffed. 'That's obvious, ain't it?'

David looked perplexed. 'Not to me, it's not.'

'It's the houses. They don't want 'em.'

'Who don't?' Clare said.

'That lot.' He pointed in the direction of the village that lay far below them at the foot of the hill.

'Why not?'

'Not posh enough for 'em. Bunch of snobs the lot of 'em. It's alright for them to live in their fancy mansions. But woe betide any of us who've got the nerve to want to live where we was born. Time was the kids round here could move into one of the cottages or get a job on the land and a tied house that went with it. Not these days – they're all holiday cottages or second homes for city types.'

David said, 'And some of the city types object to the houses.'

'What planet do you people live on? Course they do.'

Clare's heart sank. She'd been worried enough already about stepping into Beth's shoes. But now it looked as if those shoes were none too comfortable. She was already beginning to regret persuading David to take this job and they hadn't even stuck a trowel in the ground yet.

As site offices went, this one was a bloody mess. Clare stood alone in the Portakabin surveying her new domain. Aside from her and David, the only people who'd been in here in the last month were the police. And either Beth Kinsella was the crazy woman that David seemed to think she was or the Gloucestershire police were

27

less than particular about the state in which they left their crime scenes. Open box files containing the completed context sheets that would tell them what every layer, pit and post hole on the site were lay strewn across the trestle tables that served as desks. And a seemingly random assortment of seed trays and plastic boxes that had been pressed into service to dry the finds on were teetering at unlikely angles on the wooden shelving that lined the walls. It looked as if the place had been burgled.

If this was Beth Kinsella's idea of how to run a dig, they were going to have an even more difficult job on their hands than she'd thought. And to cap it all she didn't even have any staff yet to help her sort it out. They'd picked up the job so fast there hadn't been time to recruit anyone, and given the reason Beth's dig had come to such an abrupt halt, Clare suspected it wasn't going to be easy to pull a team together.

She puffed out her cheeks. *One thing at a time, Clare.* Before she could even begin to contemplate trying to hire anyone she needed to get the site office into some sort of order. Then she might have a better idea of what the real size of the task was. Focusing her attention first on the thick layer of dried mud that carpeted the floor, she searched in vain for a broom. In the end she found a brush and hand shovel in the back of the tool shed, and a floor cloth and bucket from beneath the sink of the euphemistically named 'comfort unit'. But it took her the best part of an hour – and the application of a not insignificant amount of elbow grease to remove the worst of the muck from the tattered lino. She'd spent the rest of the morning rehousing the record sheets into their respective box files and ring binders, then bagging up all the bits of bone, pot and metalwork and filing them neatly into several trays that now lay on the desk in front of her.

Feeling distinctly pleased with her efforts she settled down to reward herself with lunch in the shape of a somewhat unappetising egg and tomato sandwich purchased from a petrol station on the interminable journey to site from her flat in Salisbury. She'd just taken her first bite when she heard a car pull up outside. Reluctantly shoving her sandwich back into its packet, she stood up. But before she could get as far as the door it flew open, clattering back against the flimsy Portakabin wall. A burly, ruddy-cheeked man in his mid-fifties thrust himself into the Portakabin.

'Can I help you?'

'You can if you're able to tell me where I'll find Clare Hills.'

She had no idea who he was, but she'd already decided she wasn't warming to him. 'You're speaking to her.'

He looked her up and down, as if weighing up a slightly unsatisfactory purchase. 'You! Christ, are your lot all cut from the same cloth?'

Clare could feel her face flush. 'Look, I'm not sure who you are, but maybe you should start by telling me what business you've got charging in here like this.'

'I'm the bloke who's paying your wages, love.'

'You're Paul Marshall?' She'd thought the voice sounded familiar and now she knew why.

'That's right. And this is my development. So I'd like to know why exactly you're sitting on your arse doing sweet Fanny Adams when you should be out there digging.'

'I appreciate your desire to get on with the job, Mr Marshall, but we've only just taken possession of the Portakabins.'

'Not my problem, love. You're being paid to do a job. Time is money. Sodding archaeologists have already cost me a bloody fortune, and I've had police and journos crawling all over this place because of that mad cow.' He waved his hands vaguely in the direction of the copse.

Clare was so stunned that for a moment she couldn't quite believe what she was hearing. 'You mean Dr Kinsella.'

'That's right. Mad as a box of sodding frogs. Trying to convince anyone that would listen that this place was some sort of bloody temple or some such. Bailsgrove a temple! Load of total bollocks. That never bothers the press, though, does it?'

'Well, I grant you Dr Kinsella's investigations were at an early stage, but we really don't know what we might find here as yet.'

He took a step closer to her and Clare instinctively took a step back. 'Listen, don't go getting any bloody ideas. That mad bitch topping herself has put this development back months. I'm paying you to be in and out of here like that' – he clicked his fingers – 'and you'd best make sure you are or you won't get a penny out of me, not a sodding penny.'

Clare's every impulse was to tell him to take his job and shove it, but she was only too well aware that the contract with Marshall Construction was the only thing that gave the institute half a chance of staying afloat. She took in a deep breath before replying, 'I do understand your concerns, Mr Marshall. The institute is always very mindful of the need for efficiency on commercial developments.'

'Glad to hear it. But talk is cheap. I can't see anyone out there with buckets and spades. Doesn't look much like you're doing anything about it to me.'

'Well, no. Because of the urgency of getting things rolling here, we wanted to get access to site as soon as we could, but that's meant we haven't had time to pull our additional team members together yet. We'd like to keep as many of the team as local as possible.' Marshall glowered at her. 'It will save time in the long run.'

For the first time Marshall's face softened into something approaching a smile. 'Well, maybe that's something I can help you with. Anything to get you off your arses.' He reached inside his suit jacket and pulled out his mobile. 'Neil Fuller – he was the Kinsella woman's assistant. As far as I could make out he seemed reasonably sane for one of your lot. This is his number.'

Clare plugged his details into her own phone.

Marshall turned as if to go, then hesitated for a moment. 'And remember what I said. I expect to see progress here. A nice quiet site, no press and no police. You lot give me any trouble and I can easy enough find another unit who will do what's needed.'

David slathered his poppadom in lime pickle and smiled. 'This was a good idea, Sal.'

'Well, neither of us has time to cook. And we've both got to eat. This place is only ten minutes' drive from the station, and I figured a quick Indian before I need to get back to work was the only way we were going to get to see one another.'

David's disappointment was obvious. 'Really, have you got to go back in tonight?'

Sally gave him a look. 'Don't start. You know that with Morgan still off I'm stretched.'

David knew only too well what Sally's boss being off meant. DCI Morgan had been off sick for the last two months. And he'd barely seen her since. David felt for the bloke; he was only in his early fifties and he'd had a heart attack. Opinion seemed to be that it was the stress of the job that had triggered it. And that was what worried him. Sal might be young and considerably fitter than Morgan, but if she had to carry on doing her job and his for much longer she was going to end up in the same boat as her boss.

'You can't keep doing two jobs, Sal. How much longer is this going to go on for?'

She scowled at him. 'For as long as it takes.'

'You're going to make yourself ill at this rate. You've got to say something. Can't you speak to someone about it?'

Sally laid her spoon down and stared at him. 'Really? That might be the way it works with your lot, but it's not in my world. Do you really want me to commit career suicide?'

'You know that's not what I meant.' He leant towards her, placing his hand on hers. 'It's just that I can see how tired you look.' As soon as the words were out of his mouth he regretted them. Sally glared at him. She withdrew her hand and took a sip of her lassi. 'Well, if you can't ask anyone, is there any word on whether Morgan's coming back or not?'

She took another sip of her lassi before answering. 'Nope. From the little they said when it happened I'd say it's not when but if.'

David knew when he was on a hiding to nothing. 'Tell you what, next time you get a free evening I'll cook for you. Three courses, all your favourites.'

Sally pushed the last remaining sherd of poppadom around her plate. 'I won't be much fun. I'll probably just want to sleep.'

'Well, first you can eat and then you can sleep. Absolutely no fun required.'

Finally, she looked up at him and smiled. 'OK. You've got a deal. Mind you, I can't promise when it'll be.' David reached out and touched her arm. This time Sally reciprocated and placed her hand on his. 'Thank you.'

By the time David was digging into his lamb bhuna, Sally seemed to have regained a little of her old energy.

She dabbed her lips with her napkin. 'Oh, I meant to say, I had a word with an old mate of mine from the Gloucestershire force about that Beth Kinsella business.'

David looked up. 'What did they say?'

'By the sound of it, for once things were pretty much like they said in the papers. The Kinsella woman seems to have been having a bit of a rough time of it. Lost her job. Split up with her boyfriend. Then when she began work at Bailsgrove she started making all sorts of claims about the place having been some sort of ancient temple. By all accounts the developer paying her wages didn't take too kindly to the interest that drummed up in the papers.'

'Paul Marshall.'

Sally nodded. 'That's right. He threatened not to pay her if she went to the media again. But by the sound of it he needn't have worried. By then they'd lost interest anyway because everybody else they spoke to seems to have reckoned there was nothing there to find. So he calmed down a bit. Next thing you know a bunch of crystal danglers find her hanging from a tree in the woods above the site. There were all sorts of wooden carvings smeared with animal blood strung up from the branches. And there was this dead hare with its guts splattered all round the place. Mark said it was really spooky stuff.'

David said, 'Mark . . . ?'

'Sorry, Mark Stone, he's a DCI up there. I met him when I was doing my probation. He's a bit of a high-flyer. He's alright, though. Not one of the corporate bullshit brigade.'

David just nodded. There was no need to mention she wasn't the only woman he'd spoken to recently who apparently had a high opinion of DCI Stone. It seemed his life was destined to be full of unfortunate coincidences.

Sally said, 'He's a pretty solid sort of bloke. But it really seemed to have shaken him. He said that the hare was right in front of Beth. Its head had been smashed in and there was a length of baler twine round its neck. It had been garrotted and then its throat had been cut. It was total overkill. She must have completely lost it before she killed herself.'

'Not much doubt that it was suicide, then?'

She shook her head. 'Mark reckons not, but the coroner recorded a narrative verdict at the inquest.'

'What does that mean?'

He must have looked as concerned as he felt about the thought that the coroner hadn't entirely agreed with the fabulous DCI Stone's opinion because Sally smiled and said, 'Don't worry. You haven't got another Hungerbourne on your hands. The coroner can only return a verdict of suicide if it's proven beyond reasonable doubt.'

'And he didn't think this was?' David took a swig of his beer.

'No, but only because she hadn't left any sort of note or message. These days people will often text someone or post something on social media.'

David nearly spat out his beer. 'You're joking?'

Sally shook her head. 'Happens all the time. But not with Beth. And the coroner said there was no evidence that she'd been depressed or worried.'

'But surely anyone would have been depressed if they'd lost their job, broken up with their partner and been threatened by their new boss.'

Sally raised an eyebrow. 'You'd think, wouldn't you, but the coroner didn't agree. He said he thought it was probably suicide, but as there was no note and no one who gave evidence noticed she'd been a bit low he couldn't be sure beyond reasonable doubt.'

David wiped his plate with the last piece of his naan. 'If you ask me, that says more about the people she had around her. No wonder she wanted to end it all.'

CHAPTER FOUR

'He didn't sound keen, but at least he agreed to come and talk to me about it.' Clare couldn't hide her disappointment. She'd been counting on Neil Fuller to help her pick up where Beth had left off. Things would be twice as difficult without him. But Jo had somehow managed to wangle her way out of her commitments at the university for a few days, and Clare was glad of it. Even the most insurmountable problems always seemed more manageable when Jo was around.

Jo said, 'Is this Fuller guy nuts?'

'What do you mean?'

'With every unit in the country – correction, Europe – letting people go, where's he gonna find another offer like this?'

'I know, but the whole Beth thing must have been a bit traumatic for him. He sounded pretty shaken up by it.'

'Was he there when they found her?'

Clare shook her head. 'On-site, but according to Neil it was Crabby who actually found her.'

Jo looked at her quizzically. 'Crabby?'

'The local Druid. It was May Day; he'd gone up to the copse with a group of pagans to perform some sort of Beltane ceremony. But Neil said that he was the one who'd called the ambulance – Crabby was in too much shock.'

Jo made her way to the window and, prising open the Venetian blinds with her thumb and forefinger, peered out at the rain lashing the hillside. 'I guess it must have been pretty grim.'

'I wouldn't have thought that sort of thing would have bothered you.'

'Well, that's where you'd be wrong. I'm strictly a long-dead kind of gal. I only like them when they're bones, desiccated, mummified or frozen.' Jo leant forward across the desk towards Clare. 'In fact, so long as you swear not to tell David, I'll tell you something.'

Clare laughed. 'Deal.'

'I pass out if I see real, fresh blood.'

'You're joking.'

'Nope.'

'But how have you managed all these years?'

'For one thing, unlike some folks, I avoid chasing around after headcases with guns.'

Clare's recollection of her encounter with the wrong end of a loaded shotgun was only too fresh in her memory. Her work with the Hart Unit had been a godsend since her husband Stephen's death in a car crash, but it had certainly had its hairier moments. It had taken several months after the incident at Hungerbourne before she'd been able to sleep through the night without being woken by the image of David's apparently lifeless body being dumped inside the tea hut.

Jo swung round. 'Are you OK?' She knelt down in front of Clare. 'I'm sorry. I didn't think.'

Clare waved away her concern. 'Ignore me. I'm just being a wuss.'

'Are you still getting flashbacks?'

'No, not really. Not any more. It's just that I can't seem to shake the idea that this is Beth's office.'

'Jeez, next you're gonna be telling me you think this place is haunted.'

Clare remained silent.

But Jo couldn't suppress a snort of laughter. 'No. Really? You think this Portakabin has Beth's restless spirit roaming around it? And I always had you down as a cool-headed, rational kind of gal.'

'For your information, I don't actually believe in ghosts, but I still don't feel comfortable working a stone's throw from where Beth's body was found.'

'I get that. From the way she was found she must have been kind of troubled. But if we're going to make this work we've just got to treat it like any other dig. What happened here was real sad. Worse than sad. Beth must have been desperate to take her own life. But it's our job to pick up the pieces and make sure the job she started here gets finished.'

'You mean we should think of this as some kind of tribute to her.'

'I guess, if that's the way you want to look at it. But either way there's a site here that deserves to be given our full attention and we're kind of running behind schedule.'

Clare nodded, gesticulating towards the trays full of small plastic bags and mud-smeared ring binders. 'And our best hope of getting to grips with this lot is if I can somehow persuade Neil Fuller that it's in his best interests to come and work for us.'

'Honestly, David, it will be cheaper. If Jo and I have to keep commuting up from Salisbury every day the fuel bill alone will blow the budget.' And Clare could have added, *I'm not sure I'm up to a four-hour commute to Bailsgrove and back every day.* But thankfully he conceded the point quickly enough and she shoved her mobile back into her bag.

What she hadn't told him was that she had in fact already booked the only two single rooms that the King's Arms in Bailsgrove possessed for what she hoped would be the duration of the dig. As her mum would say, what he didn't know wouldn't hurt him. And she found herself rather looking forward to spending a few weeks in the Cotswolds with Jo for company.

But as she climbed out of Little Blue, her trusty but aged Fiesta, and scanned up and down the tightly packed row of Victorian terraced houses, she knew that if she was unsuccessful in her mission today they might as well pack up and leave Gloucestershire now. And that would mean saying goodbye to the Hart Unit. She was in search of number 46 – home to Neil Fuller. It didn't take her long to find it. From somewhere behind the peeling paint of the once pillar-box red front door she could hear a baby wailing.

He must have been waiting for her, because almost the instant she knocked, the door opened. She was greeted by the man himself, one arm shoved into a battered denim jacket and the other thrust towards her in a handshake. 'Hiya, you must be Clare. Sorry about the racket. She's teething.' He turned and yelled behind him, 'See you later, Sadie. Not sure how long I'll be,' before swinging the door to behind him.

He was younger than she'd expected – early thirties at most – with a shock of ginger hair and a few days' stubble that almost passed for a beard. He had bags around his eyes, but she guessed that excessive tiredness was only to be expected with a young baby. As they made their way up the street towards her car he kept up a constant stream of chit-chat, with Clare barely able to get a word in.

Strapping himself into his seat, he turned to face her. 'I really appreciate you coming all this way – my car's in dry dock at the moment. The exhaust is shot.' He hesitated, clearly embarrassed. 'Things have been a bit tight since the plug was pulled on the dig.'

'No problem. After everything that's happened it's good of you to agree to come and show me the ropes – we'll pay you for your time, of course.'

He said, 'No worries.' But Clare couldn't help noticing the look of relief on his face.

His tone was more upbeat than she'd been expecting after their phone conversation and she began to wonder whether his reluctance to return to the dig had more to do with not having the cash to repair his car and get to site than any deep-seated trauma.

When they got to Bailsgrove it didn't take him long to get stuck in. He started by taking Clare through the site recording system that Beth had used, before unfurling a series of pencil-drawn plans and placing them on the desk in front of her.

He weighed down their corners with plastic bags full of finds. And stepping back from the desk he looked around him, then broke into a broad smile. 'You know, I was really nervous about coming back here. I thought it might stir up the chaos of it all again. But now you've got it all in order, I don't know, it just seems sort of like everything is back to normal again. Beth would have been horrified by the state the police left this lot in.'

Clare wasn't sure whether to be relieved that it wasn't Beth who'd left the place as she'd found it or horrified at the thought that it had been the police.

She said, 'It looks from what I've seen so far as if she was a good record keeper.'

'Meticulous. You might almost say fanatical.'

She smiled. 'There are worse faults for an archaeologist to have. Beth's painstaking approach is certainly going to help us pick up where she left off.'

Neil ran his hand over the opaque surface of the drafting film, which she could see now was the main plan of the site. 'These are the evaluation trenches. Beth was convinced she'd picked something up on the geophysical survey that looked like an enclosure ditch, but to be honest I could never see it.' He pointed to two trenches towards the top of the plan. 'That's why they were positioned here.'

'To see if you could locate the ditch.'

He nodded. 'That's right. But we drew a complete blank in this first one. Not a feature in sight. And certainly no sign of a ditch. And we'd only just opened up the second when . . . well, you know.'

Clare could see that despite what he'd said earlier this still wasn't easy for him. 'From what I can see it looks like you had plenty of finds, though.'

'True enough. We had the usual handful of medieval pot and the odd flint flake or two. But it's all pretty run-of-the-mill stuff for round here.'

'I noticed there's quite a lot of animal bone, though. And I'm not a ceramics specialist, but it looked to me as if there was a fair bit of Iron Age pot in there too.'

'Maybe so, but not as much as Beth would have liked.'

'Oh?' Clare looked at him.

'Forget it. I shouldn't have said anything.'

'Please, Neil. I'm going to have to take this site on now and given everything that's happened I need to learn everything I can about what happened before I arrived.'

He gazed out of the window towards the copse on the hill high above them. What was he thinking? It was difficult to tell.

Eventually he turned towards her. 'OK.'

She pulled out the two tattered chairs from beneath the desk and gestured for them both to sit down. It seemed odd somehow, inviting him to sit down as a guest in an office he was more familiar with than she was.

Neil plonked himself down with a sigh and sat for several long minutes, staring down at his hands which were clasped firmly together in his lap. 'I suppose you've got a right to know, but it feels like I'm being disloyal.'

'To Beth.'

He looked up and nodded. 'Beth and me, we went way back. She was my tutor at Sheffield. She was brilliant. I don't just mean great to know sort of brilliant; I mean she was genuinely intellectually brilliant. She spoke so fast in lectures sometimes you could barely understand what she was saying, but you could feel the energy flying around the room. She was so alive.' He stopped short as if suddenly aware of what he'd just said.

He smiled. 'I know. Ironic, isn't it, given what happened. But she used to hold us spellbound in her Celtic studies classes – it was the one session you could guarantee people would leave the union bar for. And she was a brilliant excavator too. My first dig was with her. At Wrackley Cop.'

Clare said, 'I've heard of that. It's a hill fort, isn't it?'

He nodded. 'Up in the Peak District. Without Beth I'd never have got into this game in the first place.'

41

'She sounds inspiring.'

'She was. She was so passionate about everything – like it really mattered to her. Like it was personal. Maybe in the end that was the problem.'

'How do you mean?'

He raised his eyes towards the ceiling, avoiding her gaze. 'Look, I'm not sure—'

'Neil, I'm not here to judge anyone. I just want to know what we've got ourselves into here. Was there something Beth was involved in that I should know about?'

He shook his head. 'No, it wasn't like that. It's just that Beth was so soaked in the world of the Celts and the Iron Age that she took things a bit far sometimes.'

'You mean she was making it up.'

'She wouldn't have seen it like that. She would have said everyone else wasn't reading the evidence right. She was convinced this place was the site of an Iron Age shrine.'

'Wow, she genuinely thought it was a temple! Marshall told me she did, but I thought he was having me on.'

'Well, it would have been "wow" if there'd been a scrap of evidence to support it. But the less we found, the more convinced Beth was that she was in the right place. She'd found some reference in a journal article from 1800 and God knows when to a Latin inscription that was turfed up around here somewhere. She reckoned it proved the place had been a sacred site before the Romans arrived. After that everything we found just made her more convinced she was right.'

'It must have made her difficult to work with.'

'I never had any complaints. It wasn't as if she asked us to tamper with the records or anything. But not everyone thought like me.'

'Did some of the rest of the team have a problem with her?'

'Not here – our lot all loved her. She wasn't like some site directors; she'd get stuck in with the rest of us. But . . .'

He hesitated.

'But what?'

'Well, I'm not sure exactly what went on, but I don't think she left Sheffield by choice.'

'You mean the university sacked her.'

'Look, like I say I don't know all of the facts, but she ended up running a tinpot commercial dig in the middle of nowhere when she'd spent most of her career pulling in massive research grants and shaking hands with vice-chancellors. I bumped into Stuart Craig a few months back at a conference. He wouldn't say exactly what had gone on, but he reckoned the way Beth had acted had made things very difficult for the department.'

'I've heard of him. He's a lecturer at Sheffield, isn't he?'

He nodded. 'He was. He was a junior lecturer when I was an undergrad. Good bloke. He seemed really cut up about what happened and I didn't like to push him. But I can't blame him. He was more than just Beth's colleague. They'd been an item for years before she got the push. So it can't have helped his career much. And Beth seemed to blame him for what happened – that's why they split. But he's done really well for himself since. They promoted him to reader after she left. And now he's landed a job as head of department at Bristol.'

Clare said, 'I know it's a lot to ask, Neil, given how close you were to Beth, but is there any way you'd consider coming back and working for me here on the dig? I could really do with someone who knows the area – and the site. I'm not sure exactly what Beth was paying you, but we could offer you the going rate with a bit on top for fuel for the car journey.'

He grimaced. 'I'd like to say yes.'

A sudden thought struck her. 'If getting your car fixed is all that's stopping you from saying yes, don't let that stop you. I'll sub you the money.'

'I might not be able to pay it back all at once.'

'Don't worry, we'll work something out. What do you say?'

He hesitated for a second before smiling and sticking out a hand. 'You've got yourself a deal.'

Clare nearly shook his hand off. 'Thank you so much, Neil. I really appreciate it.'

He laughed. 'You don't have to thank me. I could do with the money. And I figure the least I can do is finish the job I started.' He looked her straight in the eye. 'You know, Clare, I never met anyone who didn't have time for Beth. She was so committed. Put her heart and soul into everything she did. But she was her own worst enemy. She made it very difficult for people sometimes. Towards the end it wasn't commitment, it was obsession. She just wouldn't let go.'

'Thanks for coming over, Margaret, I really appreciate it.' Clare handed Margaret a mug of tea.

David thought the least Clare could do was thank him too, particularly as he'd driven all the way up from Salisbury after back-to-back tutorials. And he'd had to persuade a colleague to cover his afternoon lecture – for which a large favour would no doubt be extracted at a later date. But for once he managed to hold his tongue. The three of them were jammed into the grandly named but microscopically proportioned welfare unit. In truth it was little more than a miniature Portakabin with a sink, fridge, microwave and the tiniest table David had ever seen, behind which he was now jammed with Clare and

Professor Margaret Bockford seated either side of him.

Margaret, sporting her familiar site attire of baggy green cardigan and purple Doc Martens, peered over the top of her spectacles and offered a beatific smile. 'Not at all. It's lovely to have an excuse to come and see you both. It's only a short hop from Oxford. But what is this all about?'

'And why the hurry?' David asked.

Clare offered an apologetic smile. 'Sorry about that. The dig team are due on-site tomorrow and there's a couple of things I really needed to discuss with you both before we start digging.'

David couldn't disguise his surprise. 'I'm impressed. I didn't think you'd manage to pull a team together this fast.'

'It wasn't too difficult once I'd got Neil Fuller on board. It didn't take him long to persuade most of Beth's old crew that they should come back to site.'

David asked, 'How'd you manage that? Jo seemed to think Fuller was still a bit wibbly about it all when I spoke to her a couple of days ago.'

Margaret glared reprovingly at David over her spectacles. 'I think we'd all be somewhat "wibbly" if we'd been on-site when our much-respected director's body was found hanging not two minutes from where we were working, wouldn't we?'

'Margaret's got a point, David. And once I met Neil it was pretty obvious his reluctance had as much to do with his car being off the road as anything else. So I subbed him the cost of a new exhaust and he was good to go.'

'Christ, Clare, we're not a charity. We're almost broke as it is.'

'Don't worry. I knew what you'd say so I paid for it out of my own pocket. And it was worth every penny – Neil's been brilliant. Without him we wouldn't have a team.'

David raised a hand in a gesture of surrender. He knew

when he was beaten. 'Fair enough. I'll take your word for it.'

He glanced down at his watch. He'd arranged to meet Sal back at her place in Devizes at seven and at this rate he'd be hard-pressed to make it.

Clare took the hint. She opened up her laptop. After a couple of taps of the keys she positioned it so both he and Margaret could see the screen. In front of them was a fuzzy grey image with a selection of ill-defined, slightly darker splodges splattered across its surface.

He said, 'I can see it's a magnetometer survey, but what's it meant to be of?'

'It's the site. According to Neil, Beth was convinced there was an Iron Age shrine here somewhere.'

David let out a long, low sigh. Iron Age shrines were as rare as hen's teeth and normally the prospect of digging one would have made his year. But right now what they needed to do was to get in, dig the site and get out again. The last thing they needed was something that would take months to dig and be a bloody nightmare to keep a lid on. It was so good to see Clare excited by something again. The last couple of years since Stephen's death had been tough on her. But he couldn't afford for her to get carried away on some wild goose chase looking for a long-lost Iron Age temple.

To his relief Clare sounded matter-of-fact. 'The trenches that are open at the moment were positioned to see what this is.' She pointed at one of the darker splodges that seemed to be a little longer than the others. 'What do you make of it?'

He scoffed. 'I think she must have had bloody good eyesight!'

Margaret removed her glasses and peered at the image in front of them. 'Maybe. But I'm not so sure, David. There might be something there. Do you see?' She pointed a finger at an elongated dark splodge running close to one side of the image.

Clare said, 'And now you see why I needed to speak to you. But there's something else. Neil told me that Beth had found a journal article that she reckoned proved this place was a shrine site well before the Romans arrived. So I had a look through her site diaries and found a reference to this.'

With a few more strokes of the keys a scanned image of a journal article appeared in front of them. From the typeface it was obviously of some antiquity.

David asked, 'What's this from?'

Clare said, 'The Transactions of the Bristol and Gloucestershire Archaeological Society for 1877.'

In the middle of the page was a line drawing of what appeared to be one half of a slab of stone with parts of an inscription on it. It was obvious that the other half must have contained more of the text.

Margaret leant forward. 'Now that is interesting.'

David asked, 'Where was it found?'

'Difficult to say for sure. According to this account it was "happened upon in the garden of Bailsgrove vicarage" when the new vicar took over the living. But the story he had from the housekeeper was that the previous incumbent had found it "somewhere near the foot of Bailsgrove hill".'

David said, 'Thoroughly reliable source, then.'

Margaret said, 'You shouldn't be so quick to dismiss these old accounts, David. There's often more than a grain of truth in them.'

Clare said, 'That's all very well. But what do you make of the inscription on it? I don't read Latin.'

David said, 'It looks like a dedication to Mercury.'

'But Mercury was a Roman deity.' Clare sounded almost deflated. 'Beth was wrong, then.'

Margaret shook her head, 'Not necessarily. The Romans had

a habit of twinning their gods with those of the native Brits. You know Bath was originally called Aquae Sulis.' Clare nodded. 'Well, Sulis was a local water deity, but in the temple they built at the spring site, the Romans worshipped her as Sulis Minerva.'

Clare said, 'A sort of Romano-British mash-up.'

Margaret said, 'If you like.'

David said, 'Some might call it identity theft.'

In his opinion the Romans were much overrated and the best thing they ever did was bugger off home. It was just a shame that it had taken them four hundred years to do it.

Margaret was obviously of a different mind. She turned towards Clare, studiously ignoring his remark. 'The thing is, Mercury is one of the gods that is frequently twinned with local deities. In his case it's often Lugh, the native sky god.'

'So, Beth might have been on to something.'

Margaret said, 'It's possible.'

David said, 'Oh, come on. It's hardly proven beyond doubt, is it? We don't know for sure that thing' – he jabbed his finger at the drawing – 'actually came from anywhere near Bailsgrove, let alone this site. And even if it did and there was an Iron Age shrine somewhere near Bailsgrove, there's no hard evidence to suggest it was here.'

Margaret cast him a withering look. 'It's always wise to keep an open mind about these things. And there's only one way we're going to find out. Clare here needs to get on and dig it.'

'Well, that at least we can all agree on.'

As David stepped down from the welfare unit, Margaret placed a hand on his shoulder and leant down to whisper in his ear. He was expecting a lecture on his attitude to Romano-British relations, but instead Margaret's concerns were somewhat more grounded in the present. 'I do hope you're not intending to let Clare pay for that exhaust, David. You know she's not as financially well-placed as either of us. If you don't reimburse her, I will.'

He could feel himself flush from head to toe. He'd never even considered the fact that since Stephen's death Clare had been struggling financially.

Once they were out of earshot of Clare, he turned to face Margaret and took her hand in his. 'Don't worry, Margaret. I'll look after her.'

'You just see you do, Dr Barbrook.'

CHAPTER FIVE

The wall was moving. At least that's what it felt like to Jack Tyler as he slithered down it. He hit the pavement with a bump and sat, legs splayed out across the alleyway, head lolling forward against his chest.

He hadn't been as wrecked as this in he couldn't remember how long. But right at the moment he couldn't remember much. It had been a good night. That much he knew. He'd bumped into an old mate who'd stood him a few pints. The only stroke of luck he'd had in a very long time.

He let out a belch. There was no way he was going to be sick. He always felt like shit the next day when he threw up. With a huge force of will he lifted his head up, gulped in air and hiccupped. And in so doing cracked the back of his skull against the solid Victorian brickwork behind him.

Lifting his hand to rub the back of his head, he succeeded only in grazing his knuckles on the masonry. 'Shit.'

He slumped down, closing his eyes, resigning himself to a night sleeping it off in the alley. As he drifted towards semi-consciousness he was vaguely aware of the sound of footsteps approaching. The adrenalin surge was enough to shoot him bolt upright and, bracing himself against the wall, he managed to clamber into a standing position.

Peering at the half-hidden figure in the shadow cast by the street lamp, he brandished the bottle of WKD he'd been clutching, splattering his trainers with the last dregs of its contents in the process. 'You can keep your hands off my wallet, you bassshtard . . .'

'No need for that, Jack.'

The voice was familiar. Who was it? The harder he tried to squeeze his eyeballs into focus, the blurrier the figure became. Mesmerised by the hypnotic motion of his own shadow swaying back and forth in the phosphorescent glow of the street light he tried, without success, to steady himself. Who did that voice belong to?

The figure lunged towards him. But before he could do anything he felt an arm being slipped around his waist, then his own arm being lifted upwards and draped around a pair of bony shoulders. His every instinct was to resist, but his head was spinning and it was all he could do to stop himself from throwing up.

'Come on, my ol' lover, you're in a right state. Let's get you home.'

Jack opened his eyes and looked up to see the familiar yellow stain on the ceiling above him. He wasn't sure how he'd got here, but he was lying on the settee in the living room of his flat. He ran his tongue around his mouth. It felt like someone had taken sandpaper to it. A near empty glass of water and an open box of paracetamol were sitting on the coffee table. He touched his hand gingerly to the back of his head and felt a lump the size of an egg. He had a vague memory of cracking it against something hard. He sat up cautiously, his head banging fit to burst. The bowl from the kitchen sink was lying on the floor next to the sofa. A sudden whiff of its contents made him scramble over the end of the sofa and dive for the toilet.

He was still kneeling in front of it with his head down the pan when the doorbell went. He tried to ignore it, but they weren't giving up. He hauled himself to his feet and turned on the cold tap, splashing his face with water, then shoving his mouth under it and gratefully gulping down the cooling liquid. The bell rang again.

'Keep your hair on.' He grabbed a towel, rubbing it across his mouth before dragging his unwilling carcass back into the living room.

He opened the front door just as his visitor started hammering on the other side.

They stopped mid-knock. 'Hello, Jack.'

'What do you want?'

'You've changed your tune. You were the one who wanted to talk to me last time, remember? Aren't you going to invite me in?'

Jack gestured for his visitor to sit. 'Does this mean you've been thinking about what I said?'

'You could say that.'

Jack breathed a sigh of relief. Maybe his luck really was changing. 'Look, I don't know about you, but I could murder a tea.'

'Not for me. But you go ahead. I can see why you'd be in need of one.' The visitor pointed towards the bowl. 'You never could hold your drink.'

Ignoring the comment, Jack made his way into the kitchen. As much as he welcomed the change of mind, he could do without the crap that went with it. He flicked on the kettle, grabbed a mug from the worktop and swilled it out under the tap. However shit he might feel right now, he needed to get his head together. He had to make sure he played this right – it might be his only chance. He dredged his memory. What exactly had he said last time they'd met? He stirred the tea bag, trying to make some sort of order of his thoughts.

He sniffed at the milk carton, splashed some into his mug and, still trying to replay the scene in his head, headed towards the living room. Stepping through the door he looked up, momentarily confused. Where was his visitor?

He sensed rather than saw the movement behind him. And then came the crashing blow that propelled his scalding mug of tea across the living room carpet and him into oblivion.

CHAPTER SIX

'Let's take a look at that, Malcolm.' Malcolm stood aside and Clare stepped into the trench. Kneeling down, she examined the shallow hole in front of her. As she deftly scraped her trowel through the soft, dark earth she was sure she could feel Malcolm's eyes boring into her back. He seemed a decent sort of bloke. But he was a hardened digger, with over two decades' experience on commercial dig sites. And here she was in charge of him, and twenty of his equally experienced colleagues. She remembered reading an article somewhere about impostor syndrome and now she began to understand what it felt like.

Blowing out her cheeks, she tried to focus on the task in hand. The hole in front of her looked like some kind of shallow pit, but the soil in it was loose, offering no resistance to her trowel. And mixed into it were small lumps of limestone – just like the surrounding bedrock. She was nearly at the bottom now and it was obvious that there was absolutely nothing in it.

She rocked back on her heels. 'Have you had any finds out of it?'

Malcolm pointed to the small plastic tray that sat on the side of the trench. 'Just that.' In the tray was a small, nondescript piece of blue plastic.

'Where did it come from?'

'About halfway up the fill.'

No chance it had found its way there accidentally then. Clare stood up and stretched her back.

'Thanks, Malcolm. Just finish recording it and then go and give Steve a hand over on his cutting.'

She clambered out of the trench and made her way disconsolately back towards the Portakabin. Malcolm's was the third pit like this that they'd found so far. With absolutely no sign of finds except some modern tat and looking for all the world as if they had been dug yesterday. Which she suspected was uncomfortably close to the truth. Why could things never be simple? As if Paul Marshall wasn't enough to cope with, now it looked as if someone had been messing about with the site before they'd taken it over. What sort of messing about she couldn't prove for sure, but she had a damn good idea.

When she got to the office, she found Neil already there, poring over a folder full of context sheets.

He looked up. 'You look like you could do with a brew.'

'I wouldn't say no.'

'What's up?'

She plonked herself down at her desk. 'We've now got three of those bloody pits.'

'Empty?'

'Not quite, unfortunately. This one had modern plastic in it.'

'Ah.'

'Ah indeed.'

'I did say Beth didn't miss much.'

She nodded in the direction of the sheaf of context sheets he held in his hands. 'I know, and there's nothing in the records to show that she'd spotted any of them before she' – Clare hesitated, groping for the right words – 'finished on-site.'

Neil shook his head. 'No. I did check.'

'So did I.'

If there was no record of the pits being there when the site had been closed down, they must have been dug and then backfilled since. Which meant it looked like they'd had illegal metal detectorists on the site. Or, as they were rather too glamorously known in the trade, nighthawks. In reality the people who dealt in such things were anything but glamorous.

Neil sighed. 'Well, there's nothing much we can do about it now.'

'Not about the damage that's already been done, maybe, but we need to make sure it doesn't happen again.'

'You don't want to start messing with nighthawks, Clare. They're a nasty bunch of fuckers.' Then, suddenly seeming to think better of his choice of language, he added, 'Sorry.'

Clare wasn't sure why but somewhere along the line Neil seemed to have gained the impression that she was what her mum would call 'posh'. It was true that life as a solicitor's wife had polished away her last remaining Essex comp vowels. But deep down inside there was still more than a touch of the girl from the council estate. A fact that, though she rarely shared it, she was secretly rather proud of.

She waved his apology away and smiled. 'It's alright, I happen to think your choice of language is spot on. And I have absolutely no intention of trying to take them on single-handed.'

'Thank Christ for that. I was on a Roman site over in the Forest of Dean a few years back when one of my mates nipped back to site one night to pick up some kit he'd forgotten. He got beaten to a pulp with a pickaxe handle by the bastards.'

'You're not making me feel any better about this, Neil.'

'Tell you what, I'll go and make you that cuppa.'

Once he'd left the office and was out of earshot, Clare retrieved her mobile from the pocket of her combat trousers. Scrolling through her contacts, she found the number she was looking for. She thought she was going to be out of luck, but just as she was about to ring off a male voice answered. 'Mark Stone.'

'DCI Stone.' She stumbled over her words, momentarily uncertain of how she should address him. 'Mark. It's Clare Hills – from the Bailsgrove dig site.'

'Yes, I remember. What can I do for you, Clare?'

Was it her imagination or did he seem somewhat cheerier than she imagined the average police officer sounded? Sally would have you believe they were being run ragged most of the time and barely had time to deal with serious crime, let alone take random phone calls from a virtual stranger. Well, if he was in a good mood, the least she could do was take advantage of it. 'I was wondering when you had the dig site sealed off if there had been any sort of unusual activity.'

'Not that I'm aware of.' He sounded more cautious now. 'Why, have you had some sort of problem?'

'You could say that. There seems to have been some illegal metal detecting on-site between the time Beth stopped digging and when we took over. There's no way of knowing exactly what they've taken, but of course that's not the most important thing – they've wrecked a large area of the site.'

She was sure she could hear him sighing on the other end of the phone. 'I'm really sorry to hear that, but there's not much we can do. After all, you said yourself that there's no way of knowing what's been taken.'

'But they must have done this while you had the site sealed off. I don't understand how it could have happened.'

He laughed. 'I'm not exactly sure "sealed off" is the right way to put it. It was an unexplained death, not a murder enquiry. As soon as we'd had SOCO out there and they'd done their bit we locked the place up and left site.'

She couldn't believe what she was hearing. 'You mean you just left it? With no one there to protect it?'

'Look, I know the site is important to you, Mrs Hills, but nothing much has come from it, has it? Not as far as we could make out from what the dig team said when we arrived.'

'Well, no, not yet maybe. But that doesn't mean it doesn't need protecting – who's to say what we might find.'

There was no mistaking it; this time Clare could hear an audible sigh on the other end of the line. 'Correct me if I'm wrong, Mrs Hills, but it's not a legally protected monument, is it?'

'No, that's true, it's not Scheduled. But that doesn't mean it might not be important. And if it does prove to be as significant as Dr Kinsella thought it was it could be Scheduled in the future.' Even to her ears she was beginning to sound desperate.

'I wish you every success with your dig, Mrs Hills, I really do, but I'm afraid our resources don't stretch to protecting every last patch of earth in Gloucestershire. If you have any trouble – any threats, any actual evidence of theft by metal detectorists or anyone else – then do get in touch with us.' And with that the line went dead.

* * *

Clare closed her eyes and turned her face towards the early summer sunshine. After her failure to get Gloucestershire's finest to take the destruction of chunks of the site seriously, she'd decided to award herself an end-of-shift glass of Sancerre. To her surprise and relief she'd found that she was the only person taking advantage of the King's Arms' beer garden.

She rubbed at the back of her neck. The last few weeks had taken more out of her than she'd realised. She hadn't appreciated how much of a strain the responsibility of being a site director would prove. It was one thing to stand in for a day or two when David wasn't around, but having to sort out everything from hiring the JCB to making sure there was enough toilet roll in the Portaloo was quite another.

Still, on the plus side, she hadn't had much time to think. And avoiding thinking was something she'd become particularly adept at since Stephen's death. It had only been just over two years since his car crash. But her life today was unrecognisable now from the way things had been before his death. She sometimes wondered what he'd make of her if he met her now. Looking down at her mud-splattered moleskin trousers and scuffed steel toe capped boots, she suspected he wouldn't have approved. She was about as far away from the image of the immaculately groomed wife of a successful solicitor as it was possible to imagine.

She ran her fingers through her hair and took a swig – Stephen would have thought rather too large a swig – of her wine. Well, he'd left her with no choice, hadn't he? It was Stephen who'd managed to pour virtually every penny they'd possessed into what his friend and colleague James – his executor – had described as 'ill-judged' property deals without even bothering to mention it to her. The only visible means of support he'd left her with had been a tiny photographic gallery in Richmond.

She'd always loved photography. She was beguiled by the potential that a camera held to capture the essence of a moment, or the memory of a place. Stephen had presented her with the shop out of the blue as a present for their tenth anniversary. But as grateful as she'd been at the time, it had always been more of a self-indulgent hobby than a viable business. When he'd given it to her she'd felt guilty because she'd found herself wondering whether his gift had been his way of acknowledging that there was something missing in her life – in their marriage – that neither of them had been able to bring themselves to discuss.

Whatever his motivation, she was grateful that he'd had the foresight to put it in her name. It was all she'd had left to fall back on after his death. So when David had offered her a job she'd jumped at the chance.

The trouble was, if she was being honest with herself, most of the time she was happier now than she could ever remember having been with Stephen. Not that she hadn't loved him; she had. And she had no doubt at all that he'd loved her. But that hadn't been quite enough. And despite the odd moment of self-doubt, since she'd accepted David's offer she hadn't had a moment's regret. But now she could never quite escape the feeling that part of the reason for Stephen's 'accident' was that he'd known all along that there had been something missing.

Her thoughts turned back to the present and her conversation with Mark Stone. She'd been annoyed, maybe even a little angry, that he was less than interested in the site being a target for nighthawks. But her overwhelming feeling when she'd heard the line go dead was one of disappointment. Not with his casual disregard for the nation's heritage, but that he'd called her Mrs Hills. And for some reason that she wasn't sure she was ready to delve into just yet, she'd had an overwhelming urge to let him know that there was no longer a Mr Hills.

'Don't bother, I'll find her myself.' The shrill female voice punctured the early afternoon tranquillity.

Clare finished pushing the small plastic label into the side of the trench and looked up. The voice had come from the direction of the welfare unit. She straightened up from where she'd been squatting to see a woman of later middle years, clad in a Barbour and wide-brimmed hat, striding purposefully towards her. Clare had stayed on-site to finish marking up the section when everyone else had gone for tea, so that Neil could head down into Gloucester to buy some drafting film. It had been a long, hot and decidedly unproductive day and she'd been looking forward to a mug of what laughingly passed for tea. But judging from the expression on the woman's face it didn't look likely she was going to get one any time soon. Reluctantly she climbed out of the trench and pinned what she fervently hoped was a directorial smile in place.

The woman waved a hand in the direction of the Portakabins. 'They tell me you're in charge here.' Clare glanced over to see Jo standing in front of the site huts with her arms spread wide in a gesture of silent apology. Clare opened her mouth to reply but didn't get the chance. 'It's an utter disgrace. You should be ashamed of yourself.'

Clare could feel her cheeks reddening. She had no idea who this woman was, much less what it was she was supposed to have done. She took in a deep breath and stuck out a hand in what she trusted would be construed as a friendly gesture.

'I'm Clare Hills, the dig director. And you would be . . .'

'Foggarty, Mrs Sheila Foggarty. Parish councillor. And I want to know what you think you're doing opening this site up again.'

'I'm doing my job, Mrs Foggarty. Our team are excavating here to ensure the site is properly explored and recorded ahead of the housing development.'

'Exactly! After all the effort poor Beth went to. She knew that this site was too important to build on.'

'I know that Beth believed this site may have been significant in the Iron Age, but I'm afraid so far we've found remarkably little evidence to back up her claims.'

'How much is Paul Marshall paying you?'

'I really don't think that's any of your business, Mrs Foggarty.'

'I think it's very much the business of a parish councillor to know if so-called archaeologists are taking backhanders from developers to keep quiet about what they've found in my parish.'

Clare couldn't contain herself any longer. 'Now, look here. I can see you're very upset, but whatever you might like to believe we're a perfectly respectable archaeology unit. And we're doing our best to do a professional job under difficult circumstances.'

Sheila Foggarty clearly didn't share Clare's appraisal of the situation. 'Then why are you working for a cowboy like Paul Marshall, whose only desire is to profit from the destruction of our countryside?'

'Beth worked for Paul Marshall too, Mrs Foggarty.'

'Yes, but she was only doing it to protect the site. To show everyone that it was too important to build on.'

Clare was tempted to say that if that was true, Beth had entirely failed in her mission, but she knew that would only make matters worse. 'The Hart Archaeological Research Institute is part of the University of Salisbury – our very reason for existing is to discover and investigate important archaeological sites. What makes you so sure we don't want to do our best by the archaeology and by Beth

Kinsella? If Beth was right and this place really is some sort of Iron Age shrine, we will find out.'

For a moment Sheila Foggarty stood staring at her, hands rammed into the pockets of her Barbour, as if considering something. 'Well, if that's the case you might be interested in this.' She retrieved a folded sheet of A4 paper from the pocket of her jacket and shoved it at Clare.

Clare took the paper without a word and studied it, trying to make sense of what she was looking at. It was a printout of a lot from an online auction site. It showed a photograph of what it claimed was an Iron Age sword. She was no expert on Celtic weaponry, but it looked fairly convincing from what she remembered from textbooks and museums. If it was a fake someone had done a halfway decent job. She glanced down at the description. It said it came from a nineteenth-century collection of material from in and around the area of Bailsgrove in Gloucestershire. It didn't prove that Bailsgrove had been a shrine of any kind, but she knew that if it had really come from somewhere in Bailsgrove it would certainly add weight to Beth's theory.

She looked up. 'You realise that this might not be real. It's not uncommon for dealers to give a false provenance to fake artefacts to lure customers in.'

'Does it look fake to you, Mrs Hills?'

'Well, on first appearances it does look about right but it's impossible to tell without seeing it in the flesh. But even if it is what it claims to be, it's not necessarily from Bailsgrove. And I'm sorry to say that one sword doesn't make a shrine.'

'Oh, that's not the only one. There's plenty of other material on the same website that comes from Bailsgrove.'

'I'm really sorry, Mrs Foggarty, but I'm afraid that on its own this doesn't prove anything.'

'So much for safeguarding the nation's heritage. If you had any interest at all in protecting this site you'd want to find out more about this.' Snatching the paper out of Clare's hand, she turned and marched back in the direction of the site entrance. As she strode towards the gate she half turned and waved the sheet in Clare's direction. 'And don't think I won't write to the vice chancellor about your attitude, young woman. It's shameful, truly shameful.'

David swung the Land Rover in through the field gate, narrowly missing the woman in the waxed jacket. Stopping, he flung open his door, turning towards her to apologise, but she'd already stormed past him shaking her head and muttering, 'Appalling. Simply appalling.'

He could swear he'd heard her say something about contacting the vice chancellor. What the hell was going on? He'd driven up from Salisbury in the hope of a few hours' respite from the Runt, who seemed to be positively revelling in the financial straits in which the Hart Unit currently found itself. Anyone would think that he wanted them to fail – and of course they'd be right. Nothing would please the little shit more than being able to present the dean with an excuse to eject David from the department.

'Hi, David. Fancy a brew?'

Clare sounded distinctly fed up, and she looked knackered as she trudged downslope towards him. He hoped he wasn't going to live to regret putting her in sole charge of the excavations. He knew that technically she was perfectly capable – if truth be told, he sometimes thought more capable than he was – of directing her own dig. But it looked as if the added knowledge that, unless this excavation went to plan, the unit would have to close was weighing on her more heavily than he'd expected.

65

'Love one.' He nodded in the direction of the lane down which the woman in the Barbour had disappeared. 'What was all that about?'

'I'm tempted to say "don't ask". But unfortunately I think there's something you need to know.'

He didn't like the sound of this one little bit. It was obvious that Clare was finding things tough. But with the teaching commitments Muir had piled on him this year there was no way he had the capacity to take Bailsgrove on as well. However difficult she was finding it, she was just going to have to stand on her own two feet with this one. At least Jo was going to be around some of the time – though she had teaching commitments of her own. Maybe he could give Margaret a call and get her to drop by now and then to keep an eye on things.

A few minutes later the two of them were sitting clutching mugs of tepid brown liquid in the site office.

'So, what is it you need to tell me?'

Clare put her mug down and reached over to extract three context sheets from the ring binder on her desk. She spread them out in front of him. 'Take a look at those.'

David examined them. 'Three pits. So what?'

'Three pits with absolutely no finds in them except for some modern plastic. And none of them with any record of having been there when Beth was working on the site.'

'So Beth wasn't the world's best archaeologist. We all miss things from time to time.' He hesitated. 'And we do know that things weren't quite right with Beth. After all, she did kill herself.'

David sincerely hoped that was true. Ever since Sally had mentioned the narrative verdict at the inquest he'd been worried about the prospect of leaving Clare up here on her own if there was even the slightest possibility that Beth's death was less than entirely straightforward. He'd toyed with the idea of mentioning it to Clare, or at least to Jo. But if he told Jo she would only tell Clare. And in the end he'd decided he was worrying about nothing. If the police weren't concerned, then all he'd succeed in doing by mentioning it would be to make Clare more nervous about the place than she already was. But there would be no harm in making that call to Margaret even if he didn't tell her about the inquest.

Clare said, 'Beth Kinsella's mental health may have been in a questionable state before her death, but none of her team seem to think it ever affected the way she dug. Neil says she was a brilliant excavator – it was just that she sometimes took her interpretation of what she found a bit far.'

David snorted. 'Made things up, you mean!'

Clare shrugged her shoulders. 'Whatever. What's important is that it didn't affect her ability to recognise an archaeological feature. And more to the point, from what I've seen, the team we've got digging out there are bloody good at their jobs. There's no way they'd have missed something like this.'

'So, what are you saying? Someone deliberately vandalised the site before we started work here?'

'That woman you nearly mowed down' – David wasn't entirely happy with that description but now didn't seem the moment to argue about it – 'is Sheila Foggarty. She lives locally. She says she's a parish councillor.'

'She sounded to me like she was saying quite a lot of things, not all of them entirely complimentary.'

'No. In fact she was bloody rude. But that's not important.'

'It might be if she ends up writing to the vice chancellor.' Clare's face reddened. 'What was she so upset about?'

'Us. Or more specifically us working for Paul Marshall. She's convinced we've sold out to him and we're only in it for the money.'

David raised an eyebrow.

Clare said, 'Yes, well, I know we need the money. But that doesn't mean we'll go to any lengths to get it, does it? Anyway, what she thinks of our ethics is of no consequence. But what she showed me might be.'

He was beginning to lose patience now. Where exactly was all of this leading? 'What?'

'It was a screenshot of an Internet auction site selling what they claim is an Iron Age sword.'

David said, 'So? I'm as opposed to selling antiquities online as you are, but what exactly has this got to do with us?'

'It came from Bailsgrove.'

'You've seen plenty of those sites, Clare. Half of them give fake locations and the other half are flogging replicas.'

Clare nodded. 'I know. But there are a good many dealers selling real metal detector finds advertised on the net too. And not all of the vendors are too fussy about how they've come by them.'

She glanced down in the direction of the context sheets. David pulled the sheets towards him again and reread them.

He looked up at her. 'Are you saying you genuinely think the sword could have come from this site?'

'It's got to be a possibility, hasn't it?'

He looked up at her. 'But you've found more than one of these pits.'

'And according to Sheila Foggarty there's more than the sword being advertised on the web as coming from Bailsgrove.'

David sat back in his seat and rubbed his forehead. 'Jesus Christ, Clare. That's all we need – nighthawks on the site.'

She nodded. 'I'm sorry, David, but I thought you needed to know.'

'Yes, of course,' he replied. But he was barely listening any more. What on earth was he going to do? How could he leave Clare here on her own to deal with this? Anything could happen.

'What are we going to do, David? We can't just let them waltz in here and strip the site.'

'You have no idea what these people can be like, Clare. The sort of people that take finds from excavations haven't been given a metal detector by their granny for their birthday.'

'I know that, David. Neil has been telling me about some trouble he had on another site.'

Great. She hadn't known Neil Fuller two minutes and now he was suddenly the fount of all bloody wisdom. Sometimes it seemed she'd listen to anyone except for him. 'Look, Clare, we don't do anything. You tell the police and then you let them handle it from there.'

Clare sat tight-lipped.

'Promise me, Clare.'

There was a determined look in those hazel eyes that he recognised only too well from their student days.

So he was all the more astonished when she raised her hands in the air in a gesture of surrender. 'OK, I give in. The right thing to do is contact the police.'

CHAPTER SEVEN

'Before you ask, I'd say somewhere between twenty-four and thirty-six hours ago.'

The jowly, time-wearied features of the medical examiner were in sharp contrast to those of the ashen-faced cadaver of the young man on the metal trolley that lay between them. Mid to late twenties, Frank had said. Sally had had little doubt he'd been drinking before he died, even before Frank had confirmed it from the tests he'd run. The stench of it managed to overpower the unpleasant whiff of the examination room. There was no sign of illegal substance abuse and none of the tell-tale needle marks. But from his build and muscle development Sally had already known this one wasn't going to turn out to be drug-related. That at least gave her something to be grateful for. She'd seen enough of those to last her a lifetime when she'd been a young beat copper in Bristol.

'You can put the sheet down now, Frank! I've seen a dead body before,' Sally said.

'But they're all different, you see. This particular example has been struck down from behind with something heavy.' The rotund little Welshman swung his arms above his head theatrically, miming the way in which the fatal blow had been dealt. 'Left what you might call a lasting impression on him.' He smiled, clearly satisfied with his humorous offering.

'Couldn't he just have fallen backwards and hit his head on something?'

'You tell me. I'm the medical examiner, not SOCO. Did they find any blood spatter at the scene?'

Sally shrugged. 'I'm still waiting for the report.'

'Well, patience is a virtue.' He paused then winked at her. 'So they tell me.'

He washed his hands at a small stainless-steel sink in the corner of the room before turning to face her. 'Fancy a cuppa? I might be able to stretch to a slice of malt loaf if you're lucky.'

As long as Sally had known him, Frank Barlow's office had suffered from a slightly unsettling odour that sat somewhere between mouldy fruit cake and Milton fluid. It was a cramped affair on the ground floor, with a window that gave onto a view of bumpers and exhaust pipes in the car park. But Frank wasn't a man to grumble. Instead he found solace in food and drink.

His desk was jammed up against the wall and they were sitting knee-to-knee eating buttered malt loaf.

'How's it going with Morgan off?'

Sally shrugged her shoulders and munched on a mouthful.

Frank peered over the thick frames of his glasses. 'You look knackered, girl.'

'Thanks, Frank. You always know how to make a girl feel better.'

He shrugged. 'Just being honest. I wouldn't want to end up with another one to process.'

She smiled wearily. 'Any chance this one will turn out to be an accidental?'

He screwed up his nose. 'I'd not be counting that particular chicken if I were you.'

'What makes you say that?'

'There's something about the positioning of the fracture. It's very high up on the back of the head. Don't suppose he was found at the bottom of a flight of stairs by any chance?'

Sally shook her head. 'Next to his settee on his living room floor. Why?'

'It's the only way I can think he might've received a blow to the cranium like that without someone else being involved.' He rubbed his fleshy chin. 'Long shot, though. If he'd fallen down stairs I'd have expected multiple contusions as a minimum. He has sustained another minor blow to the back of his head. But I'd expect to see fractured limbs and probably the odd broken rib if it was a fall.'

'No sign?'

'Nope. Nothing except broken skin on the knuckles of his right hand, and one small and one large donk on the bonce.' He took a slurp from his tea before setting down his mug on top of the jumble of papers and cardboard folders that occupied his desk.

Sally smiled. 'There you go again, Frank, blinding me with science.'

'Well, whether it's a depressed fracture of the cranium or a donk on the bonce, the blow that killed him wasn't self-inflicted. And from what you've said about where he was found it only confirms my conclusions. It most definitely wasn't accidental. So, Sally my girl, it seems congratulations are in order. It looks like you're going to be heading up a murder inquiry.'

* * *

Sitting curled up on the sofa in the living room of her Salisbury flat with her laptop in front of her and a large glass of Sancerre by her side, Clare was feeling almost human again after her shower. She'd thought about staying on at Bailsgrove this weekend to keep an eye on the site, but she was shattered, and in the end she'd decided that David had a point. An encounter with a bunch of pickaxe-wielding thugs was not her idea of a fun night out. And, just as importantly, if she did run into them there was no way she was going to be able to stop them on her own. So instead she'd asked Neil to install a couple of battery-operated wildlife cams on-site in the hope that if the nighthawks did show their faces they might at least have some sort of evidence.

The mood David had been in, she hadn't wanted to tell him that she'd already spoken to the police and they'd been less than interested. As far as she knew he'd never met Mark Stone, but despite that for some reason he already seemed to have taken exception to him.

It suddenly struck her that maybe Sally knew Mark. For once she wished that she'd listened a bit more closely when David had been chuntering on about Sally. She knew that she came from Bristol. Was she imagining it or had he told her that she'd been in the Gloucestershire force before she transferred to Wiltshire? If so, it was possible Sally had worked with Mark Stone, or at least come across him. Clare smiled. Maybe Sally had worked rather more closely with him than David would have liked. She banished the thought as soon as it had arrived; something about David suffering from the green-eyed monster over Sally made her feel distinctly queasy.

She took a sip of her wine and fired up the laptop. It had been a long week and it wasn't finished yet. She'd already done what David had asked and contacted the police. Even if she'd done it before she'd told him, they had a problem. Though she'd be happy if he never discovered that particular detail. And she'd come to terms with the fact that she wasn't going to be able to tackle the nighthawks single-handed on-site. But that didn't mean she had any intention of sitting back and doing nothing. She was responsible for what happened at Bailsgrove and she was damned if she was going to have Sheila Foggarty or anyone else accusing her of not taking her responsibilities seriously.

Apart from anything else, she'd only just started getting back on her feet financially after Stephen's death. And if the unit went under she'd be out of a job. The only real skills she had were as an archaeologist, and the way the construction industry was going every archaeology unit in the country was laying people off. The complexities of her husband's ill-judged property dealings had meant that he'd not only left a trail of debt behind him but also some legally dubious investments that had meant his estate had only recently finished going through probate. But there was one thing he had done that she'd had cause to be grateful for over the last couple of years. He'd appointed his friend and fellow solicitor James as his executor and not her.

At the time she'd felt more than a little hurt by the decision. She'd never really taken to James when Stephen was alive. Looking back now she could see that maybe she'd even been a touch jealous of the amount of time the two men had spent together, at work and on the golf course. But he'd shouldered the bulk of the responsibility of sorting Stephen's estate out without a hint of complaint and, frankly, without his legal know-how she would have been sunk.

She typed the words 'Bailsgrove' and 'Iron Age sword' into the search engine and the page that Sheila Foggarty had shown her popped up. There were already a couple of bids on the sword. She searched the auction site for other items from Bailsgrove and it didn't take her long to find what she was looking for. There was a whole scree of them; most of them smaller items than the sword, but all metalwork and all looking as if they were in pretty good condition. If what Sheila Foggarty had said about these coming from their site was true, then there was every chance that Beth Kinsella had been right. Bailsgrove could very well have been an Iron Age shrine, or at the very least a major site of some kind. From the research she'd already done she knew that swords didn't pop up just anywhere; as well as shrine sites and sanctuaries, they were found in burials. And Iron Age cemeteries were all but unheard of in this neck of the woods.

Under any other circumstances it would be a major coup for the unit. But Paul Marshall wouldn't like what it might mean one tiny little bit: there was every possibility the site would be Scheduled. And with Bailsgrove legally protected, his chances of being able to build his houses would be non-existent. He'd have a totally worthless, if stunningly beautiful, slice of Cotswold countryside on his hands. And whatever she might have told Sheila Foggarty, the uncomfortable truth was that right now Paul Marshall's money was the only thing standing between the Hart Unit and closure.

'But that's great, Sal. Isn't it?' David looked at Sally, who appeared to think it was anything but great. She looked tired and flat. He'd never seen her like this. She was normally such a bundle of energy he'd begun to worry that she might start to dwell on the twelve-year age gap between them. But this morning he'd have been hard-pressed to have said who looked older. An observation he thought it wise to keep to himself.

He continued to butter his toast. Sally was supposed to have been staying over last night. He'd planned a nice relaxing dinner, bought a bottle of good Burgundy. But the duck still sat uncooked in the fridge. And his throbbing head reminded him only too keenly that he'd ended up drinking the contents of the bottle on his own. Sally hadn't got in until the small hours.

The lack of rest didn't appear to have improved her mood. And her only reply to his comment was a snort, head down, as she continued to play with the muesli in her bowl.

'I thought you'd be pleased. Isn't this what you've been after? SIO on a murder inquiry.'

'No time. No resources. And, most importantly, no bloody suspects.'

'Isn't that how murder inquiries usually start?' David considered chancing a smile, but seeing Sally's expression thought better of it.

'Why couldn't I get a nice straightforward domestic?'

David looked up. 'I can't believe you just said that.'

She tossed her spoon into her cereal bowl, causing a splash of milk to slop onto the wooden tabletop. 'I'm sorry. But you know what I mean. It's just not how I imagined it.'

He leant across the table, covering her hand with his. 'I don't imagine the poor sod who was murdered had this in mind either.'

'I know.' Sally looked up at him and smiled. 'Ignore me. I'm just tired.'

'Anyway, if this isn't a run-of-the-mill murder and you manage to solve it, it would be a feather in your cap, wouldn't it?'

'Solve it?'

'Well, that's what detectives do, isn't it? Solve crimes.'

'You always make it sound so Holmes and Watson. Murder inquiries are more about data management than deerstalkers and calling cards.'

David tugged his forelock. 'I stand corrected. But it wouldn't hurt your promotion prospects, would it?'

'I don't suppose it would. But right now I've got more important things to worry about – like how I'm going to find a killer.'

CHAPTER EIGHT

Professor Margaret Bockford cursed under her breath. An unexpected knock on her office door was rarely a welcome occurrence. *What in heaven's name is Emma thinking of?* Her assistant was normally far too efficient to allow unexpected intruders to elude her. Once intercepted, if it was a day for receiving visitors, their presence was invariably announced via the telephone. And today, as Margaret had made Emma aware, was most definitely not a day for visitors. She had been grappling with the journal article she was writing for the best part of a month and the deadline for submission was tomorrow. Why on earth had she allowed herself to be badgered into writing the wretched thing in the first place?

She let out a deep sigh and pulled herself upright in her chair. 'Come!'

The heavy wooden door swung open to reveal a familiar figure. 'Hello, Margaret.'

A broad smile spread across Margaret's face. 'Clare. This is an unexpected pleasure.'

'Sorry to drop in unannounced. Emma told me you were busy, but I managed to persuade her I wouldn't take up too much of your time.'

Margaret closed her laptop, stood up and navigated her way round to the other side of her heavy wooden desk to greet Clare with a kiss. 'That's because Emma knows very well that you're one of the few people whose presence I welcome at any time.' And, she could have added, it was something of a relief to see her. Particularly since David had phoned last week to ask her to drop by the Bailsgrove dig to keep an eye on things. Something that, thanks to this benighted article, she had singularly failed to do. 'Now tell me, to what do I owe the pleasure?'

'I was hoping I might be able to pick your brains.'

'Nothing too technical, I hope. I've been trying to write a paper on socio-economic relations between the Roman military and the native British population in the first century AD for the best part of a month and I'm beginning to fear the well has run dry.'

'You're safe with me, then. I was wondering if you could give me a little bit of background on Beth Kinsella.'

'Now that I can manage.' She gestured towards the door. 'I could do with some air. Shall we take a turn around the quad?'

There was something about the quality of the light as it caressed the honeyed limestone of Breakspear College's quad that Margaret had always found calming, even in the most trying of circumstances. And today the Oxford college where she'd spent almost her entire academic career was showing itself to best advantage. She guided Clare to a wooden bench on the far side of the immaculately tended grass square.

Clare inhaled deeply. 'It's beautiful here, Margaret. So tranquil.'

'Don't let appearances deceive you, Clare. Underneath its serene exterior this place is a snake pit.' She laughed. 'But there's no denying I do love it. Now what exactly did you want to know about Beth?'

'Picking up her excavations where she left off is proving to be trickier than I'd anticipated. I'm beginning to wonder how much reliance I can place on her records. What was she like?'

Margaret sat, hands folded neatly in her lap, considering for a moment. 'If I had to sum Beth Kinsella up in one word I think it would be intense.'

'In what way?'

'Well, for a start, from the very first time I met her when she was a doctoral student it was obvious she was unflinchingly focused on her research.'

Clare looked at her quizzically. 'Aren't all research students focused on their research?'

Margaret laughed. 'Oh, you'd be surprised. There are a good many who are full of rip-roaring enthusiasm right up until the moment they actually have to begin to get stuck in and do some genuine hands-on research. Then suddenly almost anything seems to be more appealing than spending all their waking hours in the dark recesses of a museum store or surveying a windswept hill fort in the teeth of a howling gale.'

'But Beth wasn't like that.'

Margaret shook her head. 'No, she couldn't get enough of her subject. In fact, that was how I first got to know her. She pestered the living daylights out of me at every conference I attended. I have to confess after a while I got heartily sick of it. I began to avoid her.'

Clare looked shocked. 'You mean she was some sort of stalker.'

'I wouldn't put it quite like that, though she didn't really mix much with the other post-grads. No, she was more a sort of academic groupie. And it wasn't just me. She was like a sponge. She would hang around questioning anyone who appeared to know anything at all about the Iron Age and Celtic studies.'

'So, she was genuinely committed to her subject, then.'

'Unquestionably, but one can take commitment too far. Look at how she chose to end her life.'

'Before her suicide, would you have said she was obsessive?'

Margaret considered for a moment. 'You have to remember most of what I've been talking about was the best part of a quarter of a century ago. But no, I don't think I would. She wasn't what David would so eloquently refer to as "a nutter". At least not in her student days. I bumped into her at various events in the intervening years, and of course I've read most of her work since then. And there's no doubting the brilliance of her academic work. But I never really knew her on a personal level. I'm not sure that many people did. She was very' – she hesitated, searching for the right word – 'well, intense. And very private.' She sat silently for a moment, allowing her gaze to drift across the quad to the lilac-blue wisteria nodding its agreement in the late afternoon breeze. 'I am certain of one thing, though – something must have happened to make her leave her post at Sheffield.'

Clare looked at her quizzically. 'What makes you say that?'

'Well, she'd been in the department there for years. She was one of their leading lights. And then suddenly, completely out of the blue, she upped and left with absolutely no explanation.'

'Left or was asked to leave?'

Margaret shook her head. 'I really don't know. The university seemed to think very highly of her – or at least of the research ratings she brought the department. But she never did have any truck with academic politicking and intrigue. She was only interested in her work. So it's possible she told someone in the university hierarchy one too many home truths. On the other hand, if she really believed Bailsgrove was a shrine site it's not beyond the bounds of possibility that she resigned simply in order to be able to dig there and prove it.'

Clare's astonishment was obvious. 'Do you really think that's possible? That she might have given up an established academic position just to dig at Bailsgrove? I know postdocs at Salisbury who'd kill for a full-time teaching post.'

'From what I remember of Beth, I certainly wouldn't discount the idea.' She glanced down at her watch. 'Well, as lovely as it's been to see you, Clare, I really must get back to that wretched paper.'

As she went to stand up, Clare placed a hand on her arm. 'There's something else, Margaret.'

There was something in her tone that Margaret found troubling. Sitting back down, she turned to face the younger woman. 'Is everything alright, my dear? It's not something to do with Stephen and his accident, is it?'

Clare shook her head. 'No, it's nothing like that. I'm no further along with finding out what really happened.'

She was relieved to hear it. She'd grown fond of Clare during their time together digging at Hungerbourne. Working alongside her, she'd come to realise that she was a talented archaeologist with a rare gift for the subject. And a gift like that was not to be wasted. Margaret knew only too well how tough it could be to forge a path in archaeology. She was a well-respected professor at one of the world's most esteemed academic institutions now, but her own upbringing had been among what today might have been described as the rural poor. Her chair at Breakspear had been hard won, and it was a world away from the secure, respectable position as a bank clerk that her own mother and father had aspired to for the young Peggy Grafton. Her own struggle had made her all the more determined to do everything in her power to ease the path of others she encountered who had a love of, and an aptitude for, the subject.

She'd never met the man, but from the bare facts she'd gleaned from Clare, it seemed to Margaret that marrying Stephen had been a mistake of massive proportions. He appeared to have been a man who had entirely disregarded the passions and potential of the woman he'd claimed to love in order to make his own life more comfortable. Such behaviour was quite simply unforgivable; a waste of talent and of a large part of her young friend's life. She would never say as much to Clare, but Stephen exiting her life was the best thing that could have happened to her. It was only regrettable that it had been in a manner that had caused her so much pain – both emotional and pecuniary.

'The thing is, Margaret, I'd really value your advice, but I'd rather David didn't know about our discussion.'

Margaret eyed her warily. 'Well, that rather depends on what you want to ask me. I can't make any promises, Clare, but I'm willing to listen.' Clare hesitated. 'Oh, for heaven's sake. You know I would never tell David unless it's something illegal or risks life and limb.' Clare just looked at her. 'You're starting to make me nervous. What on earth is it? I promise I won't tell him.'

The worry was only too clear to read on her young friend's face.

'Alright, I promise I won't say a word to David. Just tell me what's happened.'

Clare took in a deep breath. Margaret could see she was nervous. 'OK. Well, we've found a whole series of quite sizable pits on-site that Beth and her team hadn't spotted before the site was closed down.'

Margaret said, 'I grant you that's a little troubling and I'd always assumed that Beth was a better excavator than that, but sadly archaeologists who display more talent in the lecture theatre than in running an excavation are not unheard of.'

Clare looked down at her feet. 'That's not the problem, Margaret. I wish it was. We've got almost all of Beth's old dig team working with us and from what I've seen so far, they're a pretty decent bunch of diggers. Even if Beth had missed something I'm not convinced they would, and the only things we've found in those pits are a couple of bits of modern rubbish.'

Margaret was starting to understand why her young friend was so anxious. 'I'm not sure I like where this is heading, Clare. Are you telling me those pits were dug after Beth's team stopped digging on-site?'

Clare nodded. 'It gets worse, Margaret.'

Clare reached down into her bag, withdrew her laptop and started it up. Margaret sat silently, hands folded neatly together in her lap, waiting for Clare to find what she was looking for. When Clare turned the laptop screen round to show her, Margaret was confronted with the image of what gave every indication of being an Iron Age sword.

'May I?'

Clare nodded, and Margaret took hold of the laptop, holding the screen out in front of her so that she could see the image more clearly. She placed the machine on her lap and adjusted the spectacles on the bridge of her nose to allow her to read the text that accompanied the image, mouthing the word 'Bailsgrove' as she did so.

Looking up from the screen, she let out a long sigh. 'Oh Lord, Clare, this is serious!'

'Quite. And there are more of them, all claiming to be from Bailsgrove. I'd be really grateful if you could take a look at the website for me and see what you make of them.'

Back in her office thirty minutes later and having partaken of her afternoon pick-me-up of a cup of Assam with just a splash of Irish whiskey, Margaret looked up from the laptop and across her desk to where Clare sat patiently, sipping her unadulterated coffee, waiting for Margaret to deliver her verdict. 'Well, I think you're right, Clare. They definitely all look Iron Age to me. How did you find them?'

'A local resident, Sheila Foggarty, tipped me off.'

'That was good of her. It's a welcome change to see some of the members of the Great British public taking an active interest in their heritage for once.'

'I'm not entirely sure that was her only motive. She's a parish councillor and made it very clear that she's opposed to the housing development.'

'Well, whatever her motives, she seems to have done us a favour in bringing this to our attention. I can see why you're worried, Clare, but what I don't understand is why you don't want David to know about this. I really think you should tell him. After all, he's ultimately responsible for the institute.'

Clare put down her coffee cup and straightened up in her chair. 'Oh, I've already told him.'

'Then I don't understand; why all the secrecy?'

'He told me I should leave it to the police.'

Margaret smiled. 'Well, he's got a point. If this is the work of nighthawks we're in dangerous territory here. You need to report it.'

'The thing is, I have. And they weren't interested. They said there was nothing they could do unless there was some actual evidence that anything had been stolen from our site.'

'Well, I suppose I can understand that from their point of view. If there's no hard evidence that this material has come from our site, then they could never attempt to bring any sort of prosecution. What did David say when you told him what the police had said?'

'I haven't told him.' Clare hesitated. 'I spoke to them before I told David.'

'Ah, now I'm beginning to see why you don't want him to know about our conversation. I'm assuming that you neglected to mention that small detail when David told you to report this to the police?'

Clare nodded reluctantly. 'The thing is, Margaret, he'll only tell me to drop it. And how can I do that?' She pointed at the laptop screen. 'I'm not an idiot, Margaret, I know these guys could be dangerous. If this stuff is genuinely from Bailsgrove then it would make it a nationally significant site – this could be the evidence that Beth Kinsella was looking for. I really don't understand where David's coming from on this. We can't just do nothing.'

But Margaret understood exactly where David was coming from. She'd come to know David pretty well since they had first worked together at Hungerbourne. And she'd come to understand that, though he would never admit it, there was only one thing in this world that he would ever consider putting before his archaeology and that was Clare's well-being. But she also knew that Clare was right. She couldn't in all conscience sit by and do nothing if there was even the faintest possibility that a site of such importance was being destroyed by nighthawks.

'David is just being cautious, Clare. He needs to think of the welfare of everyone who works for the institute, not just the archaeology. But I agree with you, we can't just do nothing.'

With the use of the word 'we', Margaret could see a look of relief spread across Clare's face and break into the first inkling of a smile. 'But what do we do, Margaret?'

'Well, for one thing I think you're right not to tell David about this. He would only stop us. And for another you mustn't tell anyone else on-site.' The worried look returned to Clare's face as quickly as it had vanished. 'Do I take it that it's too late for that?'

Clare nodded. 'Neil Fuller, our site supervisor, already knows about the pits and I got him to set up a couple of wildlife cams on-site for security, but I haven't said anything about the website.'

'Anyone else?'

'Just the police. Oh, and I mentioned it to Jo.'

'Well, don't say anything else to Fuller and ask Jo to keep quiet about it. The last thing we want is anyone shouting about it in the local pubs. If this is what it looks like, the more people that know, the greater the danger that one of them will end up getting hurt.'

'Understood. But what do we actually do?' Clare asked.

'Well, first of all we need to establish whether these finds are real or fake. There are plenty of gullible individuals out there who wouldn't know a La Tène sword from a Sabatier. And just as many online antiquities dealers who are willing to take advantage of that fact. And we also need to establish whether there is any actual evidence of provenance.'

Across the desk from her, Clare nodded thoughtfully. 'And I'm guessing that means we need to see these things for ourselves and meet the people who are selling them.'

Margaret lowered her head and peered over the top of her glasses. 'And in that assumption you are wholly correct, Clare. If we are going to do this thing the most important part is the "we" element. Do not contemplate even for an instant attempting to do this alone. Even if these artefacts don't come from our excavation, if they're not replicas and they've been found by metal detectorists then they're almost certainly being sold illegally. Under the Treasure Act, even if they came from a ploughed field, finds like this have to be reported to the coroner, not sold to the highest bidder on an auction site. So whatever else the people behind this may be, they're clearly not worried about the forces of law and order. And that should give us both pause for thought.'

Clare leant back in her chair and smiled. She was determined to enjoy this evening. It had been an exhausting few weeks at the dig and she'd spent most of her weekends working. But this evening she felt as if someone had opened a small portal into her old world. And as much as she loved the life she was making for herself here, she was looking forward to being pampered for once.

The call from James had come completely out of the blue. He had business in Salisbury, he'd said, and would she be free for dinner on Saturday evening? His treat. For a split second she'd considered refusing. James was part of her old life and she wasn't sure that she wanted to revisit it. But what harm could it do? And he'd been such a support since Stephen's accident, it would have seemed positively rude to turn him down, particularly as she couldn't think of any good reason to do so. Besides, it would give her an excuse to dust off her little black number and get dressed up for once.

Which is why she found herself seated in a Michelin-starred restaurant in the heart of the Wiltshire countryside, sipping an exquisite Riesling.

James raised a glass. 'Cheers. To old friends.'

Clare reciprocated and, looking around her, said, 'This place is lovely. How did you find it?'

'Oh, I've brought clients here once or twice in the past. For lunches mainly, but the food is always very good. You've been down here a while now. I'm surprised you haven't discovered it yourself.'

Clare flushed. 'I don't eat out as much as I used to.' And she could have added, *When I do it's more likely to be at the little cafe at the end of my street than in a swanky restaurant.* She lowered her voice and inclined her head in the direction of the menu. 'And this is a bit out of an archaeologist's price range.'

'Well, this evening none of that is your concern. I'm going to make sure you have the best of everything. You deserve it after everything you've been through.' He paused. 'It really is lovely to see you, Clare. And you're looking so well. So whatever the pay's like, life in the trenches must suit you.'

She lifted her glass in recognition of the compliment but swiftly deposited it from whence it had come as she became uncomfortably aware of the contrast between her own work-worn fingers and his plainly manicured hands. 'Well, thank you, kind sir.'

It was clear to Clare that life was treating James exceedingly kindly at the moment. When he and Stephen had worked together he'd always been well presented, but this evening he was immaculately dressed in what was undoubtedly a hand-tailored suit. And he'd arrived to pick her up in a Lamborghini, the like of which she suspected the quiet cathedral city had rarely seen. With his lightly tanned complexion and what she'd lay good money on being handmade brogues, he looked every inch the man about town. When they'd entered together they'd turned every head in the place. And it was rather a treat to be the centre of attention for all of the right reasons for once.

Clare took a bite out of her shellfish torte. 'Oh my God, James, this is amazing.'

He smiled. 'I'm glad you're enjoying it.'

'So what have you been up to since we last met? You seem to be doing rather well for yourself if that car of yours is anything to go by.'

'I always have been a sucker for fast cars. But you're right. I've been extremely lucky. After what happened to Stephen, I guess I decided it was time to take stock of my life. I'd always thought about going it alone, but somehow I'd never gotten round to it. Stephen's death made me realise you need to get on with your life before it passes you by. You can never tell what's round the next corner.' He hesitated, dabbing his mouth with his napkin. 'I'm sorry, Clare, that was in rather poor taste. But you know what I mean.'

She raised her hand, waving his apology away. 'Don't worry, James, it's fine. Stephen's crash made me reassess my life too. It's funny, isn't it – if it hadn't been for the accident, in all likelihood Stephen and I would still be happily married and the two of you would probably still be spending your Sundays together out on the golf course.'

Even as she uttered the words she doubted the truth of them. After all, Stephen would still have lost every penny they'd possessed without even bothering to mention it to her. And she wasn't sure that even the strongest marriage was capable of surviving that level of deception.

But whatever he might be thinking, James was clearly too much of a gentleman to say anything. He nodded. 'Only goes to show you can never predict the future. I'd never have guessed that you'd end up working in archaeology. It must be a fascinating life.'

She'd lost count of the times people had said that to her over the last couple of years. And in truth it was a fascinating life, if not quite as glamorous as most people pictured it. She couldn't remember the last time a colleague had swooped into site on a helicopter bearing instantaneously produced survey data on a top-of-the-range laptop. They were more likely to arrive in a rust bucket of a van, clutching a bag of nails and a couple of balls of string.

But that was one of the things that appealed to her about it – it was real. So much of her life with Stephen had turned out to be a sham. At least now she'd learnt to recognise things for what they were, and she'd come to realise what she wanted out of life. To follow her passions, and forge a life as her own woman – however difficult that might prove to be at times.

James said, 'So I know you're based at the university in Salisbury, and this may sound like a bit of a daft question, but what exactly is it you do?'

Clare said, 'Not daft at all. At the moment I'm directing an excavation up in the Cotswolds.'

'So does that mean you're in charge of all the students, then?'

She looked at him quizzically. And then suddenly she realised what he was driving at. 'Ah, I see what you mean. No. Not on this one. This is a contract job. All of our diggers are professional archaeologists. It's ahead of a housing development.'

'But you are based at the university?'

She nodded. 'That's right. The unit I work for is based there but we take on contract jobs too, to complement our research work.' *Or to put it another way*, she thought, *to keep ourselves from going under.*

He took a sip of his wine. 'So does that mean you have to work away a lot?'

'Not always – it depends. But for this one I'm away during the week and back home at the weekends.'

He nodded. 'Seems funny to think of you calling Wiltshire home. You and Stephen were down here as undergrads, weren't you? I seem to remember him telling me he couldn't wait to get away from the place. I would have thought that life was a bit too quiet down here for you.'

It wasn't something that she'd ever stopped to think about. She and Stephen had called the house they lived in home, but it could have been anywhere. What had made it home was that they'd shared it. And she may have ended up returning to Wiltshire because of a quirk of fate, but now that James had said it she realised she did think of it as home. There was nowhere else she would rather be.

She leant back to allow the waiter to clear her plate away. 'Oh, life in the sticks can have its moments too, you know.'

He didn't look convinced. 'Well, whatever makes you happy, I suppose. And if you're in charge of your own dig that must mean you're pretty successful in your chosen career.'

She casually flicked a breadcrumb off the crisp linen table cloth. 'Well, I'm certainly enjoying it. And you get to work with the most amazing people.'

'I'm sure. Do you think you'll stay down here?'

She nodded enthusiastically. 'I'm buying a house – not that far from this place, as it happens. Up on the Downs.'

He smiled. 'I'm pleased for you, Clare. You know I didn't like to say anything at the time, but I was worried about you after Stephen's accident. You two always seemed like such a close couple. I wasn't sure how you'd cope without him. But it sounds like you've got it all planned out.'

She laughed. 'Well, I wouldn't go quite as far as that. I've no idea how I'm going to direct a site in Gloucestershire and organise a house move.'

'Well, at least that flat of yours didn't look too big. You shouldn't have too much trouble packing it all up.'

She said, 'You would think so, wouldn't you? But I haven't finished unpacking from when I moved in yet. I've still got to go through all of that stuff from Stephen's study.'

James took a sip of his water. 'Really! I thought you said you were just going to dump all of that.'

Was it a trick of the light or had the colour suddenly drained from his face?

'I know what I said. But I'm glad I didn't; there are all sorts of personal bits and pieces in there. He kept all of the birthday and anniversary cards I ever sent him, you know. They're all in there.'

'Well, you know what I said at the time. I'd be happy to go through it all for you. Or just to dump it, come to that. It can't be easy rummaging through all of those memories.'

'It's sweet of you, it really is, James. But to be honest I'm finding it sort of cathartic. I think it's helping me to lay some of my ghosts to rest.'

'Well, the offer stands. If there's anything I can do, just ask. I know that as it transpired Stephen's business judgement wasn't always the soundest. I only wish I'd discovered what he was up to sooner. If I'd known he was intending to make those investments I might have been able to stop him, to persuade him not to go through with it.'

She could see the anxiety etched into his face. She lowered her voice. 'You can't blame yourself, James. I was his wife and I had no idea what he was up to. He was a grown man. It was his choice to make those investments. No one else's. And in the end he was the one who paid the price for his decisions. I'm rebuilding my life and you've done as much as anyone to help me out of the mess that he left behind.'

'Don't judge him too harshly, Clare. I know he wasn't perfect but Stephen was a good friend to me over the years. And I know that if I'd been lucky enough to have a wife like you and anything had happened to me, he would have done everything in his power to see that you were OK. So if you change your mind, you know all you have to do is call.'

CHAPTER NINE

Clare could taste the acid welling up in her mouth. She'd enjoyed the most relaxing weekend she'd had in a long time. And it had been lovely to catch up with James again, but today was a different story. She couldn't remember feeling as anxious about anything as she did now since she couldn't remember when. Standing here high on the edge of the Cotswold scarp looking westwards across the Severn Vale, they could see all the way to the Brecon Beacons. Margaret had been right: Crickley Hill really was the most stunning viewpoint.

Margaret pointed to a spot on the far horizon. 'Magnificent, isn't it. I've always loved this view. Look, that's Sugar Loaf!'

'I don't know how you can stay so calm, Margaret. Aren't you even a tiny bit nervous?'

Margaret turned to her. 'Oh, of course I am, my dear. Half of me wants nothing more than to dash back to the car and hotfoot it back to the Spread Eagle in time for last orders. But that wouldn't get us anywhere, would it? You don't suppose I've spent my entire career floating serenely thorough the hallowed halls of Oxford without a care in the world, do you? You seem to forget it was a very different world when I first entered academia. Women, particularly young working-class women, were not always made to feel welcome. I've had to face my fair share of anxious moments over the years. And if there's one thing I've learnt during that time, it's not to dwell too much on them before the fact. It really doesn't get one anywhere. Once you've decided to do a thing, you're much better off just getting on and doing it.'

Clare smiled. There was something about being with Margaret Bockford that always made her feel that no matter how dreadful the crisis, everything would be alright. And that was a valuable commodity at this particular moment. It had taken them a while to come up with their plan, but so far things had worked out pretty well.

Clare had set up an Outlook account in the name of Emily Draper and then she'd emailed the seller on the auction site saying that she was contacting them on behalf of her mother, who was a collector and potentially interested in buying all of the items on the website that were from Bailsgrove. Clare could almost picture the pound signs lighting up in the vendor's eyes when she'd read his reply. If, he'd said, her mother was genuinely interested in purchasing all of the items he was willing to put all of the lots on hold for up to a fortnight while they negotiated a price. He wasn't quite so delighted, however, when she'd emailed back saying that they were happy to proceed on that basis, but as the sum involved was likely to be considerable, her mother wanted to examine all of the items in person before committing herself.

After a brief exchange he'd agreed to a meeting in a 'mutually convenient location'. It had been evident from the exchange that that didn't include the home or office of the vendor – who still hadn't revealed his, or for that matter her, name. In the end it had been Margaret who had suggested Crickley Hill. As the site of not one but two Iron Age hill forts, the connection had seemed to appeal to Margaret's sense of humour. But that particular nicety seemed to have entirely escaped the seller, who was more interested in knowing how many other people were likely to be around and if there were any CCTV cameras in the car park.

They'd settled on meeting in the bottom car park at eight-thirty, an hour before the park gates were due to be locked, but a time when there were guaranteed to be hardly any visitors still about.

Clare glanced down at her watch. It was eight-fifteen, and despite Margaret's advice she couldn't help feeling distinctly queasy at the thought of what they were about to do.

Her anxiety had evidently communicated itself to her 'mother', and Margaret slipped a reassuring arm through hers. 'Come along, my dear. We can't put this off any longer. You'll be fine.' She added, 'You know, David dug up here when he was an undergraduate. He told me once it was why he decided to go in for prehistory.'

'But this place was a hill fort, wasn't it? I would have thought the Iron Age was more your sort of thing than his.'

'It is, but Crickley was a Neolithic enclosure millennia before the hill fort was built. It was the site of Britain's earliest battle – the excavators found hundreds of flint arrowheads. The whole place was burnt to the ground. The first farmers didn't inhabit the peaceful rural idyll popular television might have one believe.'

Clare looked around her. With the sun's rays dancing across the tops of the tall grasses on the side slopes of the hill, it was difficult to conceive of anywhere more tranquil. How many of the dog walkers and Sunday picnickers that used this place now had any idea of the lives that had been lived and lost on this very spot over the centuries?

Clare said, 'Well, I'm hoping for a slightly more peaceful encounter this evening.'

The car park was situated in an old limestone quarry. According to Margaret, it had been quarry workers that had first accidentally encountered parts of the fort's ramparts in the 1960s. And as the two women drew closer to the lip of the quarry they could see a white van sitting on the other side of the car park from Margaret's silver Range Rover. As they approached, a balding middle-aged man with thick metal-rimmed glasses appeared from behind the van.

Margaret half turned her head towards Clare and whispered, 'Remember that number plate. It might prove useful later.'

Clare silently chanted the letters and numbers to herself, but with little confidence she would retain them. The man stubbed out the cigarette he'd been smoking and crushed it underfoot before looking up. There wasn't the hint of a smile.

He stuck out a hand towards Margaret. 'Mrs Draper.'

Margaret, hair swept back beneath a pale blue patterned headscarf and sporting outsized sunglasses to prevent any chance of recognition, looked for all the world like a cross between Audrey Hepburn and the Queen, and every inch a woman of means.

Margaret said, 'I think you have, in a manner of speaking, already met my daughter.'

Clare, who, unlike Margaret, had never put in an appearance on television and consequently, they'd agreed, ran no chance of being recognised, was clad in an open-necked white blouse and black jeans, smiled at him. In return she received only an abrupt nod. And he showed no inclination to complete the social niceties by sharing his name.

Margaret said, 'Shall we get down to business, then?'

'You want to see the finds.'

Margaret said, 'I do hope we haven't come all of this way for nothing, Mr . . .'

Still he didn't give his name. Instead he opened the double doors on the back of the transit to reveal a tartan travelling rug spread across the back half of its interior. Clare moved aside to allow Margaret to get closer. He drew back the rug to reveal a dozen bubble-wrapped objects, two the size of baseball bats, which Clare guessed must be the swords. Glancing behind him, he leant into the back of the van and began unwrapping the items one by one. As he did so, it was all Clare could do to stop her jaw from dropping open. As well as the two swords there was a clutch of what looked like elaborate but enormous bronze safety pins, a dagger with its hilt entirely covered in delicately incised geometric decoration, and a six-inch-high figure of what appeared to be a man with his arms raised high on either side of his head.

Margaret turned to face the man, the palms of her hands turned upwards. 'May I?'

He nodded, and Margaret reached into the back of the van. Lifting her sunglasses onto the top of her head, she began examining the objects one by one. When she came to the dagger, she picked it up and turned round towards the daylight.

He stepped sideways, barring her path. 'What d'you think you're doing?'

Clare held her breath. It had all been going so smoothly. But Margaret was taking enough of a risk taking her sunglasses off. What if he recognised her? And now she was facing him down.

But she needn't have worried; Margaret didn't miss a beat. 'If you want me to purchase these items I need to be sure of what I'm getting. And for that I need daylight.'

The man hesitated, grunted and then grudgingly stepped aside. As she moved the object out of the shade of the van doors, the hilt of the dagger caught a shaft of sunlight. To Clare's amazement she could see the decoration wasn't, as she'd first thought, on sheet copper but on gold. *My God, if this stuff came from Bailsgrove it was a huge discovery.* Clare could feel her heart drumming away in her chest fit to burst. But Margaret's face betrayed no hint of excitement. After turning the dagger over in her hand several times she placed it gently back in the van, this time selecting the small figure to bring into the light. From what Clare could make out it was more roughly wrought than the dagger. But even from this distance she could clearly see that the smith who'd created it had still managed to imbue the face with a lively expression. Not only his hands but his eyes were turned heavenwards, and he had tiny individually crafted ears and a perfectly formed nose. But his feet appeared to still have parts of something else attached to them. It looked very much as if he had once formed part of a larger object.

Margaret placed the figure carefully back in the van and put her sunglasses back on before turning to face the man.

He asked, 'Satisfied?'

Margaret said, 'There is no doubting the antiquity of these pieces.'

He sniffed. 'Or their quality.'

Margaret inclined her head towards him in recognition of the truth of his statement. 'Or their quality.'

The man bent as if to start rewrapping the objects, but Margaret placed a hand on his arm. 'There's one more thing I need to be sure of.'

As he straightened up Clare could see he looked distinctly unimpressed. 'And what would that be?'

'What sort of provenance do these have?'

'Provenance? Like I said on the website, they come from Bailsgrove.'

Margaret said, 'Yes, yes, I know that's what it says on the website, but what proof do you have of where they come from?'

The man's face flushed bright red from top to bottom. 'Now, look here, if you're trying to say you don't think this lot are kosher, you can sling your hook.'

He turned, flung the travel rug over the top of the objects and slammed the doors of the van. Margaret wasn't having any of it. As he started to move round to the driver's side door she blocked his way. Clare followed, but stood by helplessly, feeling totally unequipped to deal with the situation that was developing in front of her.

He stood nose to nose with Margaret and yelled, 'Get out of my way!'

But Margaret, seemingly completely unperturbed, stood her ground. And in a quiet but implacable tone said, 'I think you've mistaken my meaning.'

He leant back, arms crossed. 'I'm all ears.'

Margaret said, 'I'm a serious collector. A very serious collector. And I'm willing to pay very highly for exactly what I want. I really don't have the slightest interest in how you came by these pieces. If I did, do you really suppose I would have agreed to meet you in a car park in the middle of nowhere? But as I say, I am a serious collector. And, like all collectors of any note, what I have to be absolutely sure of is where the pieces in my collection have come from. Provenance is all. If the pieces are right and the provenance is right, I'm willing to reward the seller very handsomely. But I have my reputation to consider. I can't run the risk of diluting the quality of my collection with inferior material.'

He looked Margaret up and down, apparently considering his options. And after a few moments' deliberation he said, 'Alright. I need to get something out of the van.'

Margaret moved to one side and he retrieved an A5 envelope from his glove compartment.

Passing the envelope to Margaret, he said, 'There you go. Take a look at those. If these aren't the real McCoy I don't know what is.'

Margaret withdrew a small sheaf of paper. On them were printed a series of photos of a selection of the objects, including the sword and the figure of a man, lying in the bottom of a series of freshly dug holes. She showed them to Clare. The holes might have been anywhere, except that in a number of them you could clearly see they sat within an open trench, and in one of them you could see not only the trench but the Portakabin that was now their site office in the background.

He added, 'That number at the bottom is the GPS location. If you've got any doubts you can check it out.'

Clare reached into her pocket and brought out her phone to take a shot of the coordinates.

He grabbed her wrist and shook his head. 'No photos. If you want the GPS coordinates, write them down.'

Clare nodded and punched in the numbers from a couple of the photos, though she and Margaret were only too well aware of where the site was. Margaret stuffed the photos back into the envelope and handed it to him.

He asked, 'Satisfied now?'

Margaret nodded. 'As soon as we've checked out the coordinates we'll be back in touch to make the necessary arrangements.'

They turned and walked away. Climbing into the Range Rover, they could see him return to the back of the van to rewrap his goods. As Margaret drove past him, windows down in the late evening sunshine, they could hear him whistling what sounded for all the world like 'We're in the Money'.

'Cheers, Margaret! You were sensational. I never knew you had a thespian streak.' Clare raised her glass in congratulations.

Margaret laughed. 'Thank you, my dear. I have many streaks. The majority of which are, thankfully, little known. But don't underestimate your part in setting up our little performance.'

Clare smiled. 'We don't make a bad team, do we?'

There was no doubt in Clare's mind now about where the finds had come from. And if nighthawks had been sniffing around Bailsgrove when Beth had been digging there, had they somehow been part of the reason why Beth had taken her own life? But whatever had driven Beth to suicide, Clare was desperate to find out what Margaret had made of the artefacts. And Margaret had steadfastly refused to tell her until she'd had a drink.

Not wanting to take the chance of being overheard, they'd decided not to risk the King's Arms in Bailsgrove. Instead they now sat in the slowly descending darkness of an early summer evening in the near empty beer garden of the George Hotel in Birdlip, only a stone's throw across the valley from their rendezvous point.

Clare studied her friend as she took a leisurely sip of her whiskey.

Margaret put down her glass. 'That's better.'

'So, are they real or fake?'

'Oh, there's no doubting they're real. They are a truly remarkable collection of artefacts. It was a privilege to hold them.'

Clare couldn't hide her excitement. 'So, Beth was right. There was a shrine at Bailsgrove in the Iron Age.' Seeing the look on Margaret's face, she added, 'Or do you think it might have been some sort of high status cemetery?'

Margaret shook her head. 'The local tribe round here were the Dobunni and their graves are pretty thin on the ground. Though, curiously enough, where we're sitting now is within a spit of one of the richest of them.' She waved her hand vaguely into the rapidly cooling night air. 'Somewhere out there on Barrow Wake they found the Birdlip Lady. She was buried with a stunningly decorated mirror, a brooch and two bronze bowls.'

'But couldn't we have something similar at Bailsgrove?'

'Well, there were a couple of male burials found near here that had swords that might not be out of place with the ones we saw tonight. But I don't know of any cemeteries that have the range of artefacts to match what was on display this evening.'

And one thing was for sure, if Margaret didn't know about them, that meant they didn't exist. So Bailsgrove couldn't have been a cemetery.

'So surely it must be a shrine, then. And an important one too, if what we've seen were all offerings.' Despite being half-terrified by the prospect of Paul Marshall's reaction, the archaeologist in Clare wanted to punch the air.

But much to her dismay, Margaret shook her head again. 'Not a shrine site. Or at least these finds don't help us in establishing whether it is or isn't.'

The exasperation in Clare's voice was plain to hear. 'But I don't understand, Margaret. What other sort of site could possibly produce finds like these?'

Margaret sighed. 'That's just the problem. I really have never seen an assemblage of artefacts like this one. And most definitely not from a site in Britain. All of these finds, without exception, have been made in continental Europe.'

'In Europe! So, what are you saying? We have some kind of trading post? Like the one at Hengistbury Head, but higher status?'

'No, though it would be rather wonderful to find another site like Barry's. I'm afraid our problem is considerably bigger than that. The truth is that, much as I'd like to say otherwise, there is no way that those objects originated on our site.'

'But how can you be so sure? Maybe Bailsgrove is truly exceptional.'

'It may very well be, my dear, but those artefacts were created across the length and breadth of Europe. The closest things I've seen to that beautiful dagger and the little figure come from a chieftain's burial in Hochdorf in Germany. The geometric decoration is unmistakably Hallstatt, I'd say from around the sixth century BC. But both of the swords are La Tène. They date to the very end of the Iron Age, three or four hundred years later. And the little figure has obviously been broken off from a krater.'

Clare asked, 'A what?'

'A sort of giant punch bowl, used for mixing wine and water. It's clearly continental. Admittedly it's just conceivable that some of the brooches could have come from Britain, but I think it's highly unlikely.' She paused to take a slug of her whiskey. 'But our biggest problem, the insurmountable issue that means that whatever those photographs appeared to show, the finds can't have originated from our site, is that the figure and both of the swords have been chemically treated to prevent corrosion.'

Clare's head was spinning. 'But there were still traces of mud on the figure. I saw it for myself.'

'Exactly. And there was mud on the hilt of one of the swords too. I'm not saying that those finds have never been on our site. Those photographs prove that they have. But that is most definitely not where they started life. And nor is it where they have been until relatively recently.'

Clare lowered her voice to a whisper. 'I really don't understand what's going on now, Margaret. Why on earth would anyone go to the trouble of burying a whole collection of genuine finds, worth a fortune on the antiquities market, on an archaeological site that had police crawling all over it and then dig them up again? It doesn't make any sense.'

Margaret drained the last few drops of her drink and replaced the glass firmly on the table. 'Indeed it does not, my dear. But that is most definitely what appears to have happened.'

CHAPTER TEN

The walk from Temple Meads station to Bristol University's archaeology department was considerably longer than Clare had remembered. She'd forgotten how steep the hills were in Bristol. And with the mid-morning sunshine beating down, she realised she'd significantly overestimated the beneficial effects of the odd bit of pickaxing now that she could no longer afford a gym subscription.

Trudging uphill, she tried to conjure some sort of sense out of what they'd discovered about the auction site objects. On the plus side, it might at least mean they were less likely to suffer raids from nighthawks. Though given that they had no clue why the objects had been planted on the site in the first place, much less why they'd been dug up again, they couldn't even be certain about that. And it still left them with a substantial portion of their site that had already been wrecked.

She'd decided, and Margaret had agreed, that there was no point in involving the police. And, given the fact that David already knew someone had been digging holes in the site, there wasn't much to be gained from telling him about what they'd discovered just yet. Anyway, what would they tell him? Someone had broken in, buried some of the most spectacular finds she'd ever seen and then taken them away again.

Whatever might have been going on at Bailsgrove, she was still no closer to knowing whether Beth had been right. Had it been the centre of some sort of cult before the Romans arrived? Or was it pure fantasy? Of course, there was still that dedication to Mercury. But when all was said and done, on its own it proved nothing. And if there had ever been any evidence of a shrine on the site, there was every possibility that their man in the car park or his supplier had put paid to any trace of it.

She paused for a moment to catch her breath. Standing in front of her, securely tucked behind iron railings, was a little brick building. Across the top of its facade ran Hebrew lettering. It must be a synagogue. Set back from the road and unassuming, she wondered how many people even noticed it was here. She smiled. 'Head in the clouds, but feet on the ground.' That was what her mum used to say about her when she was a kid. And in Clare's experience it was exactly how most archaeologists spent their lives. Bringing the obscure, the overlooked, the people who lived in the cracks into the light. But often missing what stood right in front of them – in plain sight.

In the end that's why she'd come to the conclusion that she needed to do the obvious thing. If she was going to have any chance of discovering whether Bailsgrove had been a major ceremonial centre, or if it was just the product of Beth Kinsella's deranged fantasy, she needed to speak to the one person who had known her better than anyone. She glanced down at her watch. Five past eleven. She hated being late.

Ten minutes later she found herself outside the office door of Dr Stuart Craig, Beth's ex-boyfriend. She took a moment to straighten the collar of her blouse and then knocked. No reply. She waited and knocked again. Still nothing. He must have given up on her. He hadn't waited long, had he? Caught between being angry with Craig and mad at herself for being so disorganised, she headed back downstairs to reception to see if she might be able to catch him later.

But as she stood talking to the receptionist there was a tap on her shoulder. She turned to be greeted by a figure she recognised instantly from his photo on the university website.

Stuart Craig was shorter than she'd imagined, with a thick head of hair and a neatly trimmed beard. In fact, her overwhelming impression was one of neatness and control. And though she couldn't have explained why, there was something about him that reminded her of a shop window mannequin.

He offered an unpleasantly damp and clammy hand. 'I couldn't help overhearing. You must be Mrs Hills.'

'Clare, please.'

He inclined his head in recognition and gestured to the mug of coffee in his hand. 'My caffeine addiction waits for no one, I'm afraid, Clare.' He smiled. 'Shall we go up to my office?'

She would have killed for a coffee herself, but there was no way she was going to ask for one when she was the one who was late. His office, when they entered it, was anything but neat. It made David's look like the epitome of minimalist chic. In front of them was a desk with a chair on either side. But all three surfaces had been engulfed in an avalanche of papers and books. Where did he work?

He pointed to two chairs wedged tightly together between filing cabinets in one corner of the room. 'Take a seat.'

He sat down beside her, apparently oblivious to the discomfort their physical proximity was causing her. These weren't the ideal conditions in which to ask someone whether their recently deceased ex had been a genius or certifiable.

He slurped noisily at his coffee. 'So, what was it you wanted to see me about? In your email you said you'd taken over the site Beth had been working on.'

'Going through her site journals and talking to some of her staff, Beth seems to have made some claims about the site that I'm having trouble verifying at the moment.'

'You do surprise me.' Craig made no attempt to disguise the sarcasm in his voice.

'You and Beth had been colleagues for a long time before she left Sheffield.'

'No need to beat about the bush, Clare.' He smiled. 'I take it you know that Beth and me were an item.'

Clare nodded. 'Neil Fuller mentioned it.'

'Neil Fuller. What's he got to do with it?'

'He was assisting Beth on the dig.'

Craig's face flushed red from bottom to top. 'Really? Didn't take him long, did it. He always did have a bit of a thing for Beth. Even in his undergrad days. But I wouldn't have figured she would have considered him up to her sort of standards. Just goes to show what people will stoop to when they're desperate.'

From what Neil had said, she'd thought that the two men had gotten on well, but apparently not. At least not as far as Stuart Craig was concerned. 'I didn't mean to suggest there was anything going on between them. Neil's married with a young baby.'

Craig said nothing. He was obviously less than entirely

convinced. Was there a chance Clare had misjudged things? It was clear that Neil had hero-worshipped Beth. Was that all it was? He wouldn't be the first man to have an affair while his wife was at home changing the nappies.

Very little had gone the way she'd envisaged it so far today. She needed to get things back on track. 'When you and Beth were at Sheffield you worked on a number of projects together.'

'That's right.' His eyes flicked distractedly around the room as he spoke; he was barely taking in a word she was saying.

'Were you surprised when Beth killed herself, Dr Craig?'

'Yes. No. I'm not sure.'

He stood up and, pushing a pile of papers out of the way to make room for his coffee on top of one of the filing cabinets, started pacing the floor. He stopped abruptly and looked up at her.

'Do you really think Neil Fuller is a happily married man?'

How could she answer that? She'd come here with every intention of being the one asking the questions, but now the boot appeared to be firmly on the other foot. 'Yes. I think so. I haven't seen anything to suggest he's not.'

He stood in the middle of the room, staring at the carpet and nodding his head, apparently conducting some sort of internal monologue that she wasn't privy to. 'Hmm.' Then all at once he looked up and said, 'Frankly I'm not sure what Beth was or wasn't capable of. I thought I knew her; I lived with her, I worked with her and yet I don't think I ever understood her. And to be honest now I'm glad I didn't.'

'You can tell me it's none of my business, but why?'

'Because she never cared about anyone or anything except her bloody work. Her theories, her mad bloody ideas. She was always chasing the ultimate answer. Her work always came first. Do you have any idea how it feels to play second fiddle to someone who's been dead for two thousand years?' He shook his head. 'Everybody had to support Beth, understand Beth. Beth the great bloody genius.'

He slumped down in a heap in the chair next to her, his head in his hands.

Clare asked softly, 'And was she?'

He lifted his head out of his hands and stared at her. 'Was she what?'

'Was she a genius? Everyone talks about how single-minded she was, how dedicated. Even how inspiring.'

'Pah! That's got to be Fuller.'

She didn't bother trying to deny it. 'Look, I'm not here to defend Neil Fuller, or Beth Kinsella for that matter. And I don't want to pry into your private life. I'm just a jobbing archaeologist who wants to do justice to the site I'm working on. But half of it has already been dug by Beth. So, what I really need to know is, was she really brilliant? You knew her better than anyone else. Do you think her work can be relied on?'

Pulling himself upright in his chair, he got up and moved to the other side of his desk. For what felt like several long minutes he stood motionless, staring out of the window onto the broad leafy street below.

When he turned to face her, he was a picture of calm, the resentment and anger so evident before dissipated. 'When I first met Beth, one of the things that attracted me to her was her intellect. No one could be in any doubt that she had a razor-sharp mind, but she didn't shout about it. It was plain for everyone to see. I used to love working with her on projects, sharing the buzz of discovery. Being with her was energising. But as she got more recognition, things began to change. All she wanted to do was the research. She had no interest in the day-to-day stuff academics have to do. No one likes it, but we all have to knuckle down and get on with it. But Beth thought her work was too important for her to be bothered with that. It was the same at home. Everything else could go hang. She spent more time living in the Iron Age than she did in the twenty-first century.

'She was focusing more and more on Celtic death and sacrifice; it was all-consuming. And things started to get really difficult between us. Our whole house became like a shrine to the long-dead. Most people have wallpaper – we had pictures of garrotted bog bodies and chariot burials. It destroyed our relationship. The university put up with it all the time it was upping their research scores in the REF, but eventually they couldn't even get her to submit the paperwork for that. It was impacting on all of us reputationally.' He hesitated. 'And there were worries about the effect it was having on her students too. It wasn't healthy.'

Clare asked, 'So, what happened?'

'It was inevitable really. Paints – Professor Clive Painter – put up with it for as long as he could. He's been in post for years. He's a nice old boy, but he was a bit long in the tooth to be in charge of a department. In the end even he could see that the only answer was for Beth to leave the department.'

'So she was sacked.'

'As good as.'

'And that's when she took Bailsgrove on.'

He nodded. 'Not long after that. Shows how deluded she'd become. From academic stardom to a nothing contract job in the middle of Christ knows where.'

Craig obviously wasn't any sort of diplomat. But she hadn't come here to have her ego massaged. She needed answers.

She fixed a smile in place. 'When I asked you before whether you were surprised when you heard Beth had taken her own life, you didn't seem certain. But you seem to be suggesting that she wasn't entirely stable. And that her fortunes declined rather rapidly. Did her suicide really come totally out of the blue?'

He paused for a moment as if to consider something, and then shook his head. 'No, not entirely. She lived in her own little bubble. It was difficult for anyone to predict what she would do – least of all me. Even when we were living together her actions weren't always entirely rational.' He sighed. 'So as much as I'd like to be able to tell you that you can rely on Beth's work, Clare, I really don't think I can.'

Clare stood up from where she'd been trowelling and stretched her back. Removing her sun hat, she ran her fingers through her hair. She felt exhausted. She'd tried to throw herself into her work on-site since her trip to Bristol. But despite her best efforts, it hadn't worked. Her visit to see Stuart Craig had left her feeling unaccountably despondent.

From what Craig had said it sounded as if Beth had been an obsessive and more than capable of weaving her own fantasies about the site. The single-mindedness certainly chimed with what Margaret had said about her. And much though Clare would have liked to believe what Neil had told her, she was beginning to wonder if his version of Beth had been coloured by his feelings towards her. Even if what Craig had said about Beth and Neil had been born out of jealousy, there must have been something there to have sparked it in the first place.

She knew that she should feel relieved. If they were going to keep the Hart Unit afloat they needed to get in, dig the site and get out as quickly as possible. And now that it seemed there was every likelihood that there was nothing of any real significance to find at Bailsgrove, that had just become a whole lot easier. Paul Marshall would be happy, the unit would live to dig another day and she would get to keep the job she loved. Perfect.

Yet she couldn't help feeling desperately disappointed. When she'd found that reference in Beth's journal to the inscription, she'd begun to hope that maybe, just maybe, she had an Iron Age shrine on her hands. Realistically it would have been a huge challenge to dig. She would have had to put a massive amount of work in to do the site justice. And her dealings with Paul Marshall thus far had left her in no doubt that digging the thing with him breathing down their necks would have been an absolute nightmare.

But despite all that she'd allowed herself to hope that this quiet Cotswold backwater might have been a centre of worship and sacrifice before the Romans ever set foot on these islands. And to hope, too, that she'd be the person to reveal its secrets. Now, instead, it looked as if they faced the prospect of weeks of digging with nothing to show for it but blisters, a bad back and the odd visit from abusive locals. *Pull yourself together, Clare! You should be grateful you've still got a job.*

She climbed out of the trench and headed back towards the Portakabins. Out of the corner of her eye she caught sight of Malcolm on the far side of the trench, staring intently at his patch of earth. He was wearing a puzzled expression. Over the last few weeks she'd come to learn that there wasn't much in the way of archaeology that puzzled Malcolm.

Intrigued, she called across to him, 'What you got, Malc?'

He shook his head. 'I thought it was another one of those bloody pits. But now I'm not so sure. Come and take a look!'

Clare made her way over to the far side of the trench. In front of her there was a circular depression about a foot deep. As she leant over to examine it she could see there was something poking out of the surface of the soil that had yet to be removed.

Malcolm said, 'The top of it was really loose and it had a bit of old crisp packet in it. But the stuff underneath is different. More compact. Nothing like the fills of the other modern holes we've found. And now there's this.' He waved his trowel in the direction of the dark brown earth that filled the bottom of the pit.

Clare pulled out her trowel from the pocket of her moleskins and, kneeling down, started to flick the soil gently away from the slender object that lay partially buried in front of her. It was a bone. As she worked more of it began to appear, revealing a gently curved appearance. Gradually a second bone appeared just to one side and then a third, on the other side of that. All in a neat, near parallel row.

She took in a deep breath and rocked back on her heels, looking up at Malcolm. 'Are you thinking what I'm thinking?'

Malcolm raised an eyebrow. 'Ribs?'

Clare nodded. 'Still articulated. And so tiny.' She stood up. 'Can you clear up around this and get it photographed? And, Malc, keep this to yourself for the minute, would you? I need to make a couple of phone calls.'

Clare and Mark Stone were standing on the edge of the trench waiting anxiously for Jo Granski to deliver her verdict. 'Well, you were right on the money, Clare. It's an infant. From the look of it I'd guess around six months.'

Mark Stone looked distinctly unimpressed. 'Any fool can see it's a baby. The question is how long has it been here?'

'I'm an osteo-archaeologist not a miracle worker, DCI Stone. There doesn't appear to be anything else in this part of the pit to date it. So we'll need a radio carbon date before we can say for sure.'

'And how long will that take, Dr Granski?'

Jo said, 'Generally a few weeks. Could be a while longer. A little quicker maybe if we could find some extra funding.' She looked at Stone hopefully, but to no evident effect. Turning to Clare, she said, 'And you're gonna need a Ministry of Justice licence to lift it, Clare.'

Stone harrumphed. 'Do you lot always fanny around like this?'

Jo said, 'In your line of work I would've thought you'd appreciate due process, Chief Inspector.'

Clare seemed destined to play the role of peacekeeper. 'It's all sorted. I sent off the application yesterday – as soon as we found the remains. And the licence came back this morning. So there shouldn't be any delay in excavating them.'

Stone said, 'Good. I need to know whether or not I'm dealing with a murder.'

Jo said, 'Now that I can tell you. You're definitely dealing with a homicide.'

Clare and Stone opened their eyes wide in disbelief and stared at her. And at precisely the same moment, both said, 'What?'

'See that horseshoe-shaped bone right there?' She pointed towards the tiny skeleton with her trowel. 'That's the hyoid bone. From what I can see so far, I can tell you that it has a cut mark on it. It's a sure-fire sign the child's throat's been cut.'

Clare opened her mouth in shock. 'Oh my God, that's horrible. It was only a baby.'

Stone reached inside his jacket and retrieved his mobile. 'Right, I need to get SOCO over here right away.'

Clare couldn't believe this was happening. There was a murdered baby in front of her. And now her whole site was going to be closed down. From the moment she'd got here she'd known she should never have persuaded David they should take this job on. But Jo appeared to have no such worries. She just laughed.

Stone stopped, his fingers poised over his phone. 'What's so funny?'

Jo said, 'Like I say, I can't give you an exact date until we get the RC dates through, but from the condition of the bone, given it's in an alkali environment, I'd say this baby has been here a while.'

Stone looked distinctly unamused. 'How long is a while, Dr Granski?'

Jo said, 'Hard to say for sure, but in my professional judgement we're talking centuries or millennia here, not months.'

Stone said, 'And you're certain about that?'

'As certain as anyone can be.'

Stone looked at Clare. 'Well, in that case, you've just escaped having your dig shut down again by the skin of your teeth.' As he walked away he turned back and shouted over her shoulder, 'And if you'd like to avoid it happening again, Mrs Hills, I'd suggest you have a word with your colleague here about her sense of humour. Wasting police time is a criminal offence on this side of the Atlantic.'

Every digger on the site had stopped stock-still. Most of them were standing up, staring. Clare could feel her face flush from top to bottom. She wanted the ground to swallow her up. Why on earth had Jo decided it was a good idea to play verbal tag with a member of the local constabulary in front of the whole team? Mark Stone already had a lowly enough opinion of her without Jo adding to it.

As soon as Stone had climbed into his car, Clare yelled, 'What are you lot staring at? We've got work to do.'

Jo turned to her friend. 'That was a little rough on them, Clare.'

Clare maintained a studious silence, half afraid of what she might say to her friend.

'Hey, come on, what's up?' Jo reached out to put a hand on Clare's shoulder, but she brushed it aside.

The Californian pointed in the direction of the burial. 'This stuff is exciting. I know you, you'd normally be ecstatic about a find like this. We've got some sort of deliberate killing on our hands, maybe even a sacrifice.'

Clare closed her eyes and shook her head. 'Oh, just ignore me, Jo. It's been a long week. I'm just tired, that's all.'

'OK. If you say so.'

Jo sounded unconvinced. But the last thing Clare wanted right now was the third degree in front of the entire dig team. 'I tell you what, Jo, if you want to help you could finish excavating the baby burial while Malc and I start digging those two pits that Neil found this morning.'

Jo acquiesced to her suggestion readily enough. And after a few hours of channelling her energies into the archaeology, Clare had calmed down sufficiently to regret being so short with both her dig team and Jo. Glancing at her watch, she was just about to climb to her feet and call a tea break when her trowel struck something solid in the pit she was excavating. A few small scraps of what looked to the untrained eye like dog biscuit in the plastic seed tray that lay beside her attested to the presence of prehistoric pottery in the top of the pit. So she was hopeful that this one might turn out to be ancient rather than the product of their 'friend' from the Crickley car park.

It took a few minutes of careful trowelling before she'd scraped away enough of the crumbling black earth to reveal a metal object about three inches across. On first glance it resembled a small bracelet. She lifted it, carefully placing it into the palm of her hand, and began to gently brush away the loose soil with her fingers. As she did so she could see the giveaway green colouration that told her it was made of some sort of copper alloy. But set into its surface were a series of interlinked spirals and swirls, much like the ones she'd seen on the La Tène sword. But these were inlaid with red and blue enamel.

She was sitting on her heels admiring the exquisite craftsmanship when a shadow fell across her, blocking out the afternoon sunshine.

'What you got there?'

She looked up to see Crabby leaning over the section edge. She smiled. Despite David's misgivings, over the last few weeks Crabby had become a regular visitor to the dig site. She'd begun to look forward to his visits. If truth be told, she rather envied his ability to believe in a myriad of possibilities that most of humanity dismissed as nonsense.

She lifted her hand up to show him. 'It's a terret ring.'

'A what?'

'A piece from a horse harness to you and me. But this one's Iron Age.'

Crabby's eyes lit up.

Clare stood up to let him get a better look and Jo came over to join them. 'Hi, Crabby. Wow, that's gorgeous.'

As the three of them stood admiring the find, Malcolm suddenly let out a shout. 'I've got another one.'

Clare said, 'Another terret ring?'

'No, another baby burial.'

Clare and Jo looked at one another.

Crabby's gaze flitted between Malcolm and Clare. 'Another one? You didn't say you'd found a burial.'

'We only had the first one confirmed a couple of hours ago, Crabby,' Clare said defensively.

There was something about his tone that was making her nervous. Why couldn't Malcolm have waited until the tea break to make his announcement?

The Druid looked at Clare and asked quietly, 'Can I see them?'

Clare said, 'Sure,' with a greater confidence than she felt.

The three of them made their way over to the pit with the

latest find, and, perhaps sensing his earlier error, Malcolm stepped respectfully out of the way. There was no doubting what lay in front of them. It was a second child burial, maybe a little older than the first. And this time there was something distinctly disquieting about the way it was positioned. It was ringed around by large lumps of honey-coloured limestone. The back of its skull had clearly been crushed by something very heavy and it was lying face down. In an instinctive gesture, Jo crossed herself, and then seeming to realise what she'd done quickly clamped her hands firmly down by her side.

Crabby meantime appeared to be in a world of his own. He crouched down, gazing reverently at the fragile heap of tiny bones that had once been a living, breathing child. Bowing his head, he mumbled something that they couldn't quite hear.

Then, standing up, he turned to face them. 'Beth was right. This place truly is hallowed ground.'

It was days like today that made Jo remember why she'd made the decision to move to this side of the pond. Sitting in the late evening sun in the beer garden of the King's Arms, sipping gin and tonic after a hard day's digging and a good pub meal – what could possibly be more perfect?

She raised her glass. 'Happy Solstice Eve!'

Clare reciprocated the gesture. 'Do you know, the last few weeks have been such a whirl I hadn't even noticed the date.'

'Don't worry, I'd say Crabby's got it covered for all of us.'

'Oh, don't, Jo. Why did Malc have to open his big mouth when Crabby was on-site?'

Jo took a long, appreciative sip of her gin before replying. 'Seems to me it wouldn't have made much difference. Crabby was gonna find out sooner or later. And he seemed pretty chilled about it.'

'I suppose so. What did you make of that second burial? It was a bit bizarre.'

'For today, maybe, but not if it's Iron Age. When you look at places like Danebury there was some weird stuff going on back then.'

'I seem to remember they found a shrine there, didn't they?'

Jo nodded. 'Sure did. And a whole bunch of pit burials. Old grain pits, mostly. They'd reused them to make offerings in the bottom, including some folks who looked like they'd been deliberately sacrificed.'

Clare said, 'Sort of makes a shiver run down your spine, doesn't it? Thinking about what must have happened to those babies.' She paused. 'I didn't know you had religious leanings, Jo.'

Jo looked at her friend, puzzled for a second about what she meant. 'Oh, you mean the whole crossing myself thing. I guess it was just a reflex. Some habits take a long time to fade. Us Granskis are all good, honest-to-God Polish Catholics. Or at least we were until this one came along. I think I was a bit of a shock to the system.' She laughed.

'Being an atheist, you mean.'

'No, dumbo. Being gay.'

Clare opened her eyes wide. 'What?'

'Oh, come on, Clare. Don't tell me you hadn't realised.' For a moment Jo sat silently, staring at Clare. Then she leant forward and broke out into a fit of uncontrollable laughter. When she finally managed to bring herself under control she said, 'You really didn't know, did you?'

'How the hell was I supposed to know? In the two years I've known you you've never mentioned it once.'

Jo sat looking at her friend, hands on hips. 'And how many times in those two years have you told me you're straight?'

Clare blustered, 'But it was obvious. I was married to Stephen.'

'Like that makes a difference.'

Clare looked at her friend in stunned amazement. 'Really?'

Jo raised an eyebrow and smiled. 'Really. You know, sometimes, Clare, I think you're one of the smartest people I know. And then others . . .'

The two women laughed. Clare said, 'OK. I guess you might have a point.'

When the laughter had subsided, in an attempt to recover her equilibrium, Clare returned the conversation to the fate of the dead infants. 'What happened to those babies brings it all home to you, though, doesn't it?'

Jo asked, 'How do you mean?'

'Well, for one thing, that life could be pretty gruesome and bizarre at times back in the Iron Age.'

Jo shrugged. 'I guess so. But some pretty crazy shit happens today too, wouldn't you say? You only have to look at what happened to Beth to see that. And like I told Stone, there's no telling when those burials date to until we get the radio carbon dates through.'

'But you said yourself they're not modern.'

'I know what I said.'

Clare placed her glass down and stared at Jo open-mouthed. 'Are you telling me they could be?'

'Ninety per cent sure they're not. But there's always a chance.'

'I can't believe you're telling me this.'

Jo lowered her voice. 'Look, they're probably old. And in all probability very old. And if they're part of the same pit group that that terret ring came from, they're almost certainly Iron Age. But it's impossible to be certain until we get the dates back from the lab.' She looked Clare straight in the eye. 'And we couldn't afford to have the site shut down, could we?'

For a moment Clare looked as if she was going to be sick. 'But what if they are modern? That would mean . . .'

'I know what it would mean.'

'We can't just sit around for weeks waiting for the RC dates to come through if there's even the slightest possibility that those burials are recent. What if there's some sort of baby killer in Bailsgrove?'

Jo couldn't remember seeing Clare get this stressed before. Not even when someone had tried to kill them both at Hungerbourne. 'Calm down, Clare. And lower your voice! I've already been on the phone to a guy I know in the lab in Florida. He can cut us a cheap deal to get them processed real fast.' Jo could see the anxiety written on Clare's face. 'Chill out! I didn't tell him.'

Clare's relief was clear to see. 'How long will it take?'

'I can take the samples once we've finished lifting them tomorrow. If we courier them, we should have the results in three, maybe four days. The way police budgets are these days we'll probably get the dates back before the police could anyway.'

Clare took in a deep breath. 'I hope to God you're right. I don't want to think about what it might mean if you're not.'

Jo said, 'One thing's for sure: we know that at least one of those children must have been buried there before Beth died.'

Clare asked, 'How do you figure that out?'

'Well, that first grave had been cut into by modern disturbance. The cut looked just like the pits our friendly neighbourhood nighthawks had left behind. So, if they were poking round the site between the police leaving and us arriving, the baby burial must be earlier. And they were on-site as soon as Beth's body was found.'

Clare sat silently, swirling the last dregs of her Chardonnay

126

around in the bottom of her glass. She seemed to be struggling with something. Eventually she looked up at Jo. It was difficult to make out her expression in the lengthening shadows.

Clare said, 'Well, as it seems to be the evening for confessions, there's something I need to tell you about those pits.'

Thirty minutes and another gin and tonic and white wine later, the two women sat staring into near total darkness, with only a couple of bats hunting their prey in the rapidly cooling night air for company.

Clare said, 'So you see, I really don't know what to make of it, Jo. Those finds obviously couldn't have come from our site. But they were definitely there. I've seen the photos. And the people who put them there must have come within inches of digging up that first burial.'

Jo grimaced. 'That would have given them one hell of a surprise.'

Clare said, 'I suppose we have to be thankful for small mercies. And I guess it means at least our man in the car park and his friends can't have had anything to do with the baby burials. If they'd known they were there, surely they would never have run the risk of showing Margaret and me those photos.'

Jo nodded. 'But what the hell has been going on here, Clare? First Beth kills herself. Then we have a bunch of antiquities dealers planting stuff on the site just to dig it up again.'

Clare said, 'The only sense I can make of it is that they were hoping to cash in on the publicity the site got from Beth's death being splashed all over the papers. Everyone in the country knew that this place was meant to be some kind of Celtic temple.'

Jo nodded. 'I guess. And all to give the stuff they'd ripped off from Lord knows where fake provenance so they could sell them to a bunch of rich dudes who don't give a damn.'

'And in the middle of it all we've got two murdered babies.

You don't suppose any of this had anything to do with why Beth committed suicide, do you?'

Jo wasn't sure what Clare was getting at. 'What do you mean?'

'I'm not sure I know, really. Maybe the guys with the antiquities were sniffing around before she died. Or maybe if, God forbid, those two burials turn out to be modern, perhaps she knew something about them.'

'I know you said Stuart Craig thought she was a fruit loop, but do you really think Beth Kinsella could have murdered two babies?'

Clare shook her head. 'No. Or at least I don't think so. But what if she'd seen something? Or found out something that she wasn't meant to know?'

Jo said, 'You mean what if she didn't kill herself after all?'

'Or perhaps she was frightened or being threatened in some way. Maybe that's what drove her to take her own life.'

Jo took a last slug of her drink. 'I'm beginning to think ye olde English Cotswolds aren't quite so idyllic after all.' She slammed her glass down on the table. 'Come on. Let's go inside. This place is starting to give me the creeps.'

CHAPTER ELEVEN

Standing on the threshold of The Lamb, Sergeant Tom West took a last drag on his fag before surreptitiously flicking it into the gutter. He'd spent most of the last three days trawling through the CCTV footage from every camera between Jack Tyler's flat and The Market Place in Devizes. And there were more of them than he'd ever imagined possible. If his missus wanted to watch the box tonight she could bloody well do it on her own. But square-eyed though he might now be, he felt an inner glow of satisfaction. His persistence had finally paid off.

Checking through Tyler's bank account, it was obvious he'd been in money trouble. And West had discovered that he'd flogged his car a few weeks ago. Given the amount of alcohol still in his system when he'd been found and the bowl of vomit lying in the middle of the living-room floor, it didn't take Sherlock Holmes to work out that he must have been out on the tiles the night before he died.

He'd had a hunch that without a car Tyler's favoured watering hole wasn't likely to be far from home. So he'd asked Sally Treen if he could spend some time trawling through the CCTV footage in the area. She'd made it clear she thought he'd be on a hiding to nothing. Nine out of ten times shops and pubs either had dummy cameras up or they wiped the footage every few days. Tyler's neighbours claimed to have heard voices sometime after midnight, but nothing after that. There was absolutely no sign of a murder weapon and SOCO had found bugger all else of any use by way of forensic evidence. So in the end, as it was his time he was wasting, Sally had agreed.

He'd eventually struck lucky when he'd picked up an image of Jack Tyler staggering into the appropriately named Snuff Street from The Market Place on Thursday night. According to Frank Barlow, he'd died sometime on Friday morning.

From what West could make out from the grainy images, Tyler looked as if he'd been absolutely bladdered. And that tallied with what Frank had said in the autopsy report about the amount of alcohol still in his bloodstream. It didn't seem to get them very much further, but it was at least a record of the last time he'd been seen alive. Then a few minutes later someone else walked into shot. He seemed to be saying something, though West couldn't make out what. He headed towards Tyler and for a good couple of seconds glanced upwards, almost straight at the camera. Tyler tried to stagger to his feet, then the second man dragged him fully upright and appeared to be helping him out of the alleyway. After that he'd found nothing in the way of useful footage. But those few seconds where Tyler's rescuer had looked up at the camera were enough for West to get a pretty clear image of him on the freeze-frame.

When he showed it to Tyler's neighbours they claimed not to recognise the bloke. So West had started on a trawl of the pubs and bars on the Market Place side of Snuff Street. Thus far he'd had no luck. Though he did at least now know they served a decent pie in The Vaults. He wasn't altogether surprised at his lack of progress. Some of the places he'd been in so far were a bit of a long shot – all a bit upmarket for Tyler's sort.

As he stepped inside he was relieved to see that The Lamb looked like a different kettle of fish. It was a proper pub.

There were a couple of blokes sitting at a table by the fireplace. But other than that there were no more customers to take the barman's attention. 'What can I get you?'

'Better make it an orange juice. And a bag of cheese and onion while you're at it.'

'You sure, mate? You look like you could do with a pint.'

West showed him his warrant card.

'Ah, right you are then.' He handed West his drink.

West took a slurp before answering, 'Business, unfortunately.'

The barman, a stocky, straightforward-looking man in his late fifties with a crew cut, leant towards him and asked in a whisper, 'Is this to do with what happened to Jack?'

Bingo. West's face brightened, but he suppressed the urge to smile. He didn't want to give anyone the wrong impression. 'You knew Jack Tyler, then.'

He nodded. 'He used to be a regular down here.'

West echoed his words, 'Used to be?'

The barman said, 'Jack ran up against a bit of bad luck. He didn't like talking about it, but I think he lost his job a while back. We haven't seen so much of him in here since.'

'Was he in here on Thursday night a couple of weeks ago?'

Without a moment's hesitation the barman nodded.

'Are you absolutely sure? It couldn't have been another evening?'

'Positive. Like I say, we hadn't seen him in a while, but Scatter Gun were playing and Jack left no one in any doubt that he didn't think much of them.'

West asked, 'Was he normally a bit of a loudmouth?'

'I wouldn't have said so, but he'd had a few and I think his volume control was shot, if you know what I mean.'

West nodded his understanding and reached into his jacket. He placed the CCTV still of the second man on the bar. 'Do you recognise this fella?'

The barman nodded, but the apprehension was clear in his voice. 'That's Damian. Damian Kelly.'

West drained the last of his orange juice. 'He a mate of Jack's?'

'Used to be. I think Jack's done the odd bit of work for him in the past.'

West asked, 'What line of work's Mr Kelly in?'

'Builder. Sub-contracts for bigger firms mainly. But like I say Jack hadn't been in here so much lately. So I don't know what he was up to these days.'

West got the impression that the barman was trying to avoid telling him something. 'Was Mr Kelly in here on that Thursday night? The last night Jack was in here.'

The barman nodded reluctantly. 'Yes. I think he might have been.'

'You think?'

'No. I'm certain he was. Jack had come in and bought himself a couple of pints early in the evening.' He inclined his head in the direction of the pub's two other patrons sitting by the fire. 'He sat over there nursing the second one until Damian came in. Damian had been down the races in Salisbury in the afternoon and won a few quid. He stood Jack his drinks all night.'

West said, 'That was very generous of him. Does Mr Kelly often flash his money around?'

The barman reached down behind the counter and, producing a cloth, began wiping the bar down in what appeared to West to be an entirely unnecessary gesture. 'To be truthful I've never known him win before. Betting's a mug's game if you ask me. But Damian's always liked a flutter.' He looked up at West. 'You a betting man?'

West shook his head. 'Football. Swindon Town. What about you?'

'Wrong-shaped ball, mate. The blue, black and whites for me when I can get away from this place.'

West couldn't help smiling. 'Takes all sorts.' He paused. 'Did you happen to notice if Jack and Damian left at the same time on the Thursday night?'

The barman said, 'It was packed in here because we had the band on so I wouldn't normally notice. But as it happens Jack was so pissed he nearly knocked a bloke off his bar stool on his way out.'

'Any idea what time that was?'

'Can't have been long before last orders.'

West asked, 'And did Damian Kelly leave at the same time?'

A look of obvious relief spread across the barman's face. 'No. Damian and a couple of the other lads stayed behind to give me a hand clearing the glasses when we closed up.'

'Don't suppose you happen to know where Damian Kelly lives?'

With a hint of reluctance in his voice, the barman said, 'Not sure. Somewhere off Nursteed Road, I think.'

West thanked him and turned to leave, shoving his crisps into his jacket pocket alongside the photo of Damian Kelly. He stepped out into the June sunshine with a decided spring in his step. A pie, a bag of crisps and a suspect. He couldn't wait to share the good news with the DI. It was amazing what a bit of shoe leather and some good old-fashioned police work could produce.

The limestone dust coated Clare's skin like a shroud. She took a swig from her water bottle and swallowed a couple of paracetamols. She had a splitting headache, and it wasn't all the fault of last night's wine. The whole team seemed subdued. The site was unnaturally quiet in this oppressive heat. There was a storm coming and Clare wished the weather would get it over and done with.

She looked up to see Jo kneeling down by the side of the cutting. 'Is it tea break yet?'

Jo said, 'Nope. But you're in charge, boss. You can have a cup of warm brown sludge any time you damn well want.'

Clare laughed. 'I guess I can. But I need to crack on with this. We need to get this pit dug and photographed before the rain sets in.' She lowered her voice. 'How are things going at your end?'

'Just finished sampling the second one. All I need to do now is package them up and get them down to the pick-up point at the gas station. They should be winging their way to Florida by this afternoon.'

Clare nodded. She'd barely slept a wink last night. She couldn't stop thinking about the child burials. She knew Jo was probably right. She always was – which was why she was the best in the business. But as unlikely as it was, even Jo had said there was a possibility that the burials might be modern. When Clare had finally dropped off to sleep she'd dreamt about Beth Kinsella's lifeless body hanging up there in the beech grove. And when she'd woken she couldn't escape the feeling that there was something going on here at Bailsgrove that she was missing.

She stretched out her hand. 'Give us a hand up, will you?'

Jo reached down towards her, but as she was about to grab Clare's hand she stopped and pointed towards the pit that Clare had been digging. 'What's that?'

'What's what?'

Clare turned to look behind her as Jo stepped past her into the trench. Now that Jo pointed it out she could see there was a tiny light brown splodge of something just emerging from the top of the loose soil next to where her hand shovel lay.

Jo said, 'Hand me your leaf, will you?'

Clare reached into her toolbox and handed her the plasterer's leaf tool. It was an implement they normally reserved for the most delicate jobs on-site. Clare watched Jo, entranced at the skill with which she wielded it, but with growing trepidation about what it might reveal. As Jo worked, the splodge became larger and gradually took on a smooth, domed appearance.

Clare felt something cold on her skin. 'Did you feel that? I think it's starting to spit.'

Jo ignored her. Without looking up, she said, 'Grab another leaf and give me a hand, will you!'

Clare knelt down on the opposite side of the pit and within half an hour the two women had uncovered what even the untrained eye could tell was the skeleton of another infant. This one had no visible signs of injury and was lying on its side. It looked for all the world as if it was asleep.

Clare looked across at Jo. 'Three was a sacred number in the Celtic world, you know.'

Jo just nodded. 'We need to get this little one lifted before the rain sets in.'

'I'll nip down to the Portakabin and get the skeleton recording sheets and some bags.'

As she stood up she could see Crabby in full regalia striding determinedly towards them. 'Shit.'

Jo asked, 'What's up?'

'You're about to find out.'

Crabby panted to a stop beside the side of the cutting. 'Happy solstice!'

Clare smiled. 'Happy solstice, Crabby! I'm surprised you're not down at Stonehenge.'

Why, oh why, couldn't he spend his day recovering from a hangover at a stone circle like every other pagan of her acquaintance? Though, thinking about it, Crabby was probably the first real pagan she'd ever spent any time with.

'I greeted Sol at the dawn ceremony at the Rollrights this morning, but I wanted to come and say a solstice blessing for the old souls.'

He looked towards the two now empty pits where the first two infant skeletons had been found the day before, his dismay only too evident. Clare stood ramrod straight, frozen to the spot, suddenly realising that she was blocking his view to the pit behind her where Jo was still working.

'Where have they gone?'

'We finished lifting them this morning. We had to make sure they were safe, Crabby, with the weather coming.' She pointed skyward towards the thickening clouds.

Before the Druid had chance to reply, a metallic blue Mitsubishi four-by-four swung into the gateway at considerable speed. On its roof it was sporting what looked like a small satellite dish. Every head in the place turned to watch as a man in an impeccably cut dark grey suit, with shoes you could see your face in stepped out. He was followed by a stick-thin young woman in her early twenties who lost no time in retrieving a shoulder bag and a camera that looked big enough to crush her from the rear of the vehicle. She hurried after the besuited man who was heading straight for where they were standing.

Crabby held up a hand in greeting. Clare stood dumbstruck. Jo, meantime, was now standing beside her.

'Ah, there you are, Mr Crabbs.' The besuited man ran his fingers through his immaculately cut head of hair. He turned to the young woman, who was valiantly puffing her way up the slope a few yards behind him. 'Are we ready to roll, Sophie?'

The young woman nodded, withdrawing what looked like a large furry animal from the shoulder bag and slipping it over the microphone on the camera.

Clare stepped out of the trench. 'Excuse me. No one is rolling anywhere until someone explains to me exactly what's going on.'

The besuited man turned and bestowed a smile as wide as the Severn on Clare. 'Ben Jackson. Syndicated News Network. Are you one of the dig team? Is there any chance we'd be able to have a word with your boss?'

Clare drew herself up to her full five feet six and declared in what she hoped was her most confident voice, 'Clare Hills. Site director. And for the avoidance of doubt, I am the boss.'

Ben Jackson appeared to be made of Teflon. The rebuke slipped over him without a hint of recognition. 'Oh, fabulous. That makes life so much easier. We won't take up too much of your time. We're just going to film Mr Crabbs here performing his ceremony. We'll be out of your hair in no time.'

Clare glared at the Druid. 'Crabby!'

'It's like I said, Clare, I just wanted to perform a ceremony for the old souls. I got chatting with Ben and Sophie when they were up at the Rollrights filming the solstice this morning. When I mentioned I was coming up here later to say a blessing over the babies they said they'd be interested in filming it.'

Clare said simply, 'I bet they did.'

She was gobsmacked. She looked at Crabby. He appeared to be entirely without guile. Could anyone be that naive? If anyone could, Crabby could.

Crabby turned to Ben Jackson. 'I'm sorry, Ben, we're too late. They've already dug them up.'

All of a sudden Sophie let out a squeal and pointed. 'No, they haven't. Look, Ben!'

Ben Jackson turned to look and made as if to step into the trench.

Before he could get any further Jo stepped forward and placed a hand firmly on his chest. 'No, you don't, Ben.'

From the look of total incomprehension on Ben Jackson's face he clearly wasn't used to hearing the word 'no'. And, Clare suspected, most particularly not from a woman.

Clare said, 'I'm afraid we can't have just anyone careering about in the trench, Mr Jackson. This is an archaeological excavation, not a circus. I'm afraid I'm going to have to ask you to leave.'

Ben Jackson gave no indication of having heard a word she'd said, and instead, standing on tiptoes to see over Jo's shoulder, he began gesticulating wildly. 'But I can see it. You've still got one down there.'

Crabby intervened. 'Isn't that where you found that piece of horse harness yesterday?'

Clare looked at Jo, who just shrugged. There was no point in denying it. 'Yes. Yes, it is.'

Crabby murmured to himself, 'Three of them.' Then, his voice gentle, he said, 'I'd count it as a personal kindness if you'd let me say a solstice blessing, Clare. To settle the souls of the old ones.' He glanced up towards the stand of beeches crowning the top of the hill. 'There's been enough death at this place.'

For several seconds Clare just stood and looked at him. With his white sheet, staff of twisted hazel and biker boots, at first glance most people would assume he was, as David had so quaintly put it, 'away with the fairies'. But there was a quiet certainty and calm about him that Clare found impossible to refuse. And though she didn't have a religious bone in her body, there was no denying that if anywhere could benefit from a blessing right now, it was Bailsgrove.

'OK, Crabby. Jo will show you where it's safe to stand.'

Without warning, Crabby stepped forward and enfolded Clare in a bear hug. As he did so he whispered into her ear, 'Thank you. You're a good woman, Clare Hills.'

She couldn't have explained why if you'd asked her, but as Jo helped Crabby down into the trench Clare felt tears welling up in her eyes. She turned to wipe them away with the back of her hand and as she did so she found herself looking directly at Ben Jackson.

He pointed towards Crabby. 'Honestly, it won't take a minute. Then we can be on our way.'

What harm could it do? And if she said no to them filming on-site they were bound to do a piece with Crabby afterwards anyway. She could see the headlines now: 'Archaeologists refuse access to death site. More bodies found.' It would run and run. At least this way it would be a positive story.

Finally, she conceded. 'Fine. But you can't go into the trench. You'll have to film from up here.'

Ben Jackson was nodding furiously and waving Sophie towards him. 'Of course. Fabulous. Sophie, have you got that thing set up yet?'

Clare walked away, leaving Jo to invigilate the proceedings. She might as well go and get the recording sheets from the Portakabin. At least then they'd be able to get on with lifting the skeleton as soon as the news crew had gone. In the event, it took her a while to find out where Jo had put them. And when she left the office to make her way back up to the cutting she could see Ben Jackson hurrying towards her.

She asked, 'Have you got what you needed, Mr Jackson?'

'Yes, yes. Crabby was fabulous. Just fabulous. There's only one more tiny thing that would make it perfect. And then we really will get out of your hair.'

Clare was thinking they'd been in her hair for quite long enough and she wished they'd do as they'd promised and leave. But better not to rile them. She pinned on a smile. 'And what would that be, Mr Jackson?'

'Ben, please.' There was that mile-wide smile again. 'It's just that you've been so kind letting us film here. It would be great to get your views. A real expert – the person in charge of all this.'

There was no denying she was indeed 'in charge of all this', although she was beginning to feel less and less like an expert as the days wore on. But she could see that there was no getting rid of him. And Jo still looked perfectly happy chatting away with Crabby. Things couldn't have gone too badly.

'OK, Ben. As long as it won't take long.'

'Fabulous. Let's just have you back up by the side of the trench so we've got some action in the background.' He hallooed across to Sophie, who was rummaging round in the back of the four-by-four. 'Sophie, be a love and bring the kit back up, would you? Clare here is going to do a piece for us.'

When they got back up to the trench, Clare handed Jo the recording sheets and whispered, 'Everything OK?'

Jo mouthed, 'A breeze.'

Reassured, Clare turned back to Ben Jackson. 'Sorry about that. But we need to get on with the job.'

'No problem, we've taken up a lot of your time.' Waving again, he said, 'Sophie, Sophie. The wind's picking up a bit. Can you get a mic on Clare?'

After five tedious minutes of wires, microphones and power packs being passed up, down and through various items of Clare's clothing with varying degrees of embarrassment on everyone's part, Ben and Sophie declared themselves to be content with the situation. Clare was positioned in front of the trench with Jo in the background attending to her task.

Ben Jackson said, 'So just look at me, not the camera, Clare.'

She suddenly had an overwhelming urge to run screaming into the Portakabin. *Come on, pull yourself together! You've seen David do this umpteen times. How difficult can it be?* She opened her eyes wide and took in a deep breath.

Ben Jackson said, 'Ready?' Clare nodded. 'So, if you can just say your name and job title to the camera for me.'

Clare's mouth was so dry she could barely force the words from her lips. 'Clare Hills, Site Director for the Hart Archaeological Research Institute.'

'So, Clare, we're here at the Hart Unit's dig site in Bailsgrove. And we hear you've made some rather amazing discoveries. What exactly have you found here?'

Where to start? 'Well, there's some evidence to suggest that Bailsgrove was an important site before the Romans even set foot in Britain.' Ben Jackson nodded encouragingly. 'Some people think it might have been an Iron Age shrine.'

He lowered his voice to an almost reverent whisper. 'So here, lying just inches beneath our feet, you've found a Celtic temple.'

Clare said, 'Well, we might have. It's early days yet.'

'And right in front of us' – Sophie swung the camera round to focus on Jo in the trench – 'you're excavating the burial of a child.'

The camera swung back to focus on Clare. 'Err, yes.'

'And this is the third baby you've dug up so far.'

Clare nodded nervously. 'That's right.'

'Talk us through what happens to them when you find a burial, Clare?'

This didn't seem to be going too badly after all. She began to relax.

Clare launched into her subject with gusto. 'Well, as you can see we excavate them with extreme care. We're lucky to have Dr Josephine Granski on our team. Jo here is one of the world's leading human bone specialists.' Jo glanced up and smiled. Ben gestured at her to keep digging and Jo duly obliged. 'Jo records the position of every bone and photographs the burial before it's lifted. And then the remains will be taken away for detailed analysis.'

Ben Jackson said, 'We've spoken to the local Druid, Wayne Crabbs, this morning, Clare. And Mr Crabbs is concerned that the souls of these dead babies should be at peace.' Clare didn't like the way this was heading. 'How do you justify disturbing the last resting place of these children, Mrs Hills?'

Clare managed to maintain her smile. 'It's part of our job. We're here to tell their stories. By studying their bones we can help reveal the details of their short lives and discover what life was like here in the past. We can give these children a voice.'

Ben Jackson nodded. 'Is it true that one of the babies had had their throat cut, and another had been beaten to death with a rock?'

Clare wiped the sweat from her palms on the front of her moleskins. She could feel her heart pumping ten to the dozen. She took in a deep breath before answering. 'Two of the skeletons did show some signs of violence.'

'So what do you say to those who say these children have suffered enough?'

Clare could feel her colour rising. *Keep calm, just keep calm!* She struggled to control the pitch of her voice. 'But no one would have known they'd suffered a violent death unless we'd dug them up in the first place.'

'Don't you think what you're doing here is disrespectful, Mrs Hills? Digging up babies, just to build houses. Aren't you putting profit before people?'

Clare could feel the last vestiges of her self-control slipping away. 'We're just doing our job. Without our work no one would know what happened here.'

Ben Jackson leant forward and in hushed tones said, 'These children have lain here undisturbed for centuries. Wouldn't you agree that the bones of the ancient dead deserve to rest in peace, Mrs Hills?'

Clare lost it. She jabbed a finger at Ben Jackson and all but yelled at him. 'Now look here. You have absolutely no idea what you're talking about. We don't even know yet if the bones are ancient.'

Ben Jackson sensed blood. 'Are you saying these burials could be recent?'

'Well, yes. What I mean is probably not. They're almost certainly old. But we won't know for sure until we get the radio carbon dates.'

'Given recent events at Bailsgrove, Mrs Hills, shouldn't the police be informed about this?'

Clare's jaw stiffened. She almost spat the words out at him. 'We're professionals, Mr Jackson. They have been.'

'And you can confirm that Gloucestershire constabulary have allowed you to continue excavating at a potential murder scene?'

Clare said, 'For your information they were perfectly fine with it. Even if you're not.' She ripped the microphone from her T-shirt and flung it at Ben Jackson's feet. 'Now if you've got what you came for, Mr Jackson, will you kindly leave my site.'

'Christ on a bike, Clare! What on earth possessed you?'

David was standing behind his desk in the archaeology department. The moment he'd finished watching the piece about the dig on the late-night news he'd picked up the phone to Clare, demanding to see both her and Jo first thing in the morning in his office in Salisbury. Last night's debacle had been bad enough, but this morning fanned out on his desk in front of him were a host of tabloid newspapers all featuring Bailsgrove. The top one sporting the unforgettable headline, 'Death Rate Soars at Hart Unit's Bailsgrove Horror Dig'.

He plucked one from further down in the pile. 'Do you want me to read them to you? Just so you can understand what your fifteen minutes of fame has cost us. Here we go. Have a listen to this!

'"Death has revisited the ill-starred Bailsgrove dig site. Recent scene of the grisly suicide of Druidic specialist Dr Beth Kinsella, Bailsgrove has now become the scene of another bizarre pagan ritual, with local Druid and ex-biker Wayne 'Crabby' Crabbs performing rituals over what the archaeologist in charge of the excavations, Clare Hills, maintains may be modern baby burials. When asked about the burials, DCI Mark Stone of Gloucestershire constabulary refused to comment."'

Clare held up a hand. 'Please, David. I know what they say. You don't need to labour the point.'

He slapped the paper down in front of her. 'Oh, but I think I do, Clare. You're the one who insisted we take this job. If you recall our conversation at the time I was less than convinced. But I let you talk me into it because we were desperate for the money. As you so correctly pointed out, without the money from Bailsgrove the Hart Unit is finished. So you of all people should understand the consequences of what you've done.'

Jo, who up until that point had been perching precariously on a pile of boxes in the corner of the office, stood up. 'Hey, come on, David, cut Clare some slack! It wasn't all her fault.'

David turned his ire on the Californian. 'No, too damned right it wasn't, Jo. It wasn't all Clare's fault. What the bloody hell were you doing while all this was going on? Clare's only just started in this game, but I thought you'd know better with your experience. I couldn't believe what I was watching on the news last night. Not only was Clare standing there happily telling the world we could have a baby killer on the loose and the police don't seem to care, but there you were chit-chatting with that weirdo in a bed sheet as he chanted some sort of gobbledygook over a dead child.'

He turned towards the window, refusing to look at either woman for fear of what he might do. Exams finished, the scene below was quieter now, with just a few postgrad students ambling to and from the library. Increasingly over the last couple of years he'd found himself wishing he could roll the clock back. Things had seemed so much simpler when he'd been down there among them studying for his doctorate. At least until Stephen had come along. He shook his head, pushing the thought from his mind. 'I despair. Really I do.' He turned to face them, depositing himself in his chair, his anger suddenly dissipated. 'Are you two trying to deliberately sabotage our last hope of keeping the institute afloat? Because that's what it's beginning to look like from here. You pair make quite a double act, don't you?'

Clare said, 'You can't blame Jo for any of this, David. You put me in charge of Bailsgrove. It was my decision to allow the news crew onto site.'

Jo chimed in, 'That's not fair, Clare. You didn't have much choice. They invited themselves onto site.'

'I know, but I could have refused and I didn't.'

Jo said, 'You gave it a real good go.'

Clare said, 'David's right, Jo. That's not the point. I've already had Paul Marshall yelling down the phone, threatening to sue us.'

David looked on in disbelief. It was news to him.

'What were we meant to do? Have Neil and some of the team strong-arm Crabby and the news team off-site? David, what do you think the headlines would have looked like then?' She shook her head. 'That guy's a piece of work.'

David said, 'That guy's paying our wages. And it's not only Paul Marshall we've got to worry about. What about the police? How do you think they're going to feel about your little announcement to the world that some of the burials could be modern? And why the hell didn't I know about that?'

Jo shifted uncomfortably from foot to foot, playing with a loose strand of her unruly beach-blonde hair that had escaped from its ponytail. It was a disquieting sight to see Jo Granski anything but entirely grounded and confident. 'That's just a little bit of a misunderstanding, David. You know yourself you can never be one hundred per cent confident about dates until we have the radio carbon dates through.'

He asked, 'When are they due?'

Scratching her ear, Jo said confidently, 'Two days tops.'

David thought that was remarkably fast. But if Jo Granski was normally anything, it was efficient. And she possessed that rare quality amongst academics of being both well respected and well liked. So he knew that if she pulled a few strings with her colleagues they were normally only too willing to bend over backwards for her. Therefore he didn't question it. And to be frank

146

it came as something of a relief to hear that the dating side of things was at least under control. He'd had Sally on the phone this morning saying Mark Stone had been bending her ear about the TV interview. Funny how things turned out. At the moment Sally's friendship with Stone appeared to be the only thing preventing the Gloucestershire police from closing their dig down. An irony which certainly hadn't escaped Sally, who'd been less than complimentary about Clare's television debut.

He nodded. 'As soon as those dates are in I want to hear about them. And make sure you get them to DCI Stone as a priority. We can't afford any more fuck-ups.' He sat back in his chair. 'And you do realise that filming that burial without any screening was in breach of our Ministry of Justice burial licence, don't you?'

Clare and Jo looked at one another.

He plucked a printout of the burial licence from the top of his printer and threw it at Clare. 'Read the bloody paperwork! And next time you want to screw something up, try not to broadcast it on the nine o'clock news.'

CHAPTER TWELVE

Clare raised the bone china cup to her lips and breathed in the reviving smoky aroma of lapsang. 'This is lovely, Jo. But we shouldn't really be here.'

'Why the hell not?'

'With things as they are we should be back on-site.'

'You need to chill out, Clare. It'll be fine. Neil's a solid sort of dude. He knows what he's doing. And after this morning I figured we could both do with a little R and R.'

Clare smiled. 'Well, I can't disagree with you there.'

After a month's unremitting slog on the dig and David's haranguing this morning, the cathedral tearooms seemed like an oasis of calm. Clare looked at her friend. Somehow despite her ripped denim jacket and Grateful Dead T-shirt she still managed to look as if she belonged.

Clare said, 'I didn't even know this place existed.'

Jo took a sip of her coffee. 'I found it when I was doing my doctorate. I spent a lot of time in the museum archives over there.' Jo pointed across the cathedral close. 'I used to come out to stretch my legs at lunchtime and I tripped over this place.' She pointed in the direction of her plate. 'Then I got kind of addicted to their espresso cupcakes.'

'I didn't know you did your doctorate down here.'

Jo winked at her friend conspiratorially. 'There's a lot folks don't know about me.'

Clare laughed. 'Is that when you first came across David? When you did your doctorate?'

'Yes, but not because I was at the university. I did my doctorate at UCL. But most of my research was in Wessex. David helped me out with the stone tools assemblages from some burials I was looking at.'

Jo washed a bite of her cupcake down with a sip of coffee. 'You and David never talk much about being students down here.'

Clare could feel herself blush. 'I guess it doesn't come up much.'

'But you were friends when you were here, right?'

Clare studiously avoided Jo's gaze, instead letting it roam over the Gothic magnificence of the cathedral. She sipped at her tea and nodded.

Jo asked. 'This was where you met Stephen, too, wasn't it?'

Clare stuttered, 'Yes. Yes, it was.'

'So did David know Stephen as well?'

'No, not really. At least not very well. Can we talk about something else please, Jo? I don't really feel up to this right now.'

To Clare's relief Jo mistook the cause of her discomfort. 'I'm sorry, Clare. It must be difficult sometimes being round places that bring back old memories. I didn't mean to open up old wounds.'

Clare waved her concern away. 'Don't worry about it. It's just sometimes the past doesn't seem very long ago.'

And yet sometimes it seemed like a lifetime. The David back then was a very different David to the one they'd encountered this morning. But then time changed everything, didn't it?

Jo said, 'You know David asked us to tell him as soon as the radio carbon dates come through.' Clare nodded. 'I was wondering, do you think maybe we should tell him about what happened when you and Margaret met up with the antiquities guy in the parking lot? What do you say?'

Clare nearly choked on her carrot cake. 'Are you mad? David's livid with us already. If I tell him about that too he'll go ballistic.'

Jo said, 'But what if he finds out anyway? Won't that make it twice as bad?'

'How's he going to find out? Margaret won't tell him. And I'm certainly not going to. So unless you're planning to say something, there's no one else who knows.' She shook her head. 'No, David's mad as hell right now. The last thing we need to do is pour fuel on the fire. Let's just let him calm down and keep quiet until we've got a better idea of what's been going on.'

Jo didn't look convinced, but she acquiesced readily enough. 'OK. If you say so, Clare. What is it you English say? Mum's the word.'

The weather had finally broken and for the last few days Bailsgrove had resembled a disaster zone. They'd tried baling out the pits, but to no avail. As fast as they scooped and poured, the water seemed to rise again. They'd eventually abandoned all hope of digging in favour of finds washing. But twenty diggers into two Portakabins was a less than ideal equation. And as a consequence the office and the welfare unit now both looked even more of a shambles than when they'd taken the site over. To top it all they'd had Paul Marshall stomping round site muttering darkly about penalty clauses and threatening to withhold payment on their contract.

So it was to Clare's intense relief that she pulled back the curtains on her bedroom at the King's Arms to see the thick cloud being chased across the horizon by a stiff south-westerly. By the time they'd got to site the sun was starting to break through. This was more like it. Now that the university exams season was over, Jo was on-site practically full-time. And between the two of them and Neil they should be able to make decent progress. By morning break, and not without a good deal of mopping, baling and backache, everyone was digging on-site again.

Clare was standing alongside Neil, surveying the site from the top of the hill. 'It really is an extraordinary spot. We're only a couple of hundred metres from the edge of the Cotswold scarp, but you'd never know it. The lie of the land on this side of the hill makes it feel totally cut off.' She turned to Neil. 'Funny, isn't it? We always seem to think nowadays that if you're on the edge of something it's less important. But I remember David telling me once that in prehistory, places on the edge were often revered – treated as the meeting point between two worlds.'

Neil nodded. 'Beth used to have a word for it—'

Clare cut in, 'Liminal.'

'That's it. I remember now.'

As they ambled downslope Clare stopped and pointed. 'You know, Neil, I've never noticed before, but our site sits on its own little plateau. It looks as if it's been deliberately cut into the slope.'

'Or it could be they just selected a natural terrace.'

'Maybe. And then adapted it a little.' She grabbed his arm. 'Look! Do you see that dark streak running across the cutting? It seems to stretch right into the centre of the trench and then it turns at a right angle.' She started jumping up and down. 'Oh my God, Neil! It looks like a ditch. All this wet weather we've been cursing. It's found us our ditch.'

Somewhere in the distance behind her she could hear Neil saying, 'Are you sure?'

But she was halfway down slope by then. 'Jo! Jo! You've got to come and see this! We've found the ditch.'

Much to the amusement of Malcolm and the rest of the dig team, Clare came to an abrupt halt, tripping over a bucket and landing squarely at Jo's feet.

Jo helped her up. 'Are you OK? You came down there at a heck of a lick.'

Clare brushed herself down impatiently. 'Yes, yes, I'm fine.'

'What's all the hullabaloo about?'

Clare dragged Jo upslope to get the best vantage point. She pointed. 'Do you see down there, that dark line?'

Jo stared at the cutting, at first struggling to make it out. Then suddenly she clapped her hand across her mouth. 'You're right, Clare. It's a ditch. It's got to be. And it goes right round our pits.' She placed both hands on her friend's shoulders and shook her. 'You know what this means, don't you? We've found ourselves an Iron Age shrine. Do you know how rare they are, Clare? I can't believe it. This is epic.'

Clare couldn't help smiling at her friend's unbridled joy. But she knew she was going to have to prick the bubble. 'Well, to be strictly accurate we've got a ditch and some pits. We won't know if the complex is Iron Age until those radio carbon dates come back from the infants' skeletons.'

As they'd hoped, by mid-afternoon they had their answer when an email from Florida popped into Jo's inbox.

Jo hurried over to Clare, who was filling in context sheets

by the side of the cutting. 'See, I told you. First half of the first century AD.'

'Oh, thank God for that. Whatever happened to those poor little mites, it happened two thousand years ago. Have you—'

Jo interrupted her. 'Oh yes. Don't worry. First thing I did was email David. And then Mark Stone.'

'We'd better let Margaret know too. I can't wait to see her face when we tell her.' Clare tucked the ring binder she was holding under her arm and got to her feet. 'Come on, I think this deserves a cup of warm brown sludge.'

The two women strolled contentedly downhill, chatting about their discovery.

As they approached the welfare unit, Clare saw Crabby coming through the gate at the bottom of the field. 'What does he want?'

Jo sounded considerably happier about the Druid's appearance than Clare felt. 'He probably just wants to see how things are coming along.'

Clare turned away from him, trying to usher Jo into the welfare unit. 'They would've been going a damned sight better if he hadn't dragged the press into it.' Jo gave her a reproving look. 'Well, I'm just saying. Come on, I'm thirsty.'

But it was too late. There was a tap on her shoulder.

As she turned, Crabby's deep baritone intoned, 'Blessed be!'

In as cold a tone as she could muster, Clare said, 'Hi, Crabby, what can I do for you?'

Jo dug her in the ribs, and Clare returned the favour, trying to keep a straight face.

He looked first at Clare, then at Jo. 'I wanted to apologise. For what happened the other day with the TV people. If I'd known they were going to come here and cause trouble I'd never 'ave invited them here. After the kindness you showed to the old souls.

Well, I'd not blame you if you didn't want to see me again.'

Clare hesitated, but Jo stepped into the breach. 'It's the TV guys who should be ashamed of themselves, not you, Crabby. We know you were only trying to help them out. Isn't that so, Clare?'

Sensing Clare's reluctance, Crabby turned to her and, placing his hand gently on her arm, looked straight into her eyes. 'Can you forgive me, Clare?'

Clare held his gaze for a few seconds then crumbled. She reached out to give him a hug. 'Oh, Crabby, there's nothing to forgive.' Stepping back, she said, 'Come on, let's get a mug of tea and then I'm going to take you up to the trench and show you what we've found.'

Twenty minutes later the three of them were sitting together cross-legged, slurping the last of their tea by the side of the cutting.

Crabby said, 'So Beth was right all along. This place was a temple. I knew it. She'd have been so pleased at what you've done here.'

Neither Clare nor Jo knew quite what to say.

Crabby gestured in the direction of Neil, who was deftly wielding a pickaxe in the top of the newly discovered ditch. 'And she'd have been pleased you kept young Neil on too. It was Beth who gave him a second chance, you know. She told me she could always see he had something about him.'

Clare turned towards Crabby, puzzled. 'A second chance?'

He nodded. 'He was a bit of a bad lad in his younger days by all accounts. Beth told me he'd had a few problems with drugs and such when he was at college. From what I could make out, she sort of took him under her wing. That's why she took him on when she started digging and he pitched up here.'

Clare said, 'I had no idea.'

'Neil's a good lad now, though. He's sorted himself out. I didn't take much to schooling and I know some of the youngsters reckon I'm a bit lacking up 'ere.' He tapped the side of his head. 'But Neil's never been like that. He's always had time for me. We've had one or two good nights round the fire talking about the old ways over a pint of cider. He's not one to poke fun at folks just cos they're different. And he works damned 'ard too. Even if that missus of his is always giving him grief.'

Clare said, 'Is she? Neil's never mentioned anything.'

'He wouldn't, would he? Man's got his pride. She's always on at him to pack this lark in. Don't reckon there's a future in it.' Crabby shook his head. 'That's the trouble with young folk these days, it's all about the money. But Neil, he's different. Suppose that's why Beth took to him.'

Was that what had sparked Stuart Craig's apparent jealousy? Had Craig resented the time Beth had taken straightening the young Neil Fuller out? Maybe Craig's version of Beth had as much to do with the lack of attention he'd felt she'd paid him, and the time she'd invested in helping Neil as an undergrad, as it did with her obsession with the long-dead. It was beginning to seem as if everyone had known a different Beth Kinsella.

'That was a proper treat. Thank you.' Crabby sat back contentedly, his bowl now with only the faintest traces of treacle tart and vanilla ice cream clinging to its sides in front of him.

'My pleasure, Crabby. Glad you enjoyed it.'

Clare was still feeling more than a tinge of guilt over the way she'd treated Crabby when he'd turned up on-site to apologise to them earlier in the day. So by way of a peace offering, but in truth to salve her conscience, she'd asked him to join her and Jo for dinner in the King's Arms. The restaurant had been packed so the landlord had asked them if they'd mind eating in the bar.

Clare had her suspicions that the request might have had more to do with Crabby's biker's leathers than a sudden run on tables. But as Crabby seemed relieved by the suggestion she didn't argue the point. And she and Jo had passed a surprisingly enjoyable evening with him.

Jo stood up. 'Can I get you a beer?'

Crabby said, 'A pint of cider would go down a treat.'

As Jo made her way to the bar, Crabby leant towards Clare and whispered conspiratorially, 'You know, I had my doubts about young Jo when she first came here. We get a lot of Yanks 'ereabouts, and I can't always say I care for 'em much. But she's not like most of 'em, is she? She's alright.'

Clare laughed. 'There's no denying she's a one-off. But you know she really is an expert' – Clare hesitated, choosing her words carefully – 'in what she does.'

Crabby nodded furiously. 'Oh aye. I could see that right enough. The way she handled those little 'uns. To tell you the truth, Clare, it wasn't at all what I thought it'd be like. I've never been too sure about your lot digging folks up before.'

She asked, 'But you've changed your mind now?'

'Well, let's just say I'm open to persuasion. It was what you said to that pillock yesterday. You know, when you said about giving the children voices.'

'I meant it, Crabby. It's why I love this job so much. It's not about the stuff we dig up; it's all about the people.'

He nodded. 'Was that why you got so mad about those holes the metal detectorists dug?'

Clare looked up, surprised. She hadn't realised the metal detectorists' pits were common knowledge. She certainly hadn't said anything to Crabby about it.

Her astonishment must have shown, because by way of

explanation he said, 'Neil told me. Said you were worried it might have destroyed stuff on the site.'

Before she could say anything, Jo returned and distributed their drinks. For a few minutes they sat in companionable silence. But Clare noticed that Crabby wasn't making much headway with his cider, and instead was shuffling his glass round and round on its beer mat.

Eventually she said, 'Is something troubling you, Crabby?'

He pushed his pint away from him. And after a few moments he nodded. 'I don't know how to tell you this. But you girls have been so good to me. I want to be straight with you.'

It was plain for anyone to see that Crabby's anxiety was genuine enough. His normally ruddy complexion was drained of all colour, and his hands were shaking uncontrollably. He leant back in his seat and closed his eyes.

When he opened them again he stared into space and said simply, 'It was me.'

Confused, Clare asked, 'What was you, Crabby?'

He turned to face them. 'It was me what dug them holes. Or at least I put the stuff in 'em.'

Clare looked at Jo. Jo looked as dumbstruck as she did.

After a few seconds Jo said, 'But why would you want to go and do a thing like that?'

The Druid put his head in his hands. 'To stop them building on it.'

Clare said, 'But I thought you wanted them to build the houses.'

Crabby nodded. 'I do. But not there. Not on sacred ground. That hilltop's a special place. Always has been. Mum used to take me up there to the beech grove when I was a nipper. She could feel it too – I could tell she could. She was taken from us young – the big C. My old man scattered her ashes up there. He remarried, but it was never the same after Mum died. I used to go up there when him and his new missus were rowing – to be with Mum. That's when I got interested in the old ways. It made sense to me, being at one with the earth. With what had gone before. Natural like.'

Clare said softly, 'I can see that, Crabby. But I don't understand why you thought planting finds on the site was going to stop them building.'

Crabby said, 'It was Sheila's idea.'

Clare lowered her voice. 'Sheila Foggarty. The parish councillor.'

Crabby nodded. 'That's the one. We don't see eye to eye about everything, but she knows I don't want them building up there any more than she does. When Beth first started to dig on the site we figured she might find something that would stop Marshall building. She was so sure there'd been something there. But after a bit, when nothing was turning up, that's when Sheila came to see me. She reckoned if we could get enough stuff of the right sort together and plant it on-site, when Beth dug it up she'd be able to stop the houses being built. I wasn't sure at first, but Sheila convinced me. She's used to getting what she wants.' The Druid smiled. 'Except at home, that is.'

Clare asked, 'Why's that?'

Crabby said, 'Her old man is sick to death of her shenanigans. Acting the high and mighty on the parish council. Don't make him many friends round here. But then neither did selling that land. And if she manages to stop Marshall building on the site it'll cost him a bob or two.' Clare looked at him quizzically. 'He's the one as sold the plot in the first place. Marshall did a deal with him. He takes part of the profits when the houses get built.'

'Can't make for a very happy home life.'

Crabby took a long draught of his cider. 'Sometimes I think

she's doing it just to spite him. But he don't know the half of what she gets up to.'

'He doesn't know about planting the finds.'

Crabby shook his head. 'He'd 'ave her guts for garters if he found out.'

Clare said, 'What I don't understand is where you got the stuff from.'

He said, 'Was easier than you'd think. Sheila did a bit of research on the Internet to look at what sort of stuff we should be looking for. Then I went online and bid for it.'

Clare said, 'But it must have cost you a fortune. Some of that stuff came from all over Europe,' then added quickly, 'from what I can tell on the auction site.'

Crabby took a long, slow slurp of his cider and wiped his lips with the back of his hand. 'There are plenty of folks with money round 'ere as value their way of life and are willing to pay to keep it that way. Sheila organised a bit of a whip-round.'

Clare looked around at the assorted residents of Bailsgrove enjoying their evening tipples, seemingly without a care in the world. How many of them knew about what Crabby was telling them? Did everyone in the village know about what had been going on at the dig site?

Crabby said, 'I went up to the dig the afternoon after I'd planted them. I was dead pleased with myself when Beth found one of the brooches. It all seemed to be going a treat. But Beth knew there were something fishy going on right off. She brought it over to show me. I don't know how she guessed. I never did have much of a poker face. But she just looked at me and said, "This was you, Crabby, wasn't it?"

'I'll tell you straight. I didn't know what to do. But there was no point lying to her. She knew it was me alright. So I told her.

I told her everything.' He looked at the two women. 'I thought she'd never speak to me again. I was sure she was going to turn me into the police. But do you know what she did?' Both women shook their heads. 'She just turned to me and said, "Why couldn't you wait, Crabby?"'

'But the worst bit was when she told me she'd already found evidence that Bailsgrove had been an important place for the ancestors. And she would make sure there was no way it could be built on if it was the last thing she did. I tell you I didn't know what to make of it. But I looked into her eyes, and you know what, I believed her. She loved that place as much as I do. I'll never forgive myself for what I did to that place, but I really thought it was for the best.'

Clare asked, 'Did Beth say what it was she'd found?'

He shook his head. 'Nope. Never got the chance. It was the next day I found her. Up there in the grove. And, see, that's what I can't make no sense of. The day before she was so determined. And excited too, about whatever it was she'd found up there.'

Jo cut in, 'Crabby, can I get this straight. Are you telling us you don't think Beth Kinsella was suicidal?'

'The day before she died Beth was happier than I'd ever seen her. And there's something else that wasn't right.' Jo and Clare looked at one another. 'It was the hare.'

Jo said, 'Whose hair?'

Clare said, 'Not whose hair, what hare?' She had a horrible feeling she knew what Crabby was going to say. She remembered reading about it in one of the newspapers. She hadn't thought much of it at the time, except to wonder how deranged someone must be to kill one.

Jo looked confused.

Crabby turned to face Jo. 'When I found Beth there was a

dead hare lying just in front of her. There was blood all over it. Someone had hacked at its throat with a knife, its head had been bashed in and there was this bit of orange baler twine round what was left of its neck.'

Jo said, 'From what I read in the papers there were dead animals lying all over the place. What's so special about the hare?'

'I know folks say Beth was as mad as a box of frogs, but they didn't know her like I did. And even if she was, she never would've harmed a hare.'

Jo said, 'I don't get it. Why not?'

'Because,' said Clare, 'hares were sacred in the Iron Age. That's right, isn't it, Crabby?'

Crabby nodded. 'That's right. But that's not why I know Beth would never have done it. Sitting and talking with her one day about all the creatures the Druids held sacred, I knew hares were sacred animals and I said so to Beth. She just laughed and said that was right according to Caesar, but he was a Roman and what did they know? She told me hares were one of the most commonly hunted animals among the Celtic peoples. But then she laughed again and said for once maybe the Romans had it right. She didn't understand how anyone could harm a hare; they were such beautiful, gentle creatures.'

CHAPTER THIRTEEN

Speaking to the police had seemed the only possible course of action when she'd phoned this morning to arrange an appointment to see DCI Mark Stone. But now as she sat in Little Blue, rain dribbling down the windscreen, staring up at the looming post-modern monstrosity that was Stroud police station, Clare was beginning to wonder if it was such a good idea after all.

She and Jo had stayed up into the small hours of the night trying to make some sort of sense of what Crabby had told them. At least they now knew how all of that metalwork had found its way to the dig site. And they'd agreed that it must have been sheer opportunism that had drawn the nighthawks to Bailsgrove once the police had first closed it down and then abandoned it. With every newspaper in the country running the story that Beth Kinsella had claimed the site was an Iron Age temple and zero security in place, the dig site had been a sitting duck. Clare hadn't mentioned it to Jo but she still harboured suspicions that Sheila Foggarty might somehow have been involved in tipping the nighthawks off, though she didn't think she'd ever be able to prove it.

Beth's death had ensured that whatever it was that she'd discovered was likely to remain a mystery, and there was nothing to stop the development going ahead. For anyone who wanted to prevent those houses from being built, the timing of Beth's demise seemed convenient to say the least. If, as Crabby claimed, Beth hadn't killed herself, there was only one possible alternative: somebody else had. And that meant that anyone who might stand in the way of the development was a potential target. And the moment Clare and the dig team had discovered the evidence for the shrine it had put all of them in harm's way. So despite her misgivings she knew that she had no choice but to speak to the police.

When she eventually plucked up the courage to abandon the comparative comfort of her car and crossed the threshold of the police station, her surroundings reminded her of nothing so much as her old comprehensive school in Chelmsford. Inside the waiting room, even the furniture looked as if it had been there since the day the place had been built. Mark Stone's office, when she eventually got there, was spacious but overwhelmingly drab. The only feature of any note was a neatly aligned row of certificates detailing Stone's apparently manifold achievements, which hung behind him on the wall.

The man himself, seated across his desk from her, looked tired and harassed. 'Thanks for getting your colleague to send those radio carbon dates through.' He proffered a smile. 'I have to confess when I saw your television interview I was beginning to wonder whether I should have sent that SOCO team over to Bailsgrove last time we met.'

Was he teasing her? She couldn't tell. *Oh, hell.* She could feel her cheeks reddening, and she hadn't been in his office for more than a couple of minutes. 'You needn't have worried. I've never had cause to doubt Dr Granski's professional judgement yet. Jo knows what she's talking about.'

'Well, thankfully that was certainly the case on this occasion, Mrs Hills. Now, when you spoke to the desk sergeant you said you had some information relating to Beth Kinsella's death.'

It seemed they were definitely in 'Mrs Hills' not 'Clare' territory today. That wasn't a good sign. Or was that just because of the gravity of the subject matter?

She took a deep breath. 'That's right. Do you remember Crabby?'

'Crabby. Do you mean Wayne Crabbs?' Clare nodded. 'Yes. He found Beth Kinsella's body. I interviewed him afterwards.'

'Well, Crabby told me something yesterday. Something I think might be important. About Beth's death.'

He leant forward attentively. 'Go on.'

'The day before she died, Beth told Crabby something.'

He asked, 'What sort of something?'

'She told him she'd found something that would prove that the site was an Iron Age temple.'

He leant back and crossed his arms. 'Mrs Hills, if that's what you came here to tell me I'm afraid that's not news. Everyone I interviewed about Beth Kinsella said she'd told them the place was some sort of sacred site.'

Clare shook her head, unable to disguise her impatience. 'No, you don't understand. Crabby said that he was on-site with her the day before she died and Beth told him she had actually discovered something that would *prove* it. Something that would stop the houses being built.'

'And do we have any idea what this something was that she'd supposedly discovered? Or where it is now?'

'Well, no one knows, but Crabby says she was absolutely matter-of-fact about it. According to him, Beth wasn't depressed or suicidal, she was really upbeat about her discovery and what it meant.'

'Mr Crabbs gave evidence about Dr Kinsella's state of mind at the inquest, Mrs Hills. Admittedly he neglected to mention whatever astonishing discovery he now claims she'd made. But as there's no evidence of its whereabouts, or come to that its existence, I'm afraid it doesn't really materially change the facts of the case.'

Mark Stone clearly wasn't interested in anything she had to say about either Beth Kinsella or her death.

Clare struggled to maintain an even tone in her voice. 'But don't you see? Even if Beth hadn't discovered something that would stop the housing development, if other people thought she had, that would have made her a target.'

'Are you trying to suggest that Dr Kinsella was murdered to prevent her from stopping the development being built?' Mark Stone shook his head. 'That really doesn't make any sense, Mrs Hills. Beth Kinsella was working for the developer. And as far as I could establish at the time of her death, Paul Marshall's money was the only thing between her and the job centre. If anyone other than Marshall had an interest in those houses being built, it was Beth Kinsella.'

Clare was all but pleading now. 'But it doesn't work like that. I'm in exactly the same position as Beth Kinsella was. And I have just discovered something that might very well stop the housing development going ahead.'

Mark Stone's smile was a tad too beatific for Clare's tastes. 'And have you or your team been threatened in some way, Mrs

Hills? Has something happened to make you believe that your life is in danger?'

'Well, no. But there's something else you need to know about Beth's death.'

He drummed his jotter with his forefinger. She could see he was losing what little patience he had left.

'It's the hare.'

'The hare.' He raised his eyebrows.

She nodded. 'The one that was found near Beth's body. It shouldn't have been there.'

He folded his arms again and inclined his head forward in anticipation of her great revelation. 'Is that right?'

'Yes. Beth told Crabby that she loved hares and she couldn't understand how anyone could harm them. She would never have killed one.'

Mark Stone stood up. 'And yet she did. Along with a selection of crows, magpies and rabbits, all of which were also found with their throats cut or their heads smashed in.' Maybe regretting the harshness of his words, he said, 'I appreciate your taking the time to come here today, Clare. We always encourage members of the public to talk to us if they believe they have any evidence relating to a criminal offence. But as far as I can see, nothing that you've shared with me this afternoon tells us anything new. And, tragic though it is, there is not one scrap of evidence to suggest that Dr Kinsella's death was anything other than self-inflicted. She was clearly a brilliant but extremely troubled individual. I very much hope that your excavation passes without further incident. But I really don't think there's any cause for anxiety on the part of you or your team.'

The patronising sod. Clare drew in a deep breath, in a not entirely successful attempt to maintain her composure. Stone clearly had her down as some sort of interfering busybody with an over-active imagination. Well, if he thought she was going to let him off the hook that easily, he had another thing coming. He obviously had no intention of taking her seriously about Beth Kinsella's death. But if he already had her down as some sort of nutcase, what harm could it do to try to get him to at least take the other illegal activity on the site seriously? If she achieved nothing else from today's visit at least she'd be able to walk away with a clear conscience and ensure that the nighthawks weren't allowed to get away with ransacking any more ancient sites.

Stone gestured towards the door and made as if to stand up, clearly eager to be rid of her.

'There's something else I need to tell you.'

With an almost imperceptible sigh, Stone deposited himself back into his swivel chair. 'Really, Mrs Hills, and what would that be?'

'It's about the nighthawk activity on our site.'

He sighed. 'What about it? As I explained when we last spoke about this, we simply don't have the resources to offer round-the-clock protection to every square inch of the Gloucestershire countryside.'

She nodded, still struggling to maintain an even tone. 'I appreciate that, DCI Stone. But I know who was responsible. We traced them online – they were selling items they claimed were from Bailsgrove on an auction site. A colleague and I met with them.'

Stone pulled himself upright, his interest clearly peaked. 'So you have some sort of evidence that the objects they were offering for sale actually came from your site. Is that correct?'

Clare swallowed hard, suddenly realising her error. The last thing she wanted to do was to implicate Crabby in this. 'Well, the finds were on our site. And I've seen evidence – photographs – that the person we met, or his associates, were responsible for removing them from the site. And they were the same objects that were being sold online.'

'Do you have the photographs with you, Mrs Hills?'

'Well, no. I don't actually have any photographs. The dealer showed them to us when we met him. He wouldn't let us keep them. But they were definitely images of the objects as they were being dug up at the dig site at Bailsgrove.'

He looked at her doubtfully.

'Look, if you don't believe me ask Professor' – she corrected herself – 'Dame Margaret Bockford. She was with me when I met the dealer. She can corroborate what I'm saying.'

He hesitated for a moment and then his expression hardened. He looked as if he was about to dismiss her again when a thought suddenly struck her. She reached into her bag and, producing her mobile, she found the note she'd made of the GPS coordinates of the finds and the registration number of the van.

She turned the screen around to face him. 'These are the coordinates I jotted down. They were on the photos of the finds being removed from the site – I checked them out, they're all spot on for the holes we found on our dig. And that' – she pointed at the screen – 'is the registration number of the van the seller turned up in when we met him.'

She was expecting another scornful rebuke. But to her surprise he returned the phone to her and said, 'Can you email these to me?'

She nodded eagerly. 'Yes. Yes, of course.'

'Do you think you can remember what the person you met with looked like?'

'I think so. I'll certainly give it a go.'

He picked up his phone and dialled. 'Sergeant Hughes. I've got a young lady here in my office I'd like you to take a statement from.'

When the sergeant arrived, Stone said, 'Whatever you may think, Mrs Hills, we do take heritage crime seriously. But we don't have means without end.'

As she turned to go he smiled and said, 'Oh, and Clare, I wouldn't give too much credence to what Mr Crabbs has to say if I were you. I think he inhabits a different world to the rest of us.'

Somehow events had conspired to ensure that Sally had once again ended up in the smallest interview room in the station. The tiny window high up in the wall provided the only natural daylight, and rain battered its frosted surface. A recent overhaul had resulted in the walls being given a fresh lick of paint, the results of which could be seen splattered across the floor.

She had spent more of her working life behind this and a host of similar time-worn Formica tabletops than she cared to remember. She flattered herself that she was good at reading people. So when she'd first joined CID she'd assumed that interviewing suspects would come easily to her. It didn't take long for it to become painfully apparent that she was anything but a natural when it came to extracting information from recalcitrant interviewees. Some people seemed to have a gift for it. But not her.

It was a lippy kid she'd picked up for dealing in Gloucester that had changed it all. Despite three solid hours of coaxing, cajoling and questioning he'd stubbornly refused to utter a word. That is, until he'd stood up and hurled the word 'Motherfucker!' and a scalding hot cup of tea at her, swiftly followed by the table it had been standing on. She'd just about managed to stop herself from bursting into tears, but she'd been the butt of the station canteen jokes for weeks. Couldn't handle a kid. No way she was going to make it. She'd decided there and then there was no way she was going to let it happen again. So she'd read every psychology textbook she could lay her hands on and sat in on endless interviews with senior colleagues, pestering them for tips and hints until they'd become sick of it.

But it had paid off. And now here she was about to question her first suspect in her very own murder inquiry. A uniformed constable stood in the corner of the room and across the table from her sat Damian Kelly. Six feet plus with a thick head of jet-black hair and two days' growth of stubble, he didn't look like a man you'd want to cross. She could see why he'd had no trouble hauling Jack Tyler to his feet.

She took a sip of water from the plastic cup and glanced down at the Manila folder that lay open in front of her.

'Well, Mr Kelly, thank you for coming in to speak to us.'

'It seemed to me I didn't have very much choice in the matter, now did I?'

Was it the surname that was doing it or did she detect an almost imperceptible hint of an Irish accent? Sally's eyes flicked down to the paperwork in front of her. An Irish national. But it looked as if his parents had moved here when he was a kid.

'You're here voluntarily, Mr Kelly. But you are being interviewed under caution. You do not have to say anything. But it may harm your defence if you do not mention when questioned something which you later rely on in court. Anything you do say may be given in evidence.'

For the first time he looked agitated. 'Jesus, what is this? The sergeant said you just wanted to have a word about where Jack was the night before he died. Now you're arresting me!' His face was the colour of strawberry ice cream but he looked anything but cool. He was sweating profusely, and his breathing was coming in short bursts.

Sally said, 'Calm down, Mr Kelly. You're not under arrest. It's just part of the process we're required to go through when we interview someone. I'm sure you've got nothing to worry about. You're simply here to answer a few questions.'

With shaking hands, he picked up the plastic cup in front of him and took a sip of water. Then, drawing in a deep breath, he puffed out his cheeks and seemed to relax a little.

Sally asked, 'Am I right in thinking you were with Jack the evening before he died?'

He nodded. 'That's right. I bumped into Jack down at The Lamb. I was surprised to see him. He hadn't been out and about for a few weeks.'

'Would you have described yourself as a close friend of Mr Tyler's?'

He said, 'Not especially. We knocked around together sometimes. Both enjoyed a good craic, if you know what I mean.'

'And was Jack up for the craic when you saw him that night?'

He shook his head. 'He was sitting in the corner on his own with a face as long as a clock.'

'Did he say why?'

'He said bugger all until I'd poured a pint or two inside him. That loosened him up a bit.'

Sally said, 'That was very generous of you, Mr Kelly.'

'Well, he was a mate. I'd been down to Salisbury and won a few quid in the afternoon. No point in having good fortune if you don't share it around, now, is there?'

'*A mate*'. Not exactly how he'd described him a moment ago. She tucked the comment away for now.

Sally asked, 'What did Jack have to say for himself when he loosened up?'

'He was on a bit of a downer.'

'Did he say why that was exactly?'

'He'd lost his job a few weeks before.'

Sally said, 'That's rather odd, Mr Kelly. According to our records Jack Tyler hadn't worked in over a year.'

Damian Kelly paused, and Sally watched as he stared down at his hands, clasped tightly together in front of him. After a few seconds he looked up at her. 'I don't suppose it matters now the poor bastard's dead. Jack did a bit of cash-in-hand work.'

'What sort of thing?'

He said, 'All sorts of odds and sods. He did a bit of groundwork on building sites, the odd bit of gardening. He took on anything as long as it was outside. You couldn't fault the lad for trying. He's had a go at most things since he was first laid off by Western.'

There was only one 'Western' everybody had heard of in these parts. 'Western. Western Archaeology.'

He nodded. 'That's right. He was doing OK for himself until a couple of years back. Then when the building industry ground to a halt, the digging did too. Jack and a whole bunch of his mates were laid off at the same time. Poor bastards. I ask you, what use is an out-of-work archaeologist to the world?'

She had some sympathy with Damian Kelly's view, though she doubted David would have agreed. And if the Hart Unit was in as perilous a state as David had suggested, she hoped to God she wasn't going to have to find out any time soon.

'So since then he'd been working cash-in-hand. Just picking up the odd labouring job.'

He said, 'That's right. Though he had a stroke of luck four or five months ago. Bumped into some bloke he was at university with who put him onto a bit of digging work up Stroud way.'

Sally said, 'A building job.'

Kelly shook his head. 'Nah. On a dig up there somewhere. He was made up about it.'

'So, what happened?'

He shook his head again. 'I don't rightly know. Though if I had to take a guess I'd say it was probably the drink. Jack knew how to put it away when he had the chance, and it wouldn't be the first time he'd been let go for turning up to work the worse for wear after he'd tied one on the night before. All I know for sure is he got fired. Like I said, we just knocked around a bit. But what I do know is that night in the pub he'd had a skinful. And by the end of the night he was telling everyone who'd listen what a cow the woman in charge was.'

Sally couldn't believe it. This was starting to have a horribly familiar ring to it. How many women were there running digs in the Cotswolds?

'Did he happen to mention her name?'

'No, but everyone knew who he meant.'

Sally almost didn't want to ask. 'Oh? Why was that?'

'It was that mad bitch who hung herself. Some of the lads were talking about it just after it happened – when it was all over the news. And Jack was in here shouting his mouth off, saying he reckoned she'd got what she deserved.'

Sally leant in towards him. 'And Jack Tyler actually said that, did he, Mr Kelly? He said Beth Kinsella "got what she deserved".' It might mean nothing, but it was a strange turn of phrase for someone talking about a suicide.

'If that's what her name was, he did. I remember because Toby – the barman – said he thought it was a bit harsh. And I told him to ignore Jack because it was just the drink talking.'

Sally took a sip of her water and leant back. Her backside was beginning to feel numb on the hard plastic chair. She looked up at the clock. They'd only been going twenty minutes. She skimmed through her notes until she found the section she was looking for.

'Right, I think that's enough chit-chat, don't you, Mr Kelly? Let's cut to the chase. When was the last time you saw Jack Tyler alive?'

He stared down intently at the tabletop. 'I just told you. I saw him in The Lamb the night before he died.'

'So you did, Mr Kelly. But when was the last time you actually saw him?'

He glanced up at her, his gaze flitting round the room distractedly. 'I told you, it was when Jack left the pub that night.' He straightened himself up in his chair. 'Look, I don't understand what you're getting at.'

Sally stood up, walked away from him and turned. Returning to the table she folded her arms, but this time stayed standing. Reaching into the wad of papers she withdrew the still of Damian Kelly looking up at the CCTV camera and tossed it down in front of him. 'Recognise that?'

Damian Kelly drew the image towards him. His face drained of all colour. He didn't say a word.

'Well, to me that looks very much like a photo of you, Mr Kelly.'

'I can explain.'

'For your sake, Mr Kelly, I hope so. Because I'd very much like an explanation of why you claim to have last seen Jack Tyler when he left The Lamb that night – which other witnesses put at just before eleven – when we have you on camera in Snuff Street with Jack at' – she picked up the photo and made a show of reading off the time from the bottom right-hand corner – 'eleven forty-six. Three quarters of an hour later.'

Her visit to see Mark Stone might have been an unmitigated disaster as far as getting him to take her seriously about Beth's death was concerned, but work on-site was going like a dream. Not only had they found the ditch surrounding what seemed to be a group of offering pits, but by the time she'd got back from Stroud, Malcolm – who was proving to be worth his weight in gold – had spotted what appeared to be a ring ditch, though this one looked as if it was considerably smaller in its proportions than the first. She'd phoned David to tell him last night and he'd suggested bringing Jason Dempsey up from the department to get some aerial shots with the department's drone. Clare had jumped at the chance.

Now Jason – universally known as Flyboy to his colleagues – and David were standing on the side of the trench inspecting the equipment. Looking at David, head bent over the miniature aircraft, Clare thought he looked like nothing so much as an overexcited ten-year-old who'd just woken up to the best Christmas present ever.

'So how high can it go?' asked David.

Flyboy chortled. 'Way higher than the CAA regs will let us take it. So you'd better hope we never find out.'

Clare strolled towards them. 'Is this a boys-only thing or can anyone join in?'

David waved her over. 'You've got to come and see this. Look, it's got a fully functional digital SLR and you can change the settings remotely when it's flying.'

This was Clare's sort of aerial photography. A world away from her traumatic experiences on the second-hand scaffolding tower at Hungerbourne. The only good thing about her near-death experience on the forty-year-old piece of junk was that it had convinced David they should never use it again. And that was just fine by her. Any device that could take shots of the site from fifty metres up while the photographer kept their feet firmly planted on

176

the ground was the type of kit she had every intention of becoming better acquainted with. And some of the drone shots from other archaeological sites she'd seen online were truly spectacular.

She asked, 'Can I have a go?'

David said, 'Sure, Flyboy will show you how.'

Flyboy shook his head. 'No can do on this one, Dave old chum.' David winced. Clare smiled. He'd always hated having his name shortened. And, looking at the grin on Flyboy's face, she suspected he was just as well aware of the fact as she was. 'CAA regs again, I'm afraid. You need to do the training first. We can arrange that when you're back in the department. But there's nothing to stop me from showing you how it works.'

He picked up the drone and held it out towards her. When he handed it to her she nearly dropped it, the thing was so heavy.

'Bloody hell. It weighs a tonne.'

'Not quite a tonne. But it is pretty hefty. It's all of the kit that's strapped to it. It has to be pretty robust.'

David smiled. 'Shall we put it to the test?'

Thirty minutes later Clare and David were standing staring at a laptop screen in the back of David's Land Rover. Changes in the pitch of the thrumming that was coming from overhead were the result of Flyboy's acrobatic manoeuvring of the drone above the now empty cuttings.

Clare said, 'It's difficult to see from this angle with the light on the screen.'

David said, 'Don't be a half-wit all your life, Clare. Come and stand here in front of me. Then we can both see it.'

She shuffled awkwardly into position.

One hand on the mouse, David half turned to yell, 'Hey, Flyboy, can you adjust the focus on that thing?' his arm drawing her closer to him in the process.

She suddenly became uncomfortably aware of the rise and fall of his chest as they both struggled to pick out the image on the screen in front of them.

He adjusted the angle of the screen. 'That's better. There it is.' He pointed with the cursor. 'Do you see, Clare?'

She leant forward, peering at the image, grateful to have something that demanded her attention. 'Yes. Yes. It's as clear as day.'

David said, 'It's wheels within wheels.'

'A wheel within a square to be absolutely accurate,' Clare corrected him.

He laughed. 'Pedant! But there's no doubt in my mind now. That thin, circular feature looks like a foundation trench for a wall of some kind. And the square ditch around it is much larger in scale and proportion. It's exactly like the one they found on Hayling Island. Even down to the pits with the votive deposits in the *temenos*.'

'The teme what?'

'The *temenos*. The precinct that surrounded the holy of holies. When this thing was in use no one but the priest or Druid would have been allowed inside the inner part.'

'It still makes me shudder to think about what happened to those children.'

'You've got to remember it was a different world then. Their values weren't our values. And human sacrifice wasn't common. As far as we can tell it only seems to have been practised in the most dire of circumstances. Given the radio carbon dates we've got for the infant burials, there's every possibility that our infants met their fate when the Romans were first making their presence felt in these parts. Can you imagine what it must have been like when the Iron Age people round here first saw the legions marching towards them? The local population must have been scared witless. Perhaps they felt their only way out was a triple death.'

Clare said, 'You think that's why there were three infants sacrificed?'

'And all at the same time, remember. Those radio carbon dates are pretty much identical. But there was more to it than that. They were all killed in different ways.'

'Well, two of them were,' Clare corrected him. 'Jo said she couldn't find the cause of death for the third one. It could have died of natural causes. The infant mortality rate must have been sky high in the Iron Age.'

'True enough, but there is another explanation. Do you remember that chap they found in a peat bog in Cheshire in the eighties, Lindow Man?' Clare nodded. 'Well, he'd been hit on the head, garrotted and then had his throat cut. And we know from later written sources that sometimes the third mode of sacrifice was poison or drowning. They may have thought that the three deaths together somehow boosted the value of their offering to the gods.' David shook his head. 'Didn't do the poor sods any bloody good though. Within four years of Claudius invading there was a legionary fortress up the road in Gloucester.'

This place had a dark history. There weren't just the babies. There was Beth Kinsella too. They may have been separated by two thousand years, but none of them had deserved to die.

Clare shivered.

David said, 'You OK?'

'Just thinking about Beth.' He ushered her away from the back of the Land Rover and into the sunshine. 'Do you believe what happens somewhere can leave an imprint on a place, David?'

'Everything that happens somewhere shapes a place. Just as much as it shapes the people that lived and worked there.'

'And worshipped there,' Clare said.

He nodded. 'That's what it's all about for me. The way people shape things and places, and the places and things that shape people. Places make people and people make places.'

Had David deliberately misconstrued what she was saying? She looked around her at the picture-postcard-perfect Cotswold hillside. Was her imagination running away with her or had what happened here two millennia ago really left its mark in ways she didn't fully understand?

David put a hand on her shoulder. 'Come on. What you need is a cuppa.'

One of David's avowed beliefs was that there wasn't much a good strong cup of tea or a pint couldn't put right. Though there were times when she suspected he used it as a diversionary tactic. 'You go ahead. I'll be down in a minute. I want to have another look at the camera rig on the drone.'

She turned to make her way round the side of the Land Rover towards the area where Flyboy had landed the drone. But now that the thrumming overhead had ceased she could hear someone talking – arguing – on the far side of the vehicle.

It sounded like Neil. 'For fuck's sake, Sadie, I'm doing everything I can. I can't magic money out of thin fucking air.' He must be on his mobile. 'I know it's a shit job. I'm the one who has to flog my guts out at it. But it's all I know how to do. So you're just going to have to fucking put up with it.'

He was obviously having a rough time of it at home. Clare was finding it enough of a struggle getting by on her salary. She couldn't begin to imagine how tough it must be to make ends meet on the pittance they were paying Neil. The hand-to-mouth existence of a jobbing archaeologist was precarious enough without having a wife and young baby to support too. She might ask David if there was any way they could offer him a bit of work on the post-excavation side afterwards. At least then he'd know he had some job security.

The camera rig could wait for now. Neil would be mortified if he knew she'd overheard him rowing. Best leave him to it and go and get that tea David had promised her.

CHAPTER FOURTEEN

'I'm so glad you asked me over, Clare. Those aerial shots you sent over were wonderful. But there's nothing quite like seeing the site in the flesh.'

Clare said, 'I'm the one who should be thanking you. I'm really grateful you made the time to come over. I really do appreciate it, Margaret. Having you cast an expert eye over the finds has been invaluable.'

Margaret placed the sherd of pottery she'd been holding carefully back into the plastic finds bag from whence it had come. 'Nonsense. From what I can see Val here is doing a splendid job.'

The elfin Scotswoman sitting between them in the Portakabin beamed with pride. Val had been terrified when Clare had told her she'd asked Margaret over to take a look at what they'd found. Professor Margaret Bockford's reputation had evidently preceded her.

Margaret was warming to her theme. 'It's always such a help to have a finds supervisor who's both organised and knowledgeable – sadly not always the case in my experience. Now, Clare. When do I get to have a look at the site itself? Let's take a peek at this temple of yours.'

The two women leant into the gusting wind as they made their way uphill towards the trench containing the remains of the shrine, passing the descending diggers who were trudging past them in search of a hard-earned cup of tea.

Standing by the side of the cutting, surveying its contents, Margaret turned to Clare. 'Well there's no doubt about it – you've got yourself an absolutely classic Iron Age shrine site. And from what Val showed me of the finds I'd say that they tie up splendidly with the radio carbon dates you have from the infant burials. I can't tell you how excited I am about this, Clare. This really is a once-in-a-lifetime discovery.'

Clare nodded. 'I know.'

'Then why the glum face? You look like you've lost a shilling and found a sixpence.'

Clare waved her concern away. 'Oh, ignore me, Margaret. I'm just tired.'

Margaret peered over the top of her spectacles. 'I most certainly will not ignore you. I'm not a fool, Clare. As flattering as it is to be asked, I'm well aware that you had no good reason for inviting me out to see the site. You're perfectly capable of running this site on your own. And from what I've seen you've got yourself a really strong team here.'

'That's down to Beth. They were her team.'

'Don't change the subject! I want to know what it is that's troubling you.' Without warning, Margaret deposited herself onto the grass. Sitting cross-legged, she patted the ground beside her.

'Come on; tell me what this is all about. I'm not going anywhere until I've had an answer.'

Reluctantly, Clare sat down beside her. 'I don't know where to start, Margaret. Everything is such a mess.'

'Well, it can't be the excavations you're talking about. This is about as far from a mess as it's possible for one to imagine.'

'It's the nighthawking. I told the police about our meeting with the antiquities dealer.'

Margaret smiled. 'Is that all? If that's what's troubling you, it needn't. I've already received a visit from Detective Sergeant Hughes about that.'

'Really! Why didn't you mention it?'

Margaret said, 'What is there to mention? I told him exactly what happened. He was a little confused at first but he went away satisfied eventually.'

'Confused?'

'About why anyone would go to the trouble of procuring antiquities from abroad, in order to stage photographs of them being removed from an archaeological excavation and then sell them online. But once I'd told him that they were probably attempting to give them a false provenance to enhance their market value he seemed content that it was a credible explanation.'

Clare felt a wave of relief sweep through her entire body. 'Oh, thank God!'

'What is it, my dear? I really don't understand why you've worked yourself up into such a state about this.'

For what felt like an eternity Clare sat in silence, playing with a blade of grass, until Margaret eventually said, 'Well?'

Clare looked up into the older woman's soft brown eyes. 'There's something you should know, Margaret. Things aren't quite as straightforward as they seem with the nighthawking.'

Margaret let out a sound halfway between a gasp and a chuckle. 'I have to confess, Clare, "straightforward" isn't the first word that springs to mind about the little scam we unearthed.' Seeing Clare's expression, Margaret reached out a hand and placed it lightly on Clare's. 'I'm not trying to make light of your concerns, Clare. Just tell me what's happened.'

Clare nodded. 'There's a local Druid called Crabby who hangs around the site. He got to know Beth when she was digging here, and he's been pretty much a fixture while we've been here too.' Clare hesitated, unsure of Margaret's reaction. She had no idea what her views were on members of the modern pagan community. But to Clare's considerable relief, if the calmness of her response was anything to go by, they clearly didn't entirely coincide with David's. 'Anyway, Jo and I have got to know him a bit. And when we were chatting to him in the pub one night he admitted that he and one of the other locals were responsible for planting the finds on-site that ended up being sold online.'

'I don't understand, Clare. Why on earth would they do that?'

'Because they wanted to stop the houses being built and they thought that if Beth found something spectacular they'd have to halt the development.'

'But surely Beth must have realised.'

'She did, and she told them to pack it in. According to Crabby she told him she didn't need their "help" because she already had proof of the site's significance.'

'I take it Beth didn't share with this Crabby exactly what the nature of that evidence might be.'

Clare shook her head. 'No. And I can't understand what it was. I don't remember seeing anything in her site notes that suggested she'd found any hard evidence to prove the shrine was here.'

'Though whether by evidence, gut instinct or pure fluke she

was undoubtedly right.' Margaret nodded in the direction of the trench. 'Have you considered that Beth might have told Crabby that she'd found something just to persuade him to stop burying artefacts all over the site?'

She shook her head. 'To be honest, no. But that's not what's worrying me. I know Crabby shouldn't have buried those artefacts here—'

Margaret cut in, 'And presumably illicitly procured them in the first place.'

Clare didn't respond; she had no intention of complicating matters further by recounting Sheila Foggarty's involvement in all of this. 'Believe me, Margaret. If I thought for one moment Crabby would ever pull a stunt like that again I'd be the first person to stop him. But he's a good man. He cares about this place. He was just . . .' She struggled to find the right word. 'Misguided. The thing is, the moment I told the police, I realised I'd landed Crabby in it.'

'You're not thinking straight, Clare. Other than causing some minor criminal damage – which the police really aren't going to be interested in – what exactly has this new friend of yours done that's illegal? This site's not legally protected. Buying from antiquities dealers online might be considered unethical but unfortunately it's not illegal. And, more to the point, when the police came to see me about our little encounter with White Van Man, I didn't even know Crabby existed.

'So unless you or Jo are planning on telling them about his activities, as far as they're concerned White Van Man and his confederates are entirely responsible for the untoward activity on this site. And should the police ever run them to ground, they have photographs to prove it. And I for one have no intention of disabusing them of the notion.'

* * *

'I see you've finally begun to understand the gravity of the situation, Mr Kelly.'

Following the morning's interview, Damian Kelly had demanded to see a solicitor. It had taken a while to get hold of the duty solicitor. But West had finally tracked her down, and now sitting across the table from Sally alongside Damian Kelly was the all-too-familiar figure of Gemma Bates. Gemma Bates' appearance inspired little confidence in her clients. Make-up-less and overweight, her thin, obviously dyed brown hair fell lankly about her shoulders. The uninitiated would be forgiven for mistaking her for a world-weary secondary school teacher. But as Sally sat watching her lick the last of the sugar from the doughnut she'd been eating as she strolled into the station, if they did they'd be making a serious mistake.

Gemma Bates was smart, experienced and knew every trick in the book. 'How long has my client been in custody, DI Treen?'

Sally looked at her watch. 'Seven hours, Ms Bates. Though it would have been considerably less had you been able to grace us with your presence this morning.'

Gemma Bates ignored the comment and tapped her watch. 'The clock is ticking, DI Treen.'

Sally opened her case notes. 'Well, let's just see how we go, shall we? When we last spoke, Mr Kelly, I showed you this photo.' She pulled the CCTV still from her notes and, turning it through one hundred and eighty degrees, pushed it towards Kelly. 'For the tape, this is a CCTV image captured at eleven forty-six showing Damian Kelly approaching the victim—'

Gemma Bates interrupted. 'An image that you claim is of my client, DCI Treen.'

Sally gave her a withering look. 'Take a closer look, Ms Bates. Unless Mr Kelly has an identical twin, I don't think there's much doubt, do you?' She looked at Damian Kelly. 'Do you have an identical twin, Mr Kelly?'

Kelly looked nervous. He was paler than before and in the few hours since their last interview appeared to have aged several years. He mumbled, 'No. No, I don't.'

Sally said, 'Well, I think that's cleared that one up, don't you?' She stared down Gemma Bates. 'Would you like to explain what you were doing in Snuff Street with Jack Tyler at eleven forty-six, just a few hours before Jack's murder?' The word 'murder' seemed to echo round the tiny room.

Kelly got as far as saying, 'I was . . .' before Gemma Bates stuck her hand up.

'I would advise you not to say anything, Mr Kelly.'

Kelly sat silently for a couple of seconds, head down, picking at his fingernails. Sally just waited.

Then he said, 'No.' The word rang out like a gunshot. 'Why shouldn't I say my piece? I've done nothing wrong here.'

Sally wanted to punch the air. Step one – get them to talk. 'So, what were you doing in Snuff Street with Jack Tyler?'

When Kelly looked at her she could see dark rings round his eyes. 'What does it look like? I was helping out a mate.'

Sally said, 'Helping out a mate who was found dead shortly afterwards. And whom you claimed earlier not to have seen after you left The Lamb Inn that night.'

'Look, I have no idea how Jack ended up dead. But I knew this was going to happen.'

Sally said, 'Are you saying you knew Jack Tyler was going to be killed?'

Kelly yelled, 'No, you silly bitch. I mean I knew if I said I'd found Jack down a dark alley close to midnight it wasn't going to look good for me.'

Sally said, 'I'd advise you to moderate your language, Mr Kelly, unless you'd like things to look a whole lot worse for you.'

Gemma Bates pounced. 'Are you threatening my client, DI Treen?'

'No, I'm simply advising him that the law takes a dim view of suspects abusing police officers.'

At the use of the word 'suspects', Damian Kelly slumped forward on the desk, his head in his hands. 'I don't feckin' believe this.' He sat upright again. 'Look, I didn't kill Jack Tyler. When I found him in that alley he was in a right state. There was no way I was going to leave him there all night like that.'

'So you're trying to tell me you were just doing Jack Tyler a favour.'

He said, 'Finally, now you're beginning to get the picture.'

Sally glanced down at her notes. 'If that's the case maybe you could clear something up for me, Mr Kelly. Why were you heading down Snuff Street at close on midnight in the first place, heading in the opposite direction to where you live?'

He leant forward, more confident now. 'I think that's my business, don't you?'

'This is a murder inquiry, Mr Kelly. Everything is my business. Why were you heading down Snuff Street at a quarter to midnight?'

'I was going to see someone.'

'I think you found the person you were going to see, Mr Kelly. I think you were looking for Jack Tyler. And unfortunately for Jack you found him.'

He shook his head. 'No. No. No. It wasn't like that.' He turned to the solicitor. 'Does anyone else get to find out what I say here?'

Gemma Bates said, 'Not necessarily. Not unless it comes out in court.'

Kelly turned to Sally. 'I was paying a visit to someone.' He turned to the solicitor again. 'Are you sure my wife won't find out about this?'

Gemma Bates shook her head, 'Only if you're charged and it comes to court.'

He nodded. 'I was going to see a woman.'

Sally asked, 'Which woman?'

Kelly stayed silent.

'For your own sake, Mr Kelly, I advise you to give us her name.'

Gemma Bates nodded her agreement.

Kelly said, 'Jeanette. Jeanette Freeman.'

Sally asked, 'And will this Jeanette Freeman be able to corroborate your story, Mr Kelly?'

'Yes. Yes, she will. I've been going with her on and off for years.'

Sally asked, 'And she'll be able to tell us that you spent that night with her, will she?'

Kelly ran his tongue around his lips. 'Well, no.'

Sally stared him straight in the eye. 'Oh, and why is that, Mr Kelly?'

'Because Jack threw up all over me, didn't he? I couldn't turn up like that, now could I?'

'But presumably Jeanette would be able to confirm that you'd had an arrangement for you to see her that Thursday night.'

Kelly said, 'It wasn't that sort of arrangement. I didn't have to call.'

Sally said, 'That's very unfortunate for you, Mr Kelly. So, what you're actually telling me is that you have no one who can corroborate your story.'

No response.

Sally leant forward. 'Let me put an alternative suggestion to you, Mr Kelly. The reason you were in Snuff Street on that Thursday night at close on midnight was because you'd gone looking for Jack Tyler. And the CCTV footage shows beyond any doubt that you were successful. I suggest you dragged Jack back to

191

his flat and once you got there you argued with him. And at some time in the early hours of Friday morning you struck Jack Tyler and killed him.'

Damian Kelly's eyes roamed around the room. After what seemed like several long minutes he returned his gaze to Sally.

He lowered his voice, 'Look, I was on my way to see Jeanette and I found Jack. He was arseholed. I couldn't leave him there like that so I thought I'd just get him home and then I'd go on to Jeanette's place afterwards. But when I got him back to his place the bastard threw up on me. So I made sure he was OK and decided to call it a night. Satisfied?'

Before Sally had a chance to respond, there was a knock on the interview room door.

DS West stuck his head round the door. 'Can I have a minute, ma'am?' He must have seen the look on her face as she got up because he mouthed the words, 'You'll want to see this.'

Outside in the corridor, West handed her another Manila folder. She opened it. It contained a single document with an email paperclipped to the front.

'Thanks, Tom.'

Back in the interview room she resumed her seat. She spent a few minutes skimming through the report West had handed her.

Gemma Bates finally lost patience. Pointing to her watch, she said, 'Time's nearly up, DI Treen.'

Sally pulled herself upright in her chair. 'So it would seem, Ms Bates.' She turned to Damian Kelly. 'Time's not the only thing that's running out, Mr Kelly. It looks like your luck's run out too. We've just got the forensics results from the murder scene through from the lab and your prints are all over Jack Tyler's flat.'

Kelly sounded distraught. 'Of course they are. I told you I was there. I all but carried him back to his flat. And when I last saw

Jack Tyler he might have been in a state, but he was snoring like a good 'un on the sofa in his living room.'

Sally said, 'It took you long enough to tell us, though, didn't it, Mr Kelly. And that's not how we found him. And it doesn't explain why your fingerprints were also all over Jack's empty wallet. Inside and out.'

Kelly looked momentarily confused. 'Look, I've no idea how my fingerprints got onto Jack's wallet. But if you're suggesting I killed Jack Tyler for his money you're barking up the wrong tree. The bloke was skint. I already told you, I'd been paying for his drinks all night in the pub.' He sat distractedly, shaking his head. 'I don't understand it. I don't . . . Shit! I remember now.' He looked up at Sally. The desperation in his eyes clear to see. 'When we got to the lobby of Jack's block of flats we couldn't get in. You need one of those card thingies. Jack was out of it, so I had to go through his pockets to see if he had it on him. I found it in his wallet.'

Sally stood up.

He was pleading with her now. 'That's why my prints are on his wallet.'

Sally said, 'One too many changes of story, I'm afraid, Mr Kelly.' She paused. 'Damian Kelly, I'm charging you with the murder of Jack Tyler. PC Davies here will take you down to see the custody sergeant.'

It had been a week now since Clare had been to see Mark Stone. And the seven days had passed entirely without incident aside from a brief visit from the *Western Daily Press*, who wanted to run a story about the discovery of the shrine. Even the weather had been on their side. There'd been no more torrential downpours. And though the sun hadn't shone, the thick grey cloud that hung over the site did at least make taking the site photographs a little easier.

At the back of her mind she still couldn't help feeling anxious about what Crabby had told them. But she was beginning to wonder if Stone had had a point. She might have developed a soft spot for Crabby but no one could doubt that he had what might politely be described as a sideways take on reality at times.

She'd spent much of the first two nights after her excursion to Stroud lying awake worrying about what she could do to make someone take the situation seriously. Then, as she lay there tossing and turning, she realised that she only had Crabby and Sheila Foggarty's word for the fact that Beth had been opposed to the housing development. And Beth, like Clare and the Hart Unit, were being paid by Paul Marshall.

What's more, Clare also only had Crabby's word that Beth had claimed to have found something that proved the importance of the site. No one else seemed to know anything about it. Which, when she thought about it, seemed a curious state of affairs, given that Beth had previously spent so much time trying to convince the world that Bailsgrove had been a cult centre in the Iron Age. And even if Beth had made a big discovery, if she hadn't actually told anyone other than Crabby then why would anyone have had a reason for killing her? The more she thought about it, the less sense it all made.

So she'd decided to put Crabby's fantasies about dead hares behind her and concentrate firmly on the one thing she had no doubt Beth Kinsella would have given anything to be able to do – excavate Bailsgrove's Iron Age temple.

To that end she and Jo now found themselves working on the foundation trench of what David had described as the 'holy of holies' or, as Malcolm had christened it, the 'ho ho ho'. Clare had tried pointing out that there was a 'ho' too many in there, but by then it was too late. The name had stuck. She'd been tempted to mention that the name was more than a little irreverent given the nature of the site. But in the end she'd decided it was best to keep her thoughts to herself for fear of being labelled the site killjoy.

Jo was trowelling her way through a thick black layer in the top of the foundation trench. 'This stuff's solid charcoal.'

Clare got up from the bucket she was perching on by the side of the cutting and peered down. 'Looks as if we know what the wall of the ho ho ho was made of, then.'

Jo nodded. 'Uh huh. Split planks. And someone did a real thorough job of burning it down.'

Clare said, 'Makes you wonder if it was deliberate.'

Jo laughed. 'Those pesky Romans again.'

Clare said, 'Maybe. But if it was, they did us a favour. We should be able to get some decent radio carbon samples from that lot. I'll pop down to the office and get some tin foil to wrap the samples in.'

As Clare made her way downhill she could see that Malcolm was standing just outside the office door talking to someone. Thickset and wearing dark suit trousers and a white shirt with the sleeves rolled up, even standing with his back to her she could tell that whoever it was meant business. And he and Malcolm appeared to be deep in conversation.

As she drew closer she called out, 'Can I help you?'

The man spun round. It was Paul Marshall. He was waving a copy of a newspaper at her. It took her only seconds to recognise it as yesterday's copy of the *Western Daily Press*. She had the same edition sitting on the Portakabin desk, waiting for her to cut out the temple article for the team noticeboard.

'Oh yes, you can. You can tell me what the fuck you think you're playing at.'

'I don't quite follow you, Mr Marshall.'

'Well, you bloody well should. I thought I'd stopped all of this sort of bullshit when I spoke to your boss about the last lot of bollocks you splashed all over the media. But apparently I didn't make myself clear.' He walked forward until he was standing toe to toe with her. 'I won't have it. I won't take any more of this shit from you.' He threw the newspaper to the floor.

Clare stepped back and took a deep breath, trying to control her escalating heartbeat. 'If you'd like to come into my office, I'd be happy to discuss any concerns you might have, Mr Marshall.'

His face was on fire. He looked like he was about to have a heart attack.

'*Your* office!' He bellowed. 'You've got a sodding nerve. I own this site. All of it. Do you hear me? And I won't have anyone trying to tell me where I can and can't go on my own property.'

Clare said, 'I was just trying to suggest we might be more comfortable sitting down talking this through like two reasonable human beings.'

She could see an embarrassed Malcolm edging his way round Marshall and creeping back to the cutting.

Marshall jabbed a finger at her. 'I'll tell you what would make me feel more comfortable. You stopping shit-stirring and starting to do the job I'm paying you for.'

Clare drew in a deep breath. She fervently hoped she looked a whole lot more directorial than she was feeling right now.

'If by "shit-stirring" you mean speaking to the press about what we've discovered on the site, I'd have thought you would welcome the publicity. We do credit Marshall Construction as funders in the article.'

'I should sodding well hope so. I'm paying your wages, girlie, and don't you forget it. And let's get one thing straight: I'm not paying you to do my PR for me. I'm paying you to clear this site and bugger off to whatever godforsaken hole in Wiltshire you lot crawled out of.'

He bent his head down towards her until he was so close she could smell stale wine and garlic on his breath. 'Understand?'

Clare never got the chance to reply. She heard the sound of pounding feet careering down the slope behind her and then a hand appeared, it seemed out of nowhere, and gripped Marshall firmly by the arm.

Taking in huge gulps of Cotswold air, clearly out of breath, Neil said, 'Mr Marshall, I think Clare here's got the picture, don't you? We wouldn't want any more misunderstandings, now would we?'

A seemingly stunned Marshall opened his mouth as if to speak, then apparently thinking better of it, closed it again. Neil guided Marshall, still cursing under his breath, towards where his Audi was parked next to the field entrance. Clare couldn't hear what Neil was saying, but he was still talking to Marshall. And whatever he was saying seemed to be working. With a little cajoling from Neil, Marshall eventually climbed into his car. As Marshall spun the car round he lowered his window and yelled, 'You mark my words. I expect to be bringing my diggers onto site in a fortnight. Unless you lot are done by then I won't be responsible for my actions.'

Neil walked back over towards the site office. 'Are you alright?'

'Fine. At least I think so. How did you manage that?'

'Marshall's like a fire. The more fuel you throw on him, the higher the flames get.' He hesitated. 'And I don't think he likes women much. He was never too keen on Beth either.'

'Well, however you did it, thank you, Neil.' She remembered his conversation on the phone with Sadie. Maybe there was something she could do to help. 'I think you've just earned yourself a bonus.'

Was he blushing? She hadn't meant to embarrass him.

He shook his head, his eyes cast to the floor. 'Thanks, Clare. But I know the unit's strapped for cash. You can buy me a pint if you want to. I was just doing my job.' Then, picking his head up, he said, 'You know you ought to go careful around Marshall.'

Clare asked, 'What makes you say that?'

'Apart from what you saw just then?'

'That was just schoolyard bully stuff.'

He shook his head. 'I wouldn't be so sure. Some schoolyard bullies turn into full-on thugs. I know what he's like; I've dealt with him before.'

'When Beth was running the dig, you mean?'

Neil said, 'Not just then. On other sites too. He's a nasty piece of work.' He looked her straight in the eye. 'I'm serious, Clare. You don't want to cause him any more trouble than you have to.'

'We've got a nationally important site here, Neil. There's only a handful of these things known anywhere. Are you trying to tell me I should do some sort of botch job on it just to get out of Marshall's hair more quickly?'

Neil said, 'No. I'm just saying this isn't a research project, Clare. It's a commercial excavation. Nobody would blame you for just doing what's needed to get by.'

CHAPTER FIFTEEN

'The way I see it, if Neil hadn't intervened you would've found yourself in a whole heap of trouble.' Jo handed Clare her glass of Pinot and deposited herself and her rum and Coke in the corner seat opposite her.

It had been a long and difficult day and both women had been glad to retreat to the sanctuary of the King's Arms at the end of it.

'Like I told Neil, Marshall is just a schoolyard bully. He's all bark and no bite.'

Jo tucked a stray strand of her unruly blonde hair behind her ear. 'Are you sure about that, Clare? He looked pretty darn serious from where I was standing.'

Clare shook her head. 'He's all bluster. And I'm damned if I'm going to do what Neil suggests and trash the site just to placate Marshall.'

Jo said, 'Now hang on a minute, Clare. From what you told me that's not exactly what Neil was suggesting, is it? From where I'm sitting I'd say he was just trying to help out. And you've seen for yourself what Neil's like at the moment. I don't know what's eating at him, but he's been on a real downer the last couple of weeks.'

Jo opened a packet of cheese and onion crisps and proffered one to Clare.

Clare shook her head and instead took a sip of her Pinot. 'I think I might know what the problem is.'

'Oh.'

'He's having trouble on the home front. I heard him on the phone the other day having a row with Sadie.'

Jo asked, 'What about?'

'Money. Or rather the lack of it.'

Jo said, 'Ah, the age-old problem. Being a shovel bum might make you happy, but it's never gonna make you rich.'

'Only in this case it doesn't seem to be making him happy either.'

'It's tough for all of us at times. However much we love what we do.'

Clare added, 'And Neil's got no job security. When he finishes here, who knows when he'll next pick up any work. And with a young baby . . .'

Jo said, 'Well, there you go, that accounts for it.' Jo paused. 'And don't forget Beth. He'd known her for years. I know he doesn't show it, but he must have been pretty freaked about what happened.'

'True. He doesn't like to talk about it. But Beth's death does seem to have had a big impact on him.'

Jo said, 'And not just Neil. I think it hit all of them pretty hard. I had Malc down as a hard-bitten, badass digger, but when I tried talking to him about Beth he just walked away. He seemed real cut up about it.'

Clare twirled the stem of her wine glass. 'When I went to see Stuart Craig a few weeks back he reckoned Neil had a thing for Beth.'

Jo said, 'No way! But she was way older than Neil.'

'Since when did that make a difference?'

'You've got a point. And there's no denying, Beth Kinsella was a good-looking woman. And we all have our fantasies, I guess.'

Clare gave her a quizzical look.

Jo felt herself blush. *Damn!* 'I'm just saying. It doesn't mean there was anything going on. Maybe he just admired her from afar.'

'I didn't know you were such an old romantic, Dr Death.'

Jo plucked a beer mat from the table and slapped Clare across the back of her hand with it. 'Don't start with the Dr Death crap, you! I get enough of it from the students. Anyhow, either way it would explain why he was so cut up about Beth's death. And even if he didn't have a thing for her, she was his boss. And if something happened to David I'm guessing you'd be kind of cut up about it.'

This time it was Clare's turn to blush. But she swiftly changed the subject. 'The other thing Stuart Craig told me was that Beth had been sacked by Sheffield because she was an obsessive. According to Craig, their whole lives had been taken over by her obsession with Celtic death and sacrifice. He more or less said it was why they split up in the end too.'

Jo said, 'Well, she certainly seems to have been pretty single-minded about it.'

Clare leant forward. 'That's just it, Jo. Yes, she was single-minded, but everybody thought she was a fruitcake when she was going around shouting about Bailsgrove being an Iron Age temple. And now we know that's exactly what it is. Beth Kinsella was right. And in my book that doesn't make her an obsessive fantasist. It makes her a bloody good archaeologist. And if that was the case, why would she kill herself?'

There was no way Jo would ever tell her friend as much but she looked as if she'd aged ten years since she'd taken on the Bailsgrove dig. And she was worried about her.

She lowered her voice. 'Look, Clare, none of us can get inside one another's heads. No one is ever going to know what Beth Kinsella was thinking when she took her own life.'

'*If* she took her own life.'

'Don't go there, Clare! I thought we'd talked about this. Crabby's one of the good guys. And I like the dude as much as you do. But there's not a scrap of evidence that Beth's death was anything other than exactly what it looks like – a suicide.'

Clare made no reply. And Jo watched as she sat silently twirling the stem of her wine glass between her fingers, and staring fixedly into what remained of its contents.

Jo said, 'OK, Clare, I know you. There's something you're not telling me. What gives?'

Clare let out a long slow breath. 'OK. But if I tell you, you've got to promise you won't get angry with me. I did something really stupid, when I went to see Mark Stone. Something that could've landed Crabby in hot water with the police.'

'Hey, none of us like to have our ideas dismissed. But how much harm can it have done telling Stone about what Crabby said about Beth?'

Clare shook her head, but still didn't look up. 'It's not that.'

'What then?'

'Promise me you won't get angry?'

Jo raised her hands in mock surrender. 'I promise. Now just tell me what happened.'

'I told him about what Margaret and I found out when we went to meet that antiquities dealer.'

In a stage whisper, Jo said, 'You did what? What the hell were you thinking of, Clare?' She leant in towards Clare and lowered her voice. 'You know Crabby planted those finds.'

Clare looked up at her friend, 'Yes, of course. And to be honest I don't know why I said it. I was just so pissed off with Mark. I suppose I wanted him to take me seriously for once.'

'So you figured it was worth risking getting Crabby caught up in a police investigation because you thought some guy wasn't paying you enough attention. Is that what you're telling me?'

'It wasn't like that. You weren't there, Jo. He was so patronising. I was sick to death of the way he always dismisses everything I say out of hand. I wanted to show him I wasn't just some silly little woman who could be ignored. I thought if I could face him down with the evidence, I could show him he'd been wrong to just disregard what happened with the nighthawks. Then he'd have to sit up and take notice. And I didn't want the dealer to just get away with it. Who knows what other sites he and his mates are out there wrecking right now.'

Jo leant back in her chair and folded her arms. 'I see – you did all of this for entirely ethical reasons. Is that the story?'

Clare flushed. 'No. I told you I was mad at Stone. For ignoring everything I say, for not caring about the site getting wrecked, and for not being willing to even consider the possibility that Beth's death was anything other than a suicide.' She paused. 'And to be honest I was so angry that when I told Stone about the meeting with the dealer I didn't stop to think what the implications might be for Crabby, or for anyone else for that matter.'

'Please tell me you didn't actually say anything to Stone about Crabby's part in the metal detecting fiasco!'

Clare shook her head. 'Of course not. What do you think I am, Jo? I know I've been a bloody idiot. And I'm not proud of myself. But I'd never do anything to intentionally hurt Crabby.'

Jo let out a sigh. It was obvious how worried Clare was – worried and tired. The last few weeks had been difficult for all of them, but Clare had been the one shouldering the lion's share of the responsibility. 'I know.' She smiled reassuringly. 'But you've got to admit it was kind of a dumb thing to do. And that's not like you, Clare.'

Clare shook her head. 'I didn't used to think so either. But lately I'm beginning to wonder.'

A thought suddenly struck Jo. 'Did you tell the police Margaret was involved?' Clare nodded. 'You need to tell her, Clare. If they do follow it up they're bound to want to speak to her about it. And she'll be as mad as hell if they turn up on her doorstep and she knows nothing about it.'

Clare took a sip of her drink. 'I've already spoken to her. Stone sent someone round to see her after I told him. But she was alright about it. She didn't know about Crabby's involvement. So as far as the police are concerned, the dealer and his mates are the ones who planted the finds on-site. And who's going to believe them if they try to claim otherwise?'

Jo said, 'I guess so.'

Clare said, 'The thing is, Jo, I was wondering. Do you think I ought to tell Crabby?'

'Tell him what? That he trusted us and we repaid him by telling the police?'

Clare protested, 'But I didn't tell them about his part in what happened.'

Jo shook her head. 'That's not what I'm saying, Clare. There's nothing to tell. From what you say, Stone and his guys have no idea Crabby has anything to do with what happened. And the only way they're going to find out is if one of us tells them. And that's not going to happen. So if you tell Crabby all you're gonna do is make him panic.' She took a long swig from her rum and Coke. 'Oh, and make him mad as hell with us too.'

Clare said, 'I suppose you've got a point. But it just doesn't feel right dropping him in it like that and then not even having the decency to tell him what I've done.'

Jo shrugged her shoulders, 'It's your call, Clare. But in my experience guilt is never a good reason for doing anything. And telling him is just gonna make things worse.'

Clare stared down at the tabletop before letting out a long sigh. 'No. You're right, Jo. I know you are.' Looking up, she said, 'It's not worth causing more trouble than I already have just to salve my conscience.'

Jo said, 'Don't take this the wrong way, but I think you need to chill out for a while. Take a vacation. You need a break, Clare.'

'I don't know.'

'You could take this Friday off, make a long weekend of it. What's stopping you? I can cover for you on the dig, if that's what's worrying you. And I promise not to make any epic finds while you're away.'

Clare had been tempted to argue. But when she'd thought about it, she'd recognised the wisdom of Jo's words. And in the end, she'd decided to take her friend's advice and had booked herself into a bed and breakfast on the edge of the Peak District for the weekend.

Now that all of the arrangements were in place, she was surprised at how much better she felt already. And so by the time Wednesday morning came round she was already feeling significantly more content with life as she stood surveying the cuttings, mug of lukewarm tea in hand. That is until she received her first phone call of the day.

She thrust her mobile into the pocket of her moleskins and muttered, 'Damn,' under her breath.

Jo stepped out of the trench and ambled across to join her. 'What's up?'

'That was the solicitors.'

Jo frowned. 'Oh. Not more bad news about Stephen?'

'Oh, God no. Nothing like that.' She hesitated. 'It's the house.'

'What house?' Jo looked confused. She had every right to be. Clare hadn't shared her plans with anyone yet, not even Jo. Somewhere along the line she'd managed to convince herself that if she told anyone it might never happen.

'The house I'm buying.'

'You're buying a house!' Jo asked, 'Where?'

'In East Kennett.'

'That's up near Avebury, isn't it?' Jo had the look of an excited puppy dog about her.

Clare nodded. 'Yep.'

Jo frowned. 'But that's good news, isn't it? What's the problem?'

Clare smiled apologetically, 'Sorry, Jo. I didn't mean to sound so grumpy. Of course it's good news. I can't wait. But the solicitor just phoned to ask me when I'm going to be able to sign the contract. Apparently they posted it to my flat first class on Monday and the people I'm buying from are keen to get on with it. It means I'm going to have to drive back down there tonight to pick it up and sign it.'

Jo said, 'Bummer.' There was a short pause. 'But a house near Avebury, that's real neat.'

Clare grinned. 'I suppose it kind of is, isn't it?'

It already seemed like a long week and it was only Wednesday. Jo had been amazing; not only was she going to cover for her on Friday, but she'd offered to get the team started on-site on the Thursday morning so that Clare didn't have to set off from Salisbury at the crack of dawn. Despite that, by the time Clare had gone through everything she'd needed Jo to cover for her in the following day's briefing it had been gone seven. So she'd decided she might as well eat at the King's Arms before she set off. It had seemed like a good idea at the time, but when she'd finally parked up Little Blue on the street outside her flat it was already dark. And as she hauled her holdall wearily out of the boot, she was bathed in the strange orange half-light of the street lamps.

Trudging up the front steps to her ground floor flat, she mentally worked her way through her wardrobe, selecting what she was going to take with her for her weekend away. At least that was one advantage to having to come back here. She'd be able to pick up some clean clothes for her weekend away in the Peak District.

Oh, come on, Clare. Stop being so negative about this. However inconvenient it might be, once she'd signed that contract she was on her way to making this new life of hers permanent. In the two years since Stephen's death her life had been turned upside down. And despite one or two hairy moments along the way, coming back to Wiltshire was the best thing she'd ever done. Yet somehow her life here still felt a bit like a daydream. She may have had her doubts about whether she was up to it when David had first offered her the job at the Hart Unit, but that was because she hadn't been sure she really had what it takes to make it as an archaeologist. From the moment they'd first put trowel to earth and started digging together at Hungerbourne, she'd never doubted what she wanted to do with the rest of her life. It might not be a palace but buying the house was her way of finally committing to this new life.

She fumbled in her pocket for her keys and was about to insert the key in the lock when her hand touched the woodwork and the door swung open of its own volition. Had she forgotten to lock it when she'd left? The only other person who had a key was Jo – and she was safely ensconced in the King's Arms, the best part of sixty miles away.

She stepped into the hallway and called out, 'Hello. Is there anybody there?'

Christ, what a daft thing to say. She had no idea what she'd do if there was. She stood stock-still and listened. Outside in the street she heard a car honk its horn and the distant sound of music and laughter drifting from the nearby pub. But inside, nothing. As she got to the end of the hall, she stretched her hand up and felt for the light switch. It came on with a click that in the still of the evening air sounded like a gunshot, and illuminated a scene of devastation in front of her. Her living room was almost unrecognisable. Every drawer in the place had been pulled out and their contents unceremoniously dumped where they fell. The cushions from the sofa had been flung to the four corners of the room. And, worst of all, the books that had once stood neatly arranged in alphabetical order on her shelves lay strewn across the floor.

She deposited her holdall in the only gap she could find on the living room carpet and picked her way carefully through the debris towards the kitchen. It was the same story here: cupboards and drawers stood open, their contents pushed to one side or lying smashed on the floors. The only place that seemed to have escaped was the fridge. She stood there with the fridge door open, momentarily contemplating whether it would be wise to pour herself a large glass of white wine before she rang the police. Suddenly she heard a movement from somewhere behind her. It was followed swiftly by the clatter of a door smashing against a wall. She turned and scrambled over the top of the intervening detritus and down the hallway. She got to the top of the steps just in time to see the silhouette of a tall figure sprinting down the street and turning into the side alley a few doors down. There was no way she'd catch them. And she wasn't sure she'd have any idea what to do if she did.

Clare had no notion what the normal routine was when reporting a burglary to the police, but things being what they were these days she was half expecting the woman on the other end of the line to issue her with a crime number and tell her to get on with it. So it came as something of a surprise when a female police officer accompanied by a forensics team had turned up within little more than an hour. It had, as they later explained to her, been an unusually quiet couple of days in Salisbury.

She'd been told not to touch anything, but she hadn't been able to resist checking out the bedrooms to see what sort of a state they were in. And to her relief she'd discovered that, though the contents of the boxes from Stephen's study had suffered the same fate as the rest of the flat, her bedroom had at least been spared. She must have disturbed them before they'd got that far.

And that was where she was sitting now, perched awkwardly on the end of the bed alongside the policewoman.

'And as far as you can tell, that's the only thing that's been taken.'

Clare said, 'Well, it's difficult to say for sure but the TV's still here, the iPod is still sitting in its dock in the living room and I had my work laptop with me. So yes, as far as I can tell I think it's just my husband's old laptop that they've taken. But I can't imagine they'll get much for it.'

'And there's no jewellery missing?'

Clare fiddled with her wedding ring. It was the only piece of jewellery of any worth that she possessed. She'd sold all of the rest, to help finance the deposit for the house. Clare shook her head. 'No. No jewellery.'

'Have you got anyone who could stay with you tonight?'

Clare looked up, startled. 'Why, do you think they'll come back?'

The policewoman shook her head. 'No, that's highly unlikely. It's just that it can be a bit of a shock having someone break into your house and go through your personal possessions. Sometimes it takes a while to sink in.'

Clare glanced at her watch. It was nearly one in the morning. The nearest person was David. And there was no way she was going to ask him to come over at this time of night. Besides, he might have Sally with him. And Sally was the last person she wanted to see right now. 'I'll be fine, honestly. I'd rather just get on with clearing this place up.'

The police woman nodded and closed her notebook. 'OK. If you're sure. The team should be through next door soon and then we'll be out of your hair.'

'What do you think the chances are of catching whoever did this?'

'Honestly?' Clare nodded. 'Without a better description and with no CCTV down this street, I'd say slim to zero. Unless we turn someone over for something else and we happen to find your missing laptop on them, we'll probably never catch them. Nine out of ten times it's drugs-related. Whatever they find they'll flog for a pittance. But you never know your luck if we manage to turn up a decent set of prints. We'll give it our best shot.'

A man with a thick shock of grey hair wearing a white Tyvek bodysuit popped his head round the bedroom door. 'We've finished now, Jen.'

The policewoman stood up and turned to face Clare. 'Right, if you're sure you don't want us to call anyone for you we'll be on our way now. But promise me you'll bolt the front door after us when we've gone.'

Almost literally shutting the stable door after the horse had bolted. Clare resisted the urge to smile. Instead she nodded. 'And I'll get a locksmith out to replace that lock first thing tomorrow morning.'

As soon as they'd gone, Clare had bolted the front door and collapsed in an exhausted heap on her bed. Maybe she was in shock, maybe she was just knackered, but either way she slept like a baby and didn't wake until gone nine o'clock.

When she woke the first thing she did was ring Jo to tell her what had happened and let her know she probably wouldn't make it to site until late afternoon. As soon as she'd established that Clare was OK, Jo had, as usual, taken the news in her stride, though Clare had had to dissuade her from insisting on ringing David so that he could pop round to check that she was alright.

When she'd stepped out of the bedroom, Clare noticed that someone, presumably the police, had picked up her post and deposited it on the table in the hallway. On the top of the pile of junk mail sat a bulky-looking A4 envelope – the contract for the house. She picked it up and made her way through to the living room.

Package in hand, she stood in the doorway surveying the scene. Today was meant to be the next step in starting her new life, but it looked as if the fates had decreed it wasn't going to be that straightforward. She pushed aside the junk from the drawers that had been deposited on the coffee table and laid the package on it, then made her way into the kitchen.

There was glass everywhere. Most of the fragments seemed to have originated from a smashed jar of raspberry jam, half of the contents of which was now smeared in a sticky red streak that ran the front length of the under-sink cupboard. She retreated to the hallway, put on a pair of trainers, grabbed a bin bag and the dustpan and brush.

Within twenty minutes she'd managed to restore sufficient order in the kitchen to consider making herself breakfast. She hadn't been expecting to be here during the week so there was no juice in the fridge. And it was a little early to start on the white wine, tempting though it was.

In the end she settled for coffee and, depositing four heaped spoonfuls into the cafetière, which by some miracle had escaped unscathed on the kitchen counter, she filled the kettle. No milk, so no muesli. She extracted a couple of slices of wholemeal bread from her emergency supply in the freezer and inserted them into the toaster.

Fifteen minutes later, having returned the cushions to their rightful place on the sofa, she was sitting on it, legs crossed to avoid unwittingly damaging anything on the floor, munching away on her breakfast and feeling considerably better. It was going to take more than some bloody junkie to ruin the rest of her life.

After a shower and two mugs of black coffee, she set to with trying to restore some sort of order out of the chaos that surrounded her. When the locksmith turned up almost as rapidly as the police had the night before, Clare began to think that maybe the fates were feeling more kindly disposed towards her than they had been yesterday evening. Well, her mum was always telling her that you make your own luck, and she wasn't going to sit around licking her wounds. She'd soon be out of this flat for good, and in her own home – the next step in her new life. Which reminded her, she must ring her landlord to tell him about the break-in. Though on second thoughts maybe she should leave that until after she'd cleaned the place up and had the lock repaired. She didn't want to give him a heart attack. Or, worse still, end up losing her deposit when she finally moved out.

By the end of the morning, Clare had returned the living room to a state that was at least now inhabitable and the locksmith had been and gone, relieving her of a not inconsiderable sum – an expense that at the moment she could frankly have done without. With only the spare room left to tackle, she'd considered just shutting the door on it and leaving it for another day. But in the end she'd decided that as she'd have to have everything packed and ready for the move to her new house in the next few weeks she might as well get it over and done with now.

But that didn't mean she had to go through all of Stephen's stuff now. For the moment she could just put it back in its cardboard boxes and she'd deal with sorting the contents out once she was ensconced in her new home. One or two bits and pieces of Stephen's old golfing memorabilia lay broken on the floor, which made the decision not to keep them considerably easier. And, in the event, it didn't take her long to stack the paperwork into neat piles ready to return them to the boxes from whence they'd come. She was just putting the final pile into the last box when her eye was caught by several pieces of A4 paper stapled together that lay on the top of it. It was a printout of an email exchange. She placed the rest of the pile on the box and closed the lid, taping it shut.

Perching on the edge of the bed, she read and reread the printout's contents. When she'd finished, she made her way into the living room and slipped it carefully into the side pocket of her laptop bag.

CHAPTER SIXTEEN

'Hello, Margaret. I didn't expect to see you here.'

It was mid-afternoon by the time Clare arrived at Bailsgrove and the one person she hadn't been anticipating she'd encounter on-site was Margaret Bockford.

Margaret offered a wry smile, 'Well, that's a fine sort of greeting. I'm not entirely sure it should be considered a surprise to find a professor of archaeology on the site of an archaeological excavation.'

Clare flushed bright red. 'Well, no . . .'

Jo saved her any further embarrassment. 'I called her after you phoned me.'

Clare struggled to disguise her displeasure. 'Why? I told you, I'm perfectly OK. And, besides, you said you wouldn't tell anyone else.'

Jo said, 'That's not how I recall it. I actually agreed not to phone David.'

Clare turned to Margaret. 'I'm sorry, Margaret, but this has been a waste of your time. Whatever Jo has told you, I'm perfectly fine.' She held her arms out wide. 'Look – all in one piece – just fine and dandy.'

Margaret peered over the top of her spectacles and exchanged a look with Jo that Clare knew only too well. 'That remains to be seen, young lady. But I believe your friends are entitled to show some level of concern for your well-being.'

Clare sighed. 'It's not that I'm not grateful that you're both concerned, but honestly there's absolutely nothing wrong with me. The flat's all sorted now and as it turns out they barely took anything. The police think that arriving when I did, I must have disturbed them before they could take much of any real value.'

Jo stood, wide-mouthed. 'You didn't say anything about the burglars still being around when you got there.'

Clare blustered, 'No, well . . .'

Margaret said, 'I think we need to have words, young lady.' She turned to Jo. 'Is there anywhere we can go for a quiet chat?'

Jo poked her head inside the door of the welfare unit. 'Come on. In here.'

Clare couldn't quite believe this was happening to her. In the past twenty-four hours she'd single-handedly encountered a burglar, dealt with the police, cleared up the aftermath of a crime scene and signed the contract for a house purchase. And now she'd returned to the excavation that she was supposedly directing, only to find she was about to be given the third degree like some sort of recalcitrant teenager.

Margaret directed Jo and Clare to sit. Clare reluctantly followed orders, wedging herself into the corner beside Jo. She was dying for a cup of tea but with Margaret standing in front of them in full professorial mode, it somehow didn't seem like the moment to ask.

Margaret said, 'Right, that's better. Now let's get one thing straight, Clare. Jo rang me because she was concerned for your welfare. I think we'd all agree that's an acceptable and responsible attitude for a friend to take.'

Clare went to open her mouth in reply, then, thinking better of it, closed it again and settled instead for a straightforward nod.

'Good. I'm glad we've got that cleared up. I fully understand your reasons for not wanting to involve David in this. Though I'm not sure I agree with them.' She paused and Clare made as if to protest, but before Clare could utter a word Margaret waved her response away. 'But be that as it may, someone has to look at the wider picture here. Because it's quite evident that you're failing to do so. This situation has implications for all of us.' Margaret removed her glasses and, holding them in one hand, fixed Clare with a look that would have sent any undergraduate diving for cover.

Clare said, 'What wider picture? I've just had my flat burgled. How is that anybody else's concern?' Much as she respected Margaret Bockford, this was none of her bloody business.

Margaret said, 'Yes, but have you given any consideration to exactly why your flat was burgled?'

Clare was fuming now. She'd had enough. 'Because some sodding smackhead needed money for his next fix.' She took in a deep breath. 'Look, I'm sorry, Margaret, I appreciate that you and Jo were worried about me, but I'm a grown woman. I don't need mollycoddling. I was burgled. I can't lie: it wasn't pleasant to get back last night to find that. But the police have done their job. I've phoned the insurance company. They didn't even take much. It's all just fine now.'

Margaret said, 'But that's where you're wrong: it's not fine. Not fine at all.'

Clare shook her head in exasperation. In the last couple of years she'd come to know and respect Margaret Bockford; she counted her as a friend. But this was too much. Where did she get off trying to run other people's lives for them?

Jo rested a hand on Clare's forearm, but Clare instinctively withdrew it from the table. 'Look, Clare. I know you're tired. You've got a whole heap of stuff to deal with right now. And if I were you I'd be sick of everyone, me included, ignoring what I have to say and trying to tell me how to run my life. I get that. But give Margaret a break here. Just listen to what she has to say – it's important.'

Clare took in a deep breath and, inclining her head to one side, after a moment's pause folded her arms. 'Alright. I'm listening.'

Margaret said, 'Thank you. I have no wish to tell you how to lead your life, Clare. As far as I can see, aside from the odd slip-up that we're all subject to from time to time, you're fully capable of running your own life. But when Jo told me about this burglary, it troubled me.'

Clare muttered, 'I wasn't too happy about it either.'

Margaret held up her hand and nodded. 'I understand that. Now, did the police say why they thought a "smackhead" was responsible for what happened last night?'

Clare shook her head. 'Only that nine out of ten burglaries are drugs-related.'

Margaret nodded. 'Understood. But there was no particular evidence that your burglary was drugs-related.'

Clare shifted uncomfortably in her seat. 'No.'

Margaret's tone was softer now. 'My dear, has it occurred to you that your burglary might not be random?'

Clare said, 'You mean that my flat might have been targeted in some way?'

Margaret said, 'Or more precisely that *you* might have been targeted in some way.'

Clare said, 'I don't understand.'

Jo said, 'Think about everything that's been going on round here in the last few weeks, Clare. There's been a whole load of shit happening.'

Margaret glanced at Jo, 'Not quite how I would have put it, but Jo's right, Clare. There's that business with the nighthawks and Jo tells me the developer – Marshall, is it?' Clare and Jo nodded in unison. 'Marshall has been exerting considerable pressure on you to get the site finished with the minimum of fuss.'

'Are you trying to say you think that Marshall or White Van Man are responsible for turning my flat over?'

Jo said, 'Well, you said yourself there wasn't much taken.'

Clare shivered. She'd been fine about the burglary when she'd thought it was just one of life's random events, but if it wasn't quite so random, that was another matter entirely.

Clare said, 'No. They made one hell of a mess, though. They'd been through the kitchen and the living room. The police think that I disturbed them when they were in the spare bedroom. I didn't realise they were still in there until I heard something when I was in the kitchen. And the only thing they'd taken was Stephen's old laptop – but I can't imagine it's worth much. He'd had it for donkey's years.'

'Doesn't that strike you as odd, my dear? That they were only interested in the laptop. '

'I just thought it was because it was portable. But, come to think of it, they didn't touch my iPod. That was still in the living room.'

Margaret must have seen how worried Clare looked because she said, 'I'm not saying there is definitely a connection, Clare, but if the police have been following up on the information we gave them on the antiquities dealer, there's every possibility that they may be seeking to protect their interests. You corresponded with him by email before we met up with him, didn't you?'

'Yes, but under the name of Emily Draper.'

'Well, what if our White Van Man or his friends have put two and two together and worked out that Emily Draper is in fact Clare Hills, director of the Bailsgrove dig site?'

'But how is that even possible?'

Margaret said, 'Trust me, Clare, these people are no fools. They have ways and means.'

Jo cut in, 'And you have been on television and in the newspapers since you met him.'

Clare put a hand to her mouth. 'Oh shit! I never thought.'

Margaret said, 'And though we went to some lengths to disguise my appearance, we made no such efforts with you, my dear, because you hadn't been in the public eye. And in retrospect I can see that was an error of judgement on my part.'

Clare blew out her cheeks. 'On both our parts, Margaret. But even if they'd worked out who I am, and where I lived, I don't understand why they'd want to take Stephen's old laptop.'

Margaret said, 'Simple. They probably had no idea it wasn't yours. They may have thought the emails you sent to the dealer were on it.' She paused before adding, 'But we shouldn't put all of our eggs in one basket.'

Clare looked confused. 'What?'

Jo said, 'What Margaret means is that it may not be the nighthawks. After what happened here with Marshall the other day, it could have been him – or one of his stooges – trying to put the frighteners on you.'

Clare looked from Jo to Margaret and back again, unable to disguise her incredulity. 'You're not serious!' But she could see from their expressions they were. 'Marshall's just an overgrown schoolyard bully.' She hesitated. 'You really think he might have done this? But why would he take the laptop?'

Jo said, 'To make it look like a regular burglary, maybe.'

Margaret said, 'My advice to you, my dear, would be to do exactly what Jo has suggested. Get away from this place – and your flat – for a few days. Take that weekend away. And for heaven's sake don't tell anyone else where you're going.'

She'd followed their advice and driven up on the Thursday evening straight after work, but the weather hadn't looked promising. The driving rain was coming down in such torrents that the wipers on Little Blue had been beating double time all the way up the A6. And as she clambered out of the car when she arrived, visibility was barely good enough to allow her to navigate the flagstone path leading to the front door of the bed and breakfast, let alone marvel at the glories of the Peak District.

It was somewhere she had always promised herself she'd visit ever since her student days, when a homesick David had spent endless hours recounting its manifold wonders. But Stephen had never been keen. He hadn't shared her enthusiasm for the outdoors – unless it was on a golf course. And if she was being truthful with herself, he hadn't shared her enthusiasm for David either.

She'd been so shattered from her journey and the events of the last few days that after a hot bath and a cup of tea she'd flopped straight into bed. She'd prepared herself for a day of bracing walks in driving rain, but when she'd woken and flung open the curtains the rain had abated. And to her delight she could see sunshine pushing its way through the clouds. After coffee, orange juice – freshly squeezed – and a poached egg – cooked to perfection – she was feeling just about ready to face the world again.

She donned her walking boots and checked the batteries on her camera before ramming it into an already fully laden rucksack, then headed out in Little Blue. Within thirty minutes she was heading up to Wrackley Cop, the hill fort Beth Kinsella had excavated and where Neil Fuller had worked with her as a student. Margaret and Jo had been right: a few days away was exactly what she needed. Not least so that she could clear her head and concentrate on the things that really mattered.

She couldn't have explained why if she'd tried, but she knew that she had to get a better understanding of Beth Kinsella and the things that had driven her. And this time not from the people who'd known her, all of whom seemed to have such very different but definite opinions about exactly who Beth Kinsella was. She wanted to get a sense of her from the places that had shaped her.

As she climbed towards the top of the hill, the scenery was breathtaking. Surrounding two sides of the central ridge, Clare could still clearly make out the remains of what must once have been a substantial bank and, following them round, she began to find traces of a second circuit lying just outside the first. But the biggest surprise came when she crested the top of the hill. Plunging away on two sides below her was the river carving its way through the solid limestone of the valley below. The scene was dizzying, and in truth stunning, though it was a little too dizzying for Clare to stomach. She stepped back and pulling her waterproof from her rucksack, spread it on the damp grass and settled down to admire the view from a comfortable distance.

On a day like today this place was serenely beautiful; a patchwork of fields with their drystone walls dissecting the landscape. It was a photographer's dream. But Clare knew from David's tales of winter blizzards and Peak District villages marooned by snowdrifts that this place could be savage too. And when Beth had dug here, the limestone ditches had given up an unexpectedly savage secret.

Within the short stretch of the defences that she'd dug, and trapped beneath the fallen rampart for the last two thousand years, Beth had discovered the remains of nine women and children who, it seemed, had been dispatched and disposed of like so much discarded rubbish. When she'd spoken to Jo about it she'd said there had been no outward signs of violence on their bones. And Clare liked to think they might at least have had their throats cut before the many tonnes of drystone walling had entombed them.

Despite the tranquillity of the scene, she knew that in all probability dozens if not hundreds of victims of that Iron Age massacre lay in the ditches all around her. What sort of impact, she wondered, had the discovery made on Beth? Had she felt for the victims, or did she view the skeletons of those who had perished as so much data to fuel her research? Clare suspected she knew the answer, though she could never prove it. How could anyone fail to be changed by a discovery like that?

There were events in her own life that had changed her outlook on things in ways that she could never have foreseen. Stephen's death was one of them. From grief through guilt and anger, she'd been an emotional wreck for months afterwards. And there were still times, though less frequently these days, when it felt like she was taking one step forwards and two steps back. She'd managed to navigate her way through the carnage of her old life, at first with toddler steps but latterly with increasing confidence. And that had only been possible because of the help and support of those she'd had around her. She might not always show it, but she was well aware that without Jo and Margaret and of course David, she had no idea where she'd be today.

And there was another name that she could add to that list – James. Or at least until a couple of days ago she'd thought she could. She unzipped the side pocket on her rucksack and delved inside, pulling out the folded sheets of A4 paper. It was a printout of a series of emails. The same print out that she'd found when she'd been tidying up the contents of the cardboard boxes in her spare bedroom after the break-in. The name on the top of the first sheet in bold print was Stephen Hills. So there was no doubt who it had belonged to. And the email exchange was between Stephen and James Douglas – Stephen's friend and executor. The same James who had helped guide her through the Gordian entanglements of Stephen's financial arrangements after his death. And the same James, too, who only a few weeks ago had told her with utter certainty that he had known nothing about Stephen's property deals.

David had been looking forward to his afternoon of freedom as he put the pedal to what little was left of the metal on his trusty Land Rover on his journey across the border into Gloucestershire. He was feeling particularly pleased with himself as he'd managed to escape the clutches of the Runt who, even as David weaved his way through the Cotswold countryside, was delivering a motivational training session designed to encourage his colleagues to 'unleash their inner entrepreneur'. Whatever that might mean for a bunch of archaeologists who, generally speaking, had enough trouble unleashing a paper clip from the departmental stationery cupboard. Sod that for a game of soldiers on a Friday afternoon.

His good humour had diminished markedly when he'd got to site only to discover firstly that Clare had abandoned the excavation in favour of some weekend jaunt to heaven knows where. And further still when he'd heard Jo's explanation for exactly why his site director had taken it upon herself to award herself time off when the entire future of the Hart Unit depended on the dig she was supposed to be running.

Jo had tried to persuade him it wasn't a good idea to do anything rash, but by then all David could see in front of him was Paul Marshall's overweight carcass. And his ears had entirely ceased functioning.

He pulled up outside the offices of Marshall Construction, leaving the Land Rover slewed across the front steps of the building, the driver side door open. As he entered the air-conditioned lobby he scanned the room for any clues to the whereabouts of Marshall's office. The receptionist was dealing with a young man in a cheap-looking suit who appeared to be showing her a briefcase full of samples of some sort. David walked away and one by one started exploring each of the three corridors that lead off from the reception area.

The receptionist, who must somehow have escaped the clutches of the sales rep, clattered after him. 'Can I help you, sir?'

Opening a door to discover only a vacuum cleaner and a mop bucket behind it, he turned to the woman. 'You can if you can show me where Paul Marshall is?'

'Do you have an appointment with Mr Marshall, Mr . . . ?'

'Doctor. Dr David Barbrook.' The woman looked him up and down disbelievingly. He obviously didn't fit her idea of what a doctor looked like. 'No, I don't have an appointment. But I need to see him. And I need to see him now!'

'I understand you're anxious to see Mr Marshall, Dr' – she

stuttered over the word – 'Bellbrook, but he's an extremely busy man. If you'd like to come to reception I'd be happy to see when Mr Marshall might have a gap in his schedule.'

'Don't worry about that, I'll put a gap in his schedule when I find him.'

David tore off down the corridor, the hapless receptionist trailing after him, making a series of increasingly desperate appeals to his better nature as she went.

As David tore open door number four he hit the jackpot. Paul Marshall's name was emblazoned across his desk in neat metallic letters.

'Marshall. I want a word with you.'

Paul Marshall was talking on the phone. 'I'll give you a call later. Something's come up.'

'Too bloody right it has.'

Paul Marshall pushed his swivel chair away from his desk and got to his feet.

David faced him down across his desk. 'Where do you get off threatening my staff?'

'I don't know who the hell you are, but you can either get the hell out of my office or I'll get security to throw you out.' Marshall turned to the receptionist, who was hovering nervously by the door. 'How the hell did he get in here?'

'I tried to stop him, Mr Marshall, but he was very insistent. He just walked in. He said he was some sort of doctor.'

Marshall said, 'I'll deal with you later. Get security in here.' The woman scampered down the corridor.

David asked, 'Is that how you get off, Marshall, bullying women?'

'I've no idea what you're talking about. I've told you once to get out of my office, Dr whatever-your-name-is. I won't tell you a third time.'

'Barbrook, Dr David Barbrook. Ring any bells?'

'You! You've got a sodding nerve busting in here like that. You and your mob of halfwits have already cost me a small bloody fortune.'

'It'll cost you more than that if you ever threaten one of my team again, mate.'

'It's my site and I'm paying you bunch of incompetent fuckwits. I'm entitled to my money's worth and so far I've seen precious little sign that I'm getting it. And as for that useless fucking bitch you've put in charge—'

David swiped his hands across the desk, sending Marshall's phone, laptop and a large pile of filing clattering to the floor.

'Why, you bastard!' Marshall leant back and swung a round-armed punch at the side of David's head.

David saw it coming just in time and, swaying to one side, shoved the desk hard at Marshall. It sent him sprawling into the mass of scattered electrical goods and paperwork.

'I'll have you for this, Barbrook. You see if I don't.'

As David turned to leave, two uniformed security guards appeared in the doorway. Both of them looked old enough to be his father.

David said, 'Alright, lads. Nothing to see here. Mr Marshall and I were just having a little difference of opinion. I'm leaving now.'

The shorter of the two security guards stifled a grin as he peered over the desk and saw Marshall on his hands and knees trying to get to his feet. Turning back to David, he said, 'It's too late for that, son. The police are already on their way.'

CHAPTER SEVENTEEN

The weather that had looked so promising when she'd left the bed and breakfast that morning didn't last into the afternoon. As Clare picked her way back down to the car park, heavy drops of rain had begun to splash into the residue of yesterday's puddles. The afternoon called for a less exposed location.

She'd taken refuge, and the opportunity to refuel, at a nearby hostelry. It was only just past noon and she sat alone, aside from a party of elderly tourists on a day trip, playing with the avocado on her salad. As she'd driven up on the Thursday evening she hadn't been able to get Stuart Craig's description of Beth out of her head. 'She spent more time living in the Iron Age than she did in the twenty-first century.' Had that really been true? If you looked at the way she'd died you certainly might be forgiven for thinking so. But was she as irrational as Stuart Craig had made out or was she simply a woman who knew her own mind? Excavating the infant burials at Bailsgrove and just now up on Wrackley Cop, Clare had begun to wonder how anyone could fail to have sympathy for the plight of those women and children. Was it so wrong to feel for their suffering? To want to show the world what they'd gone through and why? It seemed to Clare that, whether they'd met their fate last week or two millennia ago, somebody needed to speak for them.

Clare pushed her plate to one side. Despite her attempts to focus on the mystery that was Beth Kinsella this weekend, her appetite seemed to have diminished markedly since her chat with Jo and Margaret yesterday afternoon. Was it really possible that Paul Marshall could have been responsible for the break-in at her flat? She'd told Margaret and Jo that he was no more than a school-yard bully. But what if he'd taken things further than that? Sheila Foggarty certainly didn't have any time for him, and Clare had put that down to the woman's torpedo-like focus on stopping the housing development at all costs. But Sheila Foggarty had known Marshall longer than Clare had. As had Neil. And both of them seemed to share a similarly low opinion of him.

But the alternative – that the burglary might have been carried out by the nighthawks – was an even less appealing idea. And unfortunately, given that whoever had broken in had taken the laptop as well, it seemed by far the more credible scenario.

An awful thought suddenly struck her. If the nighthawks had targeted her, what was to stop them targeting Crabby as well? She'd been assuming that she and Jo were the only ones Crabby had told about his involvement. But Crabby had said that it wasn't just Sheila Foggarty who'd shelled out the cash for the artefacts that he'd planted on the site. Several of the villagers had clubbed together to buy them. And if that was the case, the number of people who knew about Crabby's involvement might be much wider than she'd first assumed.

She made her mind up. Whatever she might have agreed with Jo, she needed to tell Crabby that she'd gone to the police with information about the antiquities dealer. He might never speak to her again, but that was a risk she'd have to take. If the nighthawks were prepared to break into her flat, who knew how much further they might go. And if she might have put him in danger's way, the least she could do was to let him know about it. But that was going to have to wait. She didn't have a phone number for Crabby – come to that, she didn't know if he possessed a phone. Did Druids have phones? She'd track him down and speak to him as soon as she got back to Bailsgrove.

But there was nothing she could do about that right now. And in the meantime there were other things she had every intention of concentrating on this weekend. Picking up her phone, she plugged Clive Painter's name into a search engine. Stuart Craig's view of Beth may have been soured by their relationship but what had her head of department made of her? Maybe he'd be able to give her a more dispassionate view of the real Beth Kinsella.

The departmental website said he'd officially retired last year, but he still had an honorary position at the university. Further down her search she came across his name again. He was giving a talk today.

Professor Emeritus Clive Painter. 2.30 p.m. St Thomas Centre, Brampton, Chesterfield. The Church Spire: its place in medieval English architecture.

Brampton couldn't be that far away, could it? And she had nothing else to do with her afternoon.

St Thomas Centre turned out not to be the dank and dreary church hall of her imagination but an ultra-modern conference venue

231

with a rustic limestone facade that she supposed the architects had thought echoed the surrounding hillsides. Clare had slipped in at the back of the room in an attempt to be inconspicuous. But looking around the half-full room she appeared to be the youngest person there by several decades.

A small, wiry man with a hairline that had long since departed, Clive Painter cut a somewhat lonely figure in his oversized gold-rimmed spectacles. He was perched behind a podium he could barely see over, surveying the cavernous auditorium. The organisers, it seemed, had been hoping for a somewhat larger audience. The main event turned out to be a pleasant enough way of whiling away a wet Friday afternoon. Painter was an animated and engaging speaker. He clearly knew his subject back to front. And as far as Clare could make out, the majority of his audience seemed to have stayed awake for the entirety of the lecture, which was a not inconsiderable achievement given the age of most of them.

As the audience drifted away and Painter busied himself packing up his laptop, Clare approached him. 'Professor Painter.'

He looked up, his trepidation evident. Maybe he'd been hoping for a quick getaway.

But when he saw Clare he smiled. 'Hello.'

She stuck out her hand. 'Clare Hills. I'm a fellow archaeologist.' Even now she still felt like a fraud when she said those words. 'I'm based down at the University of Salisbury. I noticed there's a little cafe here. I wonder, if you've got a moment, could I buy you a coffee and pick your brains about Beth Kinsella?'

There wasn't a moment's hesitation. 'How can I refuse such a charming invitation from such a pretty young woman? I'll just finish packing this lot away, and I'll be with you.'

The comment could have come over as sleazy, but there was

a gentle, old-school charm about Clive Painter that Clare found rather appealing.

They settled themselves at a table in the corner. Her with a macchiato and a glass of tap water, him – somewhat unexpectedly – with a hot chocolate with whipped cream, 'and chocolate sprinkles, please'.

Clare watched in quiet amusement as the erstwhile head of department deposited a spoonful of cream and chocolate sprinkles into his mouth with obvious relish.

Clive Painter finished licking his lips. 'Always been a weakness of mine, sugar.'

Clare said, 'There are worse weaknesses.'

He looked at her. 'So, what do you want to know about Beth?'

'I've taken over a site Beth was digging on down in Gloucestershire.'

He placed his spoon down on his saucer. 'Bailsgrove. That's it, I thought I recognised you. I saw you on the news a couple of weeks ago.'

Clare wished he hadn't. She was painfully aware it hadn't been her finest hour.

She shifted uncomfortably in her seat. 'Yes, well. This might sound a bit odd, but working on the site I suppose I've become a bit of an admirer of Beth's work.' Clare hadn't even realised it herself until the words had come out of her lips, but it was true. She'd begun to respect Beth's single-mindedness and tenacity. After all, their dig had proved her right. 'But not everyone seems to have been such a big fan.'

'Oh, really?' There was a note of surprise in his voice.

'I was talking to Stuart Craig . . .'

'Ah, Stuart. You do know that Beth and Stuart were a couple for some time, don't you?' He sipped at his hot chocolate through the remains of the cream, depositing a thin white moustache on his top lip. Despite Clare's best efforts, he must have noticed her staring at it because he plucked a paper napkin from its stainless-steel dispenser and dabbed at it.

'Yes. I gather the split was somewhat acrimonious.'

He nodded. 'At least on Stuart's part. It was always a little difficult to tell with Beth.'

'This is rather difficult, Professor Painter, but I don't know how else to say it. Stuart gave me to understand that you fired Beth.'

He sat back in her chair and stared at her wide-eyed. 'Really? Stuart said that? I know his view of Beth had somewhat soured towards the end of their relationship, but I'm surprised he would have lied.'

Clare looked at him quizzically. 'Lied? You mean you didn't sack Beth?'

He shook his head. 'No, and nor would I have done. Her research scores were all that was keeping our department afloat. Losing Beth Kinsella is a large part of why I got put out to pasture.'

'If you don't mind me asking, what happened?'

He said, 'It was her father.'

Clare couldn't hide her astonishment. 'Her father?'

He nodded. 'He wasn't well. Some form of dementia, as I understand it. She tried to give him the best care she could, but it was a struggle for her. I met him several times at various functions with Beth before he became unwell. He was a concert pianist, quite well known in his day. And a very independent man. Some might say stubborn – I suppose that's where Beth got it from.' He took a sip of his hot chocolate. 'Anyway, even when he became quite unwell he insisted on living at home. I can understand that – wanting to retain your independence. God knows I'd hate to end my days in some kind of an institution. But it put a huge strain on Beth.'

Clare said, 'Beth was caring for him.'

'Yes. And he lived out of town, down in Dronfield. Beth and Stuart were up in Walkley near the university. From what I understand she was making three, sometimes four trips a day out there.'

'That must have been difficult for her. Did it affect her work?'

'If I'm honest, it did a little. I tried to help as much as I could. I removed virtually all of her teaching commitments, which was a shame because the students loved her. But there we are; it had to be done.' He shrugged his shoulders. 'She mainly worked from home after that. And she was astonishing. She was still our star performer in the REF.'

Not, Clare thought, quite the version of Beth that Stuart Craig had presented.

Clare asked, 'So how did she come to leave Sheffield?'

'She did just that. She left. Her father had seriously deteriorated by then and, as I understand it, she had no choice but to put him in a nursing home. She was fortunate. She managed to find him one that specialised in dementia care not too far from where he used to live in Dronfield. I had hoped that would mean she'd resume her former duties in the department, but by then her relationship with Stuart had deteriorated so badly she told me she couldn't work with him any longer. And Stuart made it very clear he wasn't going anywhere until it suited him. So she left, to plough her own furrow.'

'Why the hell didn't you tell me? That's what I want to know.' David was yelling so loudly Clare was having to hold her phone away from her ear.

Clare whispered, 'What, about Marshall?'

'Speak up, Clare, I can hardly hear you!'

'That's because I had to come out into the corridor to get a decent signal, and I'm trying not to wake every other person in the place. Do you know what time it is?'

He said, 'About two-thirty.'

'That's right, David, two-thirty – in the morning. When normal people are sleeping.' Trying to shout in a whisper wasn't easy. 'What on earth are you ringing me for at this time of night?'

'I couldn't ring you before, I've just got out.'

What the hell was he talking about?

'Out of where?'

David said, 'The police station.'

'The police station!'

There was a thump on the wall next to her and a muffled voice yelled from one of the bedrooms, 'Will you keep it down!'

She reverted to whisper mode, 'Hang on a minute, David!'

She padded along the corridor to the stairwell, descended a few steps and, pulling her dressing gown tightly around her, sat down. 'OK, that's a bit better. What the hell are you doing in a police station?'

'I'm not in one any more, and anyway, that's not important.'

A sudden thought struck her. 'Are you with Sally?'

'No.' He sounded puzzled. 'Why on earth would I be with Sally?'

Had he been drinking? He didn't sound like he'd been drinking.

'Well, one: she's your girlfriend. And two: she's in the police force.' Clare paused. Had he had an accident? Maybe he was in shock. 'Are you alright, David?'

He was yelling again now. 'Of course I'm bloody alright. It's you I'm worried about.'

'Look, David, none of this is making any sense. Will you please just tell me why you called me? I'd like to get some sleep tonight.'

'Why didn't you tell me Marshall had threatened you?'

She said, 'Why do you think? Because I knew you'd react like this. Though clearly I had no idea you'd wait until the wee small hours of the morning to do it.'

'If someone threatens my site staff I want to know about it, Clare.'

'Nothing happened, David.'

David said, 'That's not the way Jo tells it. She said Neil had to strong-arm Marshall off-site.'

'That's a bit of an exaggeration, David.'

Clare didn't know what she'd have done over the last couple of years without Jo around. But why on earth had she had to go and tell David about Marshall? She should have known he was bound to overreact. It's what he did best.

David asked, 'Where are you anyway? And when are you coming back?'

'I'm in the Peak District. And if all you're worried about is getting your pound of flesh from me you needn't be. I'll be back on-site first thing Monday morning.'

She could hear him harrumphing down the phone. 'What the hell are you doing in the Peak District?'

'They're called holidays, David, most people take them.' Though in truth she knew he rarely did. 'I wanted to take a look at one of Beth's old sites – Wrackley Cop.'

'That's a hill fort, isn't it? Nothing like our site.'

She had no intention of dignifying that with a response. 'While I've been up here I've had a very informative chat with Beth's old head of department, Clive Painter.'

'While you were on Wrackley Cop.'

She said, 'No. I bumped into him at a talk he was giving.'

'Bumped into! What are you playing at, Clare? We haven't got time for you to go chasing ghosts. You've got enough on your hands trying to finish digging a site started by a madwoman.'

The derision in his voice was all too clear. She'd had enough now.

'It may have escaped your attention as you've spent so little time on-site, David, but everything Beth claimed about Bailsgrove has turned out to be true. And from what Painter told me, Beth Kinsella was anything but mad. She was a dedicated and talented professional trying to juggle her research with caring for a father who's seriously ill with dementia. Painter said he's so bad now that he's in a specialist nursing home at some place called Dronfield. But Beth was caring for him at home. And by all accounts her boyfriend was more concerned about the impact it might have on his career than anything Beth was going through. So, for your information, Beth Kinsella wasn't a lunatic. She was trying to do the right thing. She was bloody good at her job and like most women got zero sodding support from the men around her. So, if you don't mind, David, I'm tired and I really want to get some sleep.'

And with that she hung up.

CHAPTER EIGHTEEN

Paul Marshall pulled over into the gateway and climbed out of his car. The field in front of him was a building site – literally. And that was how he liked it. The business had had some lean times recently, but one way or another he'd managed to survive even when he'd seen his competitors going to the wall. And he had no intention of joining them.

A foreman in hi-vis jacket and hard hat rushed over to greet him, but he dismissed him with a flick of his hand. He had business to attend to first.

He walked into the site office. A lone workman was sitting, mug in hand, with his feet on a chair.

Marshall bellowed, 'Get out!'

The guy didn't need telling twice. He sprang to his feet and all but sprinted out of the office door, trailing tea behind him as he went.

Marshall pulled the door to behind him and twisted the lock before pulling out his phone. He pulled up the number he was looking for and waited while it rang. 'It took you long enough.'

A whispered voice said, 'I was in the middle of something. What do you want?'

'I want you to do what I'm paying you for.'

'I am.'

Marshall lowered his voice. 'That's not what it looks like from here. As I see it, our little problem is getting worse and you need to deal with it. If you want your money you're going to have to do something to earn it.'

The strain in the voice was clear. 'It's not that easy. There are complications.'

Marshall said, 'Sod complications. I've had enough of this crap. You've dealt with it once. You can do it again.'

'But it's not that simple.'

Marshall said, 'Then let me make it simple. I've had that arsehole in charge of the unit round trying to come the heavy with me. No one tries to make me look like a fucking idiot and gets away with it. No one. Do you understand?'

There was silence on the other end of the phone line.

This time he screamed, 'Do you understand!'

There was a quiet, 'Yes.'

'Then get it done!'

Jo was feeling distinctly pleased with herself. Things had been ticking along nicely on-site while Clare was away. And she'd even managed to persuade most of the team to come in and work on Saturday to try to get them back on track. They'd all seen Marshall's antics when he'd turned up on-site. And while in Malc's stated opinion they should tell him to 'Go shove it', that wasn't going to help them hit their deadline. And, more importantly, it wasn't going to help take the pressure off Clare.

Most of them were only too willing to keep going over the weekend – digging a site like this was a once-in-a-career opportunity and they wanted to make the most of it. Even the few that had initially been reluctant had been won over by Jo's promise of a bonus. Though as yet she had no idea how the unit was going to pay for it.

They'd been fortunate in that a fair chunk of the shrine looked as if it lay outside of the footprint of the development. So with a bit of luck they should be able to persuade the county archaeologist and the planning department that it wasn't under threat and didn't need excavating. But if they were going to do the site justice they still had a supersized task on their hands trying to dig the rest of the site.

It wasn't only the site they had to worry about; there were the finds too. The post-excavation team back at the university came to the sum total of two: Jo and Clare. And even if they could find the money to employ Neil for a while after the dig finished, the finds coming up now were extraordinary. They'd had more horse fittings, brooches and even a handful of Dobunnic and Roman coins. So, it was looking as if the site had continued in use even after the Romans arrived. But what they were really struggling with was the pottery. There were vast quantities of Roman pot coming up from the periphery of the site now. And if they didn't get it processed now there was no way they'd get it done back at the department.

Which was why Jo found herself, despite the glorious sunshine that had miraculously appeared after the morning showers, tucked away in the site office alongside Val, their finds supervisor, scrubbing away furiously at a bowlful of sherds of assorted Roman tableware.

Jo asked, 'Don't you ever just want to get out there and dig, Val?'

The red-headed Scot laughed. 'Och, I've done my share of pickaxing in my time. But I kind of got into this side of things when the kids were wee. I could fit in the post-exc. stuff around school hours.' She looked out at the sun blazing down on the hillside outside and touched a hand to the side of her face. 'And it has its advantages, you know. On days like today I used to end up like a pickled beetroot.'

Jo laughed and plucked a large piece of shiny red pottery out of the water, holding it up to the light. 'We must be on the edge of some sort of Romano-British settlement, the amount of this stuff we're getting. It's kinda cool when you look up close at this Samian, don't you think?'

'Alright if you like that sort of thing, I suppose. It's a bit flashy for my tastes. All mass-produced, y'know. They turned it out by the cartload. I'm keener on the handmade British stuff myself.'

'Careful, Val, your Celtic roots are showing.' Jo stood up, washing bowl in hand. 'I'm done with this lot. I'm gonna get some clean water from next door. I'll put the kettle on for tea break while I'm there.'

Jo turned to go. But before Val had time to answer there was a sudden crash, followed by a thud. Splinters of glass lay festooned across the lino.

'What the fu—' Jo halted mid-sentence.

She turned again to find Val lying slumped across the table, blood pouring from her head.

'Jesus!' She knelt down, staring in disbelief at what she saw. 'Val, are you OK? Val!'

There was no response from the elfin Scot.

Jo felt dizzy, as if she were going to faint. 'Shit, shit, shit . . .'

She stood up and staggered towards the door, managing to stand upright for long enough to yell, 'Hey guys, we need some help here!' And then promptly collapsed.

Jo opened her eyes to see Malcolm standing over her.

'You OK, Jo? You had us worried there for a minute. You just collapsed. You were clean out.'

She tried to get to her feet. 'Don't worry about me, Malc, Val's hurt. We need to get her some help.'

Malcolm said, 'Take it steady, me old. No need to worry, Neil's sorting it.'

With a steadying hand from Malcolm, Jo stood up to see Val, conscious and sitting upright, with Neil standing over her and a wad of gauze pressed against Val's temple.

Neil said, 'I think I managed to get all of the glass out. It looks a pretty clean wound. But once I've got her bandaged up we need to get her over to A & E.'

Without a moment's hesitation, Malc said, 'I'll take her.'

Neil said, 'No, you won't. She needs someone with first-aid training with her just in case.' He looked up at Jo. 'Beth paid for me to be first-aid trained.'

That explained his dexterity with the roll of bandage he was now swaddling Val's head with. Malc couldn't hide his disappointment, but he acquiesced quickly enough once he heard the explanation. She'd always suspected he harboured a bit of a soft spot for Val, and it seemed she might have been right.

Val, who thankfully now looked to have considerably more colour in her cheeks than Jo felt as if she had in hers at that moment, dug Neil swiftly in the ribs.

'What was that for?'

'I am here, y'know.'

Jo deposited herself into a chair, for fear she might fall down again. Her head still felt like cotton wool.

She must have inadvertently touched her hand to her head because Val said, 'Are you alright, Jo?'

'I'm fine. I just passed out, that's all.' She felt their collective eyes on her awaiting an explanation. 'It's the blood, OK. It's just the blood.'

Even saying the word was making her feel woozy. And she was studiously avoiding looking at the sticky red substance splattered across the tabletop in front of her.

She said, 'But Neil's right, Val, we need to get you checked out at a hospital.'

Val protested, 'Rubbish, I'll be fine. Can't you just give me the once-over, Jo? I've got to pick the kids up from school.'

Jo said, 'Don't worry about the kids, we'll sort something out. And I'm strictly bones only. I wouldn't even want me treating me. Besides, you've just seen what happened. I'd probably hit the deck again if I tried.'

Val's chuckle was cut short by a wince.

Thrusting his hand into his pocket, Neil flung Malcolm his car keys. 'Can you bring my car round, Malc, while I finish bandaging Val's head?'

Malc nodded and was out through the door almost before Neil had finished the sentence.

Jo watched as Neil expertly cocooned Val's head in swathes of bandage. 'Did you see what happened, Neil?'

Neil shook his head. 'I didn't, but it's pretty clear what did the damage.' He inclined his head towards the corner of the office where a large red brick lay on the glass-strewn lino with what appeared to be a piece of brown paper wrapped round it.

Neil said, 'Have a word with Malc. He reckons he saw someone chuck it. He was on his way down here when it happened.'

'But why would anyone do it?' Jo nodded towards the brick. 'That thing could have killed one of us.'

Neil glanced down at Val and hesitated before replying. 'It's like I told Clare, we need to get done and dusted here. It's dangerous working at Bailsgrove.'

Jo said, 'Do you think it's Marshall? He wants us gone.'

Neil said, 'Maybe, but there were threats before. When we were digging here with Beth.'

Val cut in, 'It's true, Jo. I found a note shoved under the office door when I opened up one morning telling us to clear out or face the wrath of the old souls. And someone trashed the Portaloos. That wasn't a pretty sight, let me tell you.'

Jo stood with her mouth open. 'Why didn't anyone tell the police?'

Neil said, 'We did. But they just thought it was local louts mucking about.'

'Jeez, why did any of you guys agree to come back here?'

Val looked up at her. 'Simple. There are no jobs in archaeology out there. We needed the money.'

Malcolm poked his head through the door to announce that the car was ready, and Val was duly clucked and fussed over as she was loaded gently, but still protesting, into Neil's car.

Returning to the site office, Malc and Jo flopped down into the chairs.

Malcolm said, 'I'll kill the bastard if I get my hands on them.'

'I get where you're coming from, Malc, but that's not gonna help anyone.'

Malcolm growled, 'Maybe not, but it'd make me feel a hell of a lot better.'

'Neil was saying you saw what happened.'

245

Malcolm nodded. 'Yeah, I was just on my way down to get some more finds bags when I saw it. They were hanging round outside the gate for a bit. At first I thought they'd maybe lost their dog or something. Then they just ran round to the front of the office and lobbed that thing' – he nodded towards the corner – 'in through the window. After, they legged it.'

'Did you get a good look at them?'

'Not close up. They were wearing a waxed jacket and a big floppy hat with the brim pulled down.' After a moment's pause, Malcolm added, 'Bit like that hoity-toity piece who came round shouting the odds at Clare.'

Was it possible? Had it really been Sheila Foggarty? The description could have fitted half of the middle-class inhabitants of Gloucestershire. But she was the only one who'd already picked a fight with them.

It had been one hell of a day and after what had happened none of them felt like wielding a trowel. As soon as they'd swept away the shattered glass and boarded up the broken window, Jo had told the team to pack up and go home. They'd all agreed readily enough, except Malcolm, who in a somewhat unexpected display of chivalry had insisted on hanging around until Jo had left site too. An offer she was only too grateful to accept, and in recompense for which she'd promised him a lift home.

To which end Malcolm now sat waiting in her VW campervan while she gathered her kit together. Alone in the office, she picked up the brick from the shelf where it had been safely stowed.

She'd called the police the moment Val had been dispatched to hospital. But as soon as they'd established no one had been seriously hurt, and despite Jo's protestations that they couldn't be sure until Val's head injury had been assessed, they seemed to be remarkably uninterested in the afternoon's events. There wasn't even a perceptible increase in interest when Jo had insisted on telling them that a member of staff had thought they recognised the perpetrator and given them Sheila Foggarty's name.

The voice on the end of the phone had dutifully issued Jo with a crime reference number – 'You'll need it for your insurance claim.' But when Jo had asked when they'd be sending someone round and should she wait to clear up, she'd been told to go ahead and make the place secure – they'd email details of the officer who'd been assigned in due course.

Jo got the distinct impression they weren't likely to receive a visitation from the police any time soon. But, even if they weren't interested, she wanted to know what was on that piece of brown paper. She placed the brick on the desk and slipped the brown paper carefully out from under the string. There were large red blotches of what looked like marker pen bleeding through from the other side. She turned the paper over to see just two words scrawled across its reverse: 'GET OUT!'

CHAPTER NINETEEN

Clare turned towards Margaret. 'Well, when I called you and you said you'd meet me in the Pitt Rivers Museum, I didn't realise that we'd have company.'

The two women were standing alone in front of a glass case displaying a collection of shrunken human heads – or, as the label called them, *tsantsas* – which apparently originated on the border between Ecuador and Peru. Clare had called ahead to arrange to see Margaret on her way back to Bailsgrove. She was in need of a clear head and some dispassionate advice, two things she knew she could always rely on Margaret to provide.

Margaret stood motionless, seemingly entranced by the contents of the cabinet. 'Strictly speaking, company no longer. After the heads had been taken in battle, the tribesmen would treat them to preserve them then perform a ritual to incorporate the soul of the dead warrior into their own kin groups. The idea was to capture the strength of their enemies. Once the ceremony was over the heads themselves would be discarded. Or, as almost certainly happened in the case of these chaps, traded to some poor unsuspecting white fellow who thought they still had some element of meaning attached to them. Fascinating, aren't they? I'm considering writing a paper on the comparison between these practices and head hunting in Iron Age societies.' She turned towards Clare. 'Now what can I do for you? I trust your weekend away went well. You certainly look better for it. Where did you go, by the way?'

Clare said, 'The Peak District.'

'Any reason for that particular choice of location?' Margaret smiled. 'It's where David grew up, you know.'

Clare mustered a fixed smile in response. 'I do know. But that's not why I went there.'

Margaret said, 'Oh,' in a tone that suggested she wasn't entirely convinced by Clare's denial.

Clare cleared her throat. 'No. I went there to visit Wrackley Cop.'

'Wasn't that the hill fort that Beth excavated?'

Clare nodded. 'That's right. I wanted to try to get a better understanding of the way Beth's mind worked.'

'You've been listening to David again. "Places make people and people make places."'

'No,' Clare said, just a little too defensively. 'Or at least, not entirely. I do have a mind of my own you know, Margaret.'

'I know you do, my dear. I'm only teasing. And as it happens it's an aphorism that I have a great deal of sympathy with – although it's not the whole story, of course. But the important thing is, did it help?'

'I think it did. And I met Clive Painter too. He drew a somewhat more sympathetic picture of Beth than Stuart Craig had. Did you know she spent years caring for her father, virtually single-handed?'

'No. I had no idea. But then I really didn't know her that well.'

'Anyway, that's not why I asked to see you, Margaret. I wanted to ask you what you made of this.' Clare withdrew the folded sheets of A4 from her bag and handed them to Margaret.

Margaret stood reading them intently for several minutes. Finally she looked up at Clare. 'I obviously recognise Stephen's name but who exactly is James Douglas?'

'He was a colleague of Stephen's and he was his executor. They'd known each other for years. He was the best friend Stephen had. It's James who's been helping me to unravel the mess that Stephen left our finances in.'

'Forgive me, my dear, but I don't quite understand what it is you want my opinion on.'

'James was down in Salisbury a few weeks ago. He invited me out to dinner with him. We had a lovely evening.'

'Ah, I see. You're feeling guilty for being attracted to Stephen's best friend. These things aren't unheard of, you know. It's only natural you should feel drawn to one another under the circumstances – sharing a common bond, so to speak.'

Clare blushed and shook her head. 'No. I don't think you do see, Margaret. James seems like a lovely man – though I admit I didn't have much time for him when Stephen was alive. He was as shocked as I was when Stephen's misadventures in property first came to light. When we had dinner the other evening he told me that he knew nothing about the investments Stephen was intending to make.'

'Well, these emails certainly suggest that at the very least James has an exceedingly poor memory.'

Clare nodded. 'But is that all it suggests, Margaret?'

'You mean can you trust him? I don't know, my dear. I've never met the man. Maybe he did know about the investments and he's just too embarrassed to say so. He wouldn't be the first man to try to rewrite their personal history in order to win the affections of an attractive young woman.'

Clare said, 'No. I suppose not. But he's been such a support since Stephen died. I honestly don't know where I'd be without him.'

'And if he's been dealing with Stephen's finances he's obviously not after you for your money.'

Clare snorted. 'No. I suppose that's true. And just for the record, Margaret, I've never thought of James as anything other than a friend.'

'Well, that at least makes things a little more straightforward – though it really is time you started to dip your toe back into the water, you know.'

'Margaret!'

'I know, my dear, but a ring binder full of context sheets won't keep you warm at night.' Clare laughed and the museum attendant at the end of the row coughed meaningfully. 'Well, whatever the situation is, my advice would be to have a care. He may be a reformed sinner. But at the very least he suffers from a faulty memory.' She returned the wad of papers to Clare. 'And he appears to have shown something of a lack of moral fibre in not attempting to dissuade his best friend from making these investments.'

The two women turned and began to walk towards the entrance side by side. As they neared the front door, Clare turned to Margaret and asked nervously, 'Can I ask you one more question, Margaret?'

Margaret's brow furrowed with concern. 'Of course – though I can't guarantee that I have the answer to all of life's conundrums.'

'Did you know that Jo was gay?'

'Oh, heavens yes. I thought everyone knew. I understand it was part of the reason she chose to do her PhD over here. Escaping from a broken heart – or at least so the rumour mill goes.'

'I don't believe it. I've only been away from site for a few days and now it looks like a war zone.' Clare was standing in front of the Portakabin, hands on hips, surveying the damage.

'It could've been one heck of a lot worse. According to the docs at A & E, if that brick had hit Val just a couple of inches lower it could've blinded her – or worse. And take a look at this.'

Jo led Clare into the Portakabin and removed the ragged sheet of brown paper from the filing cabinet where she'd had it under lock and key, and spread it out on the table in front of them.

Clare said, 'Well, there's no mistaking the message, is there?'

'Nope.' Jo hesitated. 'I don't like to say this, Clare, but I think we're in trouble here. Neil was saying someone wants us out of here and this proves he's right. From where I'm standing things are looking pretty gnarly. I know this site is real important, but is it really worth risking these guys' lives? Or yours, for that matter?'

Clare slumped down in her chair, head in hands. Through her fingers the bloodstains were still obvious to see on the wooden tabletop in front of her.

She drew in a long breath and hauled herself upright. 'No, no it's not. No site is worth that. But what choice do we have? If we pack it in now, that's the Hart Unit finished. And none of those poor sods out there are going to thank us for laying them off. Half of them have got families to support. And how much chance do you reckon there is of them being able to pick up another job right now?'

Jo said, 'What difference is it gonna make? The dig will be over in a couple of weeks anyhow. And they'll all be out of work.'

'All the more reason to keep going while we can. And I'm damned if I'm going to stand by and watch the Hart Unit fold and this site destroyed just because some lunatic wants us gone. We won't take any chances, though. I want all the glass in the windows in these units replaced with Perspex, and under no circumstances is anyone to be left on-site on their own.'

Her memories of what had occurred at Hungerbourne, to first Jo and then David, were far too vivid to run the risk of ever allowing the experience to be repeated.

Jo said, 'You know you won't get any arguments from me on that score. I'm fine going along with this, Clare, but don't you think it's about time you tell David?'

'What for? You told me yourself what he was like when he found out about Marshall turning up on-site shouting the odds. And he went nuts at me on the phone.'

Jo said, 'It's not the same.'

'As far as I can see it's exactly the same.'

Jo's frustration at her friend's obstinacy was obvious. 'Why don't you quit pretending and open your eyes? Everyone else can see it. Why can't you? It's because it was *you*.'

Clare could feel herself blushing. She dismissed the suggestion with a flick of her hand. 'Don't be so ridiculous, Jo. When David phoned me about the whole Marshall thing he was angry because the team had been threatened. His team. I understand that he feels a sense of responsibility towards them. But going round threatening people isn't helping anyone, is it?'

Jo raised both hands in the air. 'OK, OK. If that's the way you want to deal with it, fine.'

In all the time she'd known her this was the closest Clare had ever come to seeing Jo angry. At least with her. And she wasn't enjoying the experience.

She reached out and laid her hand on Jo's shoulder. 'Hey, I don't want to fall out over this. You are OK with us carrying on digging, aren't you?'

Jo nodded, but Clare could feel the tension in every bone of Jo's body.

Clare asked, 'And we're still OK, aren't we?'

Jo placed her hand on Clare's and smiled. 'Sure, we're OK. If we're gonna go down, we're gonna go down together.'

Clare said, 'Right, let's get to work, then.' She headed towards the doorway. 'I'm going to see if I can get Neil to do something about these windows.'

Jo said, 'You're out of luck there.'

Clare turned to face her. 'Why?'

'Neil hasn't turned up for work this morning.'

Clare asked, 'Has he phoned?'

Jo shook her head. 'Nope. I tried phoning, but his phone just went to voicemail.'

Clare said, 'That's not like him. He's normally on-site before we are.'

Jo said, 'When I spoke to Val on Saturday night she said he'd had to wait for hours with her at A & E. Maybe he's just taking the time back that he's owed.'

'Maybe. But he'd normally have phoned to let us know by now. I'm worried about him, Jo. You said yourself he seems really down at the moment. Between what happened on Saturday and how things are for him at home at the moment, if he got back late on Saturday night and got a whole load of grief from Sadie . . .'

'What?'

'Well, what if he did something daft?'

'Like what exactly?'

Clare said, 'I don't know. Crabby said he used to have a problem with drugs and booze. Maybe he's gone on a bender.' She paused. 'Can you hold the fort here for a couple more hours, Jo? I'm going to go down to Neil's place and check to see if he's OK.'

Jo said, 'Sure. But I think you're wasting your time.'

'Where the hell are you, David? It sounds like Bedlam there.'

David was standing in a queue for coffee, one hand clamped over his ear, the other on his phone, surrounded by two hundred other people equally desperate for their mid-morning caffeine fix.

'I'm in Manchester, remember, Sal, that Prehistoric Society conference I told you about.'

'Do they all have to shout so loud?'

Whatever she'd phoned about it didn't sound as if she was in a good mood.

'Are you alright, Sal? You sound a bit odd.'

Sally said, 'How very perceptive of you. As it happens I'm very far from alright. I've just got off the phone from speaking to Mark Stone.'

'Oh.'

Now he thought he knew where this was heading. He scooped up a cup of black coffee, waving aside the offer of biscuits, and retreated to a seat on a nearby windowsill.

'Oh, indeed. What the hell do you think you're playing at, David? Mark's just told me that one of his officers arrested you for common assault.'

'It wasn't as bad as it sounds, Sal. Honestly. Just a bit of a misunderstanding.'

'You seem to forget, David, I'm a serving police officer. I know exactly what common assault is. He said it was Paul Marshall. Isn't he the bloke your lot have got the contract with? The one whose money is keeping your unit afloat.'

David took a sip of his volcanically hot coffee and had immediate cause to regret it. 'Ow!'

'What was that?'

He ran his tongue over his burning lip. 'Nothing. Look, Sal, it all got a bit out of hand, that's all. When I got up to site on Friday, Jo told me Marshall had been out on-site calling the odds.'

'Isn't he entitled to do that? After all, he is paying their wages.'

'He might be, but I'm not having anyone threatening my staff. They don't get paid enough for that. He was well out of order. One of the lads had to strong-arm him off-site in the end.'

Sally said, 'That doesn't give you the right to go round hitting people though, does it? Didn't your mum ever tell you two wrongs don't make a right?'

'It wasn't like that. I just went round to his office to put him straight about a few things. He was the one who tried to throw a punch at me.'

Sally lowered her voice to a whisper. 'Do you realise how lucky you are, David? You could have ended up in court over this. You can get six months for common assault.'

David gulped. He hadn't known that. And he rather wished he didn't now.

'It's OK, Sal, I got off. I mentioned your name and they let me off with a caution.'

David could almost feel the tidal wave of fury propelling itself down the phone line. Sally's voice wasn't a whisper any more. 'You did *what*? Christ almighty, David. I don't believe this. For one thing that's called perverting the course of justice, and for another, what the hell did you think you were doing dragging me into it?'

'It's OK, Sal. He was much more understanding after that. He said he knew you when you were in the force up there. Asked to be remembered to you. Charlie Waites, I think his name was.'

'This isn't some kind of joke, David. It's my career you're screwing with here. And you do realise, don't you, that now that you've got a caution that means that you've got a criminal record. I shouldn't go applying for other jobs any time soon if I were you.'

David puffed out his cheeks. That was something else he hadn't known about.

'Look, Sal, I'm sorry. I didn't think things through. And I should never have dragged you into it. One thing just sort of led to another. I was so angry when Jo told me Marshall had been threatening Clare that I guess I just saw red.'

He knew they were the wrong words almost as soon as they'd come tumbling out of his mouth.

'Clare! Didn't you make her site director? I thought she was getting paid to take care of herself and the site. She's not a child, David. You can't do everything. And I'm sure Clare's perfectly capable of dealing with difficult men. God knows you're living proof there's enough of them about. She doesn't need some buffoon dashing round like a demented knight on a white charger clocking people on her behalf.'

He knew that he'd screwed up, and he'd screwed up really badly. But he'd had enough now. 'OK, Sal, I get the message – you can stop now. I get the message.'

There was silence on the end of the phone. For a moment he thought the line had gone dead. But then he heard a sigh.

He said, 'Anyway, never mind the rollicking. Why was your mate Mark phoning you? Surely he didn't just want to share the good news about your fuckwit of a boyfriend.'

He could hear a stifled laugh at the other end of the phone. 'Don't even begin to think you're forgiven for this, David Barbrook.' David allowed himself a smile. 'No. Do you remember that murder inquiry I'm heading up while you're careering round Gloucestershire like a half-crazed loon?'

'Yes. But what's that got to do with Mark Stone?'

Sally lowered her voice again. 'The guy we've arrested for it claims the victim had been working for Beth Kinsella. So I got Mark to check it out from his end. And it turns out he was right. Not only was he working for Kinsella but she sacked Jack Tyler for turning up to work drunk.'

'What does that mean, Sal? Has Tyler's murder got something to do with Beth Kinsella?'

'Don't go seeing reds under the bed, David. There's nothing to worry about. We were just tying up a loose end. There's no evidence to suggest Jack Tyler working for Beth was anything other than one of life's peculiar coincidences.'

But David was worrying. And he didn't like coincidences.

It had been called in by the young constable who'd been sent out to speak to one of the locals about some bit of petty vandalism up at the dig. But before he'd been able to get to his prospective interviewee he'd been stopped by a woman in her nightdress running down the middle of the street screaming at him. She'd seen it from her upstairs window in the garden next door.

Mark Stone's day had been going from bad to worse. He'd overslept. And in his blurry-eyed state he'd managed to first short out the toaster by shoving a fork into it in an attempt to retrieve a recalcitrant slice of bread, and then dollop marmalade down the front of his only clean, if somewhat creased, shirt. As it had turned out the state of his shirt hadn't been an issue because he was now standing in the back garden of number 6 Weaver's Close, Bailsgrove, clad from head to foot in a white Tyvek onesie.

He hated days like today. Somehow it was always worse when you knew the victim. And unlike Beth Kinsella's death there was no doubting that this time he was going to be investigating a murder. He'd already cordoned off the house and SOCO were in full swing.

He squatted down to take a closer look, being careful not to step into the enormous pool of blood. It was obvious even to him that his throat had been cut. Lying there on the concrete path, the life force drained from him, Wayne 'Crabby' Crabbs looked twenty years older than the last time he'd seen him. What was it he'd said to Clare Hills about him? 'He inhabits a different world to the rest of us.' Well, he certainly did now, the poor bastard.

He turned away to examine the second victim. At least this one wasn't human. One of the SOCO team was squatting down taking close-ups of it. It was a huge black bird. His sergeant – Ray – had confidently informed him it was a raven. He'd worked alongside Ray for the best part of a decade and it was the first time he'd found out the man was a twitcher. It really was a strange old morning. But what troubled Mark Stone wasn't the bird itself but what had been done to it. Its skull had been crushed with a rock that still lay nearby; its throat had been cut and there was a length of orange baler twine cutting deep into what remained of its neck.

CHAPTER TWENTY

With Jack Tyler dead and Beth Kinsella dead, it meant that two people who'd worked on the Bailsgrove excavations had met an unnatural end in the last three months. And that was two too many for David's liking.

Despite what Sally had said he just couldn't get the connection out of his head. His paper was first up in the afternoon session, but he'd been on autopilot as he'd addressed the auditorium. As soon as he'd finished he'd made his apologies and departed.

David might have had second thoughts about slithering his way through Snake Pass in the worst of the winter snows, but it was only an hour and a half down the A57 across the Pennines from Manchester to Dronfield in the summer months and today there wasn't so much as a raindrop in the air. He had no clear idea of exactly what he was going to do when he got there, but he did know that if there was anyone Beth Kinsella might have confided in it would have been her father.

From what Clare had told him, David knew Beth must have been close to him. David had spent the last few years watching his own father's gradual decline from Alzheimer's. But increasingly he'd watched from a distance. He was only too well aware of his own deficiencies in that department. He could never have cared for his father in the way that Beth had hers. And despite everything he might have said and thought about Beth Kinsella, he had to admit he admired her for it.

He knew he wouldn't have any trouble finding the place. There was only one nursing home in Dronfield that specialised in dementia care. He'd visited it with his youngest brother when they'd been trying to find somewhere for their father; somewhere comfortable enough to assuage their guilt at abandoning him to an institution.

He pulled up at the end of the gravel drive, a mass of Victorian brickwork in front of him. Dronfield Place must have been a substantial country house when it had been built in, as the plaque between the upper-storey windows proudly proclaimed, the 1880s. The addition of a sprawling modern extension had increased its capacity but diminished its impact considerably. He could see a few residents seated round tables in front of the extension's patio doors enjoying the summer sunshine. Why hadn't they chosen this place for his father? They'd looked at so many he was struggling to remember.

As soon as he entered the reception the reason came back to him. At the desk stood the not inconsiderable figure of Mrs Danks, the care home manager. Twice the girth of David and almost as tall, Mrs Danks was decidedly more drill sergeant than Florence Nightingale. And now he also recalled thinking to himself last time that he wouldn't have fancied being a resident who disagreed with her. He just hoped she didn't remember him from his previous visit.

He smiled, grateful that he'd thought to pack his Marks & Spencer blazer for the conference. 'Hi, I wonder if you can help me. I'm here to see . . .' He hesitated, suddenly aware he didn't know Beth's father's first name. 'Mr Kinsella.'

Mrs Danks hit David with a full-on laser beam of a glare. 'And you would be?'

'David. David Barker. I'm a relative of Mr Kinsella's.'

She didn't look convinced. 'I wasn't aware Mr Kinsella had any surviving relatives, now that his daughter is no longer with us.'

David supposed you must become practised in death-related euphemisms if you worked in a place like this for any length of time.

He said, 'Our side of the family had kind of lost touch with Beth's until the funeral. You know how it is. And with Beth gone I just sort of thought someone ought to come and pay Uncle a visit.'

She seemed to have accepted his explanation, because she started searching through a list on the clipboard in front of her. 'Ah. Here he is: Jeffrey Kinsella, room 27B – that's ground floor, corridor B, but you'll probably find him in the day room. I'll get someone to show you through. If I can just get you to sign in.'

He must have looked nervous. He certainly felt it.

'It's just in case of fire.'

She punched in something on the computer keyboard and a few minutes later a harassed-looking young woman, five feet nothing tall, hair drawn neatly back in a ponytail, appeared.

'Ah, there you are, Nina. Is your pager not working?'

Nina said, 'I was just seeing to Mrs Dempsey, Mrs Danks.' The lilting intonation was slight but distinct. She sounded Polish, or maybe Lithuanian – he wasn't good with accents.

'Will you show Mr Barker here to Mr Kinsella, please?'

Nina held her hand out towards the double doors. 'Come with me, please.'

Once they were safely on the other side of the doors, Nina looked up at him and smiled. 'Don't mind her.' She tilted her head back in the direction of reception. 'She's not so bad as she sounds. Her bark is more bad than her bite. It's nice that you've come to see Jeffrey. No one visits him now Beth is gone.'

'You knew Beth, then?'

'Yes. Beth, she was a good woman. Jeffrey, he is not always easy. It's often the way, you know, when they have dementia.'

Indeed, he did know. 'I understand. My father has Alzheimer's too.'

She nodded. 'It's not so surprising. It sometimes runs in families.' She suddenly seemed to realise what she had said. She touched his arm. 'Oh, I am sorry.'

'You don't have to be. I already knew.'

And in truth he did know. In the small dark hours of the night, when the demons came calling, it was one of the myriad things he lay awake worrying about. The thought terrified him. When he'd first found out he'd even briefly started looking up living wills. But when Jo had stumbled over him looking up Swiss clinics in his office one day he'd decided it was time he pulled himself together. If the fates decreed that he was destined to end up trapped in an increasingly diminishing world like his father, he should at least make the most of his faculties in the meantime.

When they got to the day room there was no sign of Jeffrey Kinsella. But they had more luck when they got to his room. Jeffrey was seated in one corner, staring fixedly out of the open window. He appeared to be listening to the birdsong.

Nina said, 'Jeffrey, you have a visitor. Your nephew has come to see you.'

David said, 'Hello, Jeffrey.'

Jeffrey turned towards him. 'Hello.'

That was a good start; at least he recognised there was someone there. On the rare occasions that he visited his father these days, an hour of total silence ensued as David desperately tried to think of something to say to the husk of the man that had brought him up. He'd learnt to take a book with him, so that he could read to him – *The Oxford Book of Romantic Verse*. From somewhere long ago David had remembered his mother telling him his father used to read to her from it when they'd first been courting. And just now and then, as David read, there would be a glimmer of recognition. Or on a good day he might take David's hand and smile.

Then Jeffrey added, 'I don't have a nephew.'

David felt an overwhelming wave of guilt rush over him.

But Nina turned to him and said, 'Don't worry. He didn't always remember Beth.'

David was just thinking that given what had happened to her maybe it was a blessing that he didn't remember her when Jeffrey said, 'Beth. Where's Beth?'

Nina said, 'Beth can't come today, Jeffrey. Your nephew David is here to see you.' Then mouthed the words, 'I'll leave you to it.'

David said, 'This is a nice room, Jeffrey.'

Jeffrey didn't reply.

Glancing over at the table in the opposite corner of the room, he saw a silver picture frame with a photo of Beth in it. David walked over and picked it up.

Jeffrey reached out as if to grab it. 'Beth! Beth!'

David handed it to him and the old man held it hard to his chest. Oh God! He wished he'd never started this.

'Jeffrey, do you remember Beth?'

The old man nodded. 'Beth brings me things.'

It hadn't even crossed his mind. The least he could have done if he was going to put him through the wringer was bring him a bar of chocolate or a bag of grapes. The truth was until he'd stepped into this room, Jeffrey Kinsella had been a way to find answers to his questions, not a real person. And he'd thought Beth had been obsessively single-minded!

'What sorts of things, Jeffrey?'

'All sorts. Nice things.'

More in desperation than in hope, David said, 'When Beth comes to see you, Jeffrey, does she talk to you about her work?'

'Beth has to work.'

David nodded. 'Yes, Beth has to work. Did' – he corrected himself – 'does Beth talk about what she does?'

Jeffrey said, 'Beth digs. She finds things.'

Smiling, David leant forwards. 'That's right, Jeffrey, Beth finds things. I find things too, Jeffrey, like Beth does. I dig them up. I work where Beth used to work.'

Jeffrey was smiling at him.

David asked, 'Does Beth talk to you about where she works, Jeffrey?'

Still clutching the picture frame to his chest, Jeffrey asked, 'When is Beth coming?'

He should never have done this. What on earth had he been thinking? It was perfectly apparent that he was going to learn the square root of bugger all from Jeffrey Kinsella. All he was doing was causing him more distress. The only thing that salved David's conscience was that Jeffrey was highly unlikely to remember that David had ever visited him.

David said, 'Beth can't come today.'

He stood up, unsure of what to say. Jeffrey Kinsella was staring up at him, his eyes almost pleading. It must be a lonely world he inhabited. As he moved towards the door, David heard movement behind him. Turning round, he saw that Jeffrey had abandoned the picture of Beth on his chair and was trying to climb onto a chair below the shelf on the far wall.

David asked, 'Do you want something, Jeffrey?'

Jeffrey pointed at the shelf.

David said, 'Don't worry. I'll get it for you.'

The shelf only had three items on it. There was a picture of an older woman bearing a striking resemblance to Beth, whom David guessed must have been her mother. Next to it was a small carriage clock of the silver wedding gift variety and at the far end was a padded brown A5 envelope. David reached up towards the picture of Jeffrey's wife, but the old man shook his head determinedly and instead pointed to the end of the shelf where the envelope lay.

David tried to hand it to Jeffrey, but he immediately pushed it away.

When David went to replace it on the shelf, the old man shook his head. 'No, no, no, no. From Beth.'

David tried to hand it to him again, but Jeffrey wasn't having any of it.

David said, 'You want me to have it.'

Jeffrey smiled at him and immediately returned to his seat, his gaze firmly fixed on the window. David might as well not have been in the room.

On the outside of the envelope someone had scrawled the word 'Bailsgrove' in thick black marker pen. David opened it to see a clear plastic finds bag containing a single small red USB stick.

David drew in a long, slow lungful of Derbyshire air. He needed this. After his trip to see Jeffrey Kinsella his head had felt like mashed potato. His mind kept replaying images of Jeffrey and his own father, each trapped in their own small and ever-diminishing worlds. He knew the moorland around Gardom's Edge like the back of his hand. As a teenager growing up in Chesterfield he used to catch the bus out to Baslow and walk up here. While his brothers were off playing cricket or chasing their latest conquest, David was picking his way between the birch trees and the tumbled Bronze Age field walls trying to imagine what life had been like for the men and women who'd lived here then. Wiltshire might be where his heart was these days but if he had a soul this was where you'd find it.

He picked his way along the top of the gargantuan curving remains of the stone bank that the adult David now knew had been built by the first farmers almost sixty centuries before he'd set foot here. Sally's phone call had panicked him. First Beth Kinsella, then Jack Tyler. How could that be a coincidence? But he needed to think straight. He didn't know how he'd survived the last few months. Had he believed in a deity, he'd have given it credit for preventing him from throttling the Runt. He'd been revelling in the imminent demise of the Hart Unit. David knew that the teaching commitments the Runt had piled on him this term had been Muir's less than subtle strategy to ensure saving the unit was as difficult as possible.

And, as a consequence, David had been forced to leave that particular responsibility entirely in Clare and Jo's hands. And capable though they were, he couldn't help feeling he'd let them down. He'd been the one accusing Clare and Jo of being irresponsible when the press had muscled their way onto site. But where had he been when they needed him? And now he'd let Sally down too. *Well, David Barbrook, it was about time you stopped feeling sorry for yourself and started taking your responsibilities seriously.*

It had taken him forty minutes to get to the top, but it took him less than twenty to scramble back down to the pub car park where he'd left the Land Rover. Grabbing his laptop bag, he shoved the envelope into the side and headed into the bar. He ordered a pint, tucked himself into a quiet corner and fired up the laptop.

Slipping the USB stick from its plastic bag, he plugged it into the laptop. There was only one folder on it, which in turn contained a single file. A video file labelled 'Bailsgrove20150413'. He double-clicked on the file. The video seemed to take an eternity to load.

When it eventually did it showed an image of two men. It must have been either last thing in the evening or early morning because the light wasn't great. But David could clearly see they were standing in front of the Portakabin on the dig site. And just as obviously the figure standing facing the camera was Paul Marshall. He was holding something out in front of him, waving it in the direction of the second, thinner man. It looked like a package of some kind. The sound quality was atrocious and David could only make out a couple of Marshall's words – 'problem' and 'last chance'. The second man seemed to be arguing, shaking his head. But David couldn't hear what he was saying. Then Marshall ripped open the package and withdrew its contents. It looked like a wad of twenty-pound notes. Marshall rippled his thumb through them, then shoved them back into what remained of the packaging. The second man started to walk away and Marshall grabbed him by the arm. Marshall swung him round and thrust the package into the pocket of the second man's denim jacket. The second man looked up towards Marshall and started to protest. David could see who it was now. It was Neil Fuller.

* * *

269

Standing in front of the cracked and peeling front door of 46 Compton Street, Clare hesitated. Next to her, the tiny weed-choked front garden was overlooked by a substantial bay window, its curtains half-drawn even at this hour. Neil and Sadie obviously weren't gardeners, but then they probably had other things on their mind at the moment.

Now that she was actually here, she was less than entirely sure exactly what she'd thought she was going to achieve by coming here. Even if Neil was here. But what harm could it do? At worst Sadie would be hacked off that his boss had come calling. At best . . . Well, she didn't know what her best scenario was, but she did know she was worried about Neil.

She knocked. But there was no reply. She tried a second time. Still no response. At least she wasn't waking the baby up. If she didn't get a reply this time she'd go. Maybe Neil was upstairs or out the back. She rapped on the knocker harder this time, and as she was about to turn and walk away the door swung open of its own accord. It had been open all along.

She stood in the doorway, taking in the scene in front of her. The hallway was uncarpeted, the cracked Minton tiles splattered with several generations of paint. Above her a bare light bulb was swinging in its light fitting.

She pushed the front door to behind her and called out, 'Hello. Is anyone in?'

There was no reply. Maybe he was out back. She walked through towards the back of the house and into the kitchen. It was unremittingly grim. There were steel bars across the only window. And there was no need to open the back door. She could see through the window that it would have been near impossible for anyone to wade through the thicket of nettles that consumed the garden. Much like the teetering stacks of unwashed plates and half-crushed beer cans that were threatening to consume the kitchen.

There was no sign of baby paraphernalia and precious little sign that anyone other than a single male inhabited the place. Had Sadie finally left him and taken the baby with her? That would explain how low he'd been the last few weeks. And from what she could see he must be in a considerably worse state than either she or Jo had imagined. It would also explain why he hadn't minded spending hours in A & E with Val on Saturday night.

But where was he? Clare really was worried now. What sort of state of mind must he be in to just walk out and leave the front door wide open? And, most importantly, what could she do about it?

Despite having spent the best part of the last two months working with him, she had no conception of what he did with himself when he wasn't – as she'd assumed at least – at home with Sadie and the baby. It suddenly struck her that other than the discussions they'd had about Beth and the Celtic world there had been precious little substance to their conversations. The whole of the rest of what she knew of him was based on Crabby's insights and the somewhat one-sided opinions of Stuart Craig.

She made her way back into the hallway. Should she go and look for him? The trouble was she didn't have the first clue where to find him. Crabby had said he'd had problems with drugs and booze when he was younger. She was relieved at least to see that so far the only signs of alcohol were the empty cans of Sainsbury's Basics bitter, and you were more likely to drown yourself than get drunk on those.

But what if he'd gone out to try to score some drugs? '*Score some drugs.*' *Listen to yourself, Clare!* She didn't have the first clue about what that really even meant. The sum total of her knowledge of drugs came from one puff on a 'herbal' cigarette in her first year, which had resulted in her feeling decidedly queasy. She was distinctly underqualified for stalking the streets of Gloucester in search of likely dealers' haunts.

There wasn't much point hanging around here, though. And he wasn't answering his phone so there was no point sending him a text message. But she could try leaving him a note.

She pushed open the lounge door. There must be something in here that she could write on. The scene was shrouded in a strange half-light. She walked to the bay window and drew back the curtains, narrowly avoiding tripping over a stack of books as she did so. The sunlight flooded in to reveal a room that retained the bones of its Victorian origins; high-ceilinged and still with its picture rail intact. But a cursory coat of white emulsion had failed to disguise the bold brown and orange swirls that chronicled the tastes of long-forgotten residents.

Clare's eye was drawn to the heavy black marble-effect overmantle that dominated the room. In the middle of it, set between two brass candlesticks, someone had taped an A4-sized colour photograph that appeared to have been torn from a book. The dog-eared photo was badly faded, but Clare could still make out the image. It showed the head and torso of a middle-aged man. His torso appeared to have been hacked away from his lower body and his skin was a decidedly unnatural chestnut hue, looking more like well-worn leather than the skin of even the most enthusiastic self-tanning aficionado. On closer examination the viewer could see that the subject of the photo was sporting a moustache and Clare could clearly make out five o'clock shadow around his chin. And just to one side, poking out from under that chin, was the end of a length of sinew, the garrotte that had helped to hasten his death. But what made the image truly extraordinary was that

Clare knew that the man in the photo had been laid to rest the best part of two thousand years ago. It was Lindow Man.

As her eyes adjusted to the bright daylight, Clare could see that between the scatter of old takeaway containers and McDonald's wrappers, every chair and surface was covered with books. All of them with pieces of paper and Post-it notes sticking out at every angle. But the same words appeared in the titles over and over again: CELTIC, GODS, MYTHS, RITUAL, SACRIFICE, DEATH.

If this was Neil's homework, my God he's been doing it thoroughly. No wonder Sadie left him; no woman could put up with this. On the walls, in no apparent order, were taped more images: some printed from the Internet, others ripped from books. There were images of the skeletons of horses, dogs and birds all in pits. Classic Iron Age offerings, every one. And then, as she turned, behind her on the wall she saw a corkboard. On it were three photos. One of each of their three child burials from Bailsgrove and beside them another, this time photocopied, image of Lindow Man. Two of the infant skeletons had a circle of red marker pen ringed round their necks, the third round its head.

She plucked a book from the top of the nearest pile. Flicking through its pages she saw image after image ringed in red marker. She opened a second, almost afraid to look. Photo upon photo of the skeletons of birds and animals. Ancient human burials in peat bogs – all ringed in red marker pen. Clare could feel the palms of her hands beginning to sweat. This was everything Stuart Craig had said about Beth and more. It was time to leave.

She headed for the door, but as she got to the hallway she heard footsteps clattering across the uneven concrete path, accompanied by the sound of heavy breathing. It was Neil – he sounded out of breath.

Before she had time to think she found herself darting up the stairs, taking them two at a time. She headed through the first door that she came to, pulling it gently closed behind her just in time to hear the front door open. It slammed shut with a jolt that shook the house. Standing stock-still, her every instinct was telling her to keep calm, to breathe, but to get out. And then she heard a quiet metallic click as he dropped the catch.

From somewhere below her she heard a muffled thud. It sounded like something heavy being dropped on the piles of bills and junk mail that had been dumped on the hallway table.

She switched her phone to vibrate and held her breath. She didn't know what was going on with Neil. But one thing she knew for sure was she had no intention of confronting him about it now.

CHAPTER TWENTY-ONE

Stone knew that the first few hours in a murder inquiry were always the most important. If the right decisions were taken at the start it could shorten an investigation by months or even years. If the wrong decisions were made it could mean a killer went undiscovered. And that could cost lives.

He could leave Ray and SOCO at Weaver's Close to get on with it. They knew the drill as well as he did. He already had family liaison on the case and they'd contacted the relatives – one brother in Surrey somewhere. You had to know where to put your resources. And his time was best spent elsewhere.

As he climbed into his Volvo he noticed a well-dressed, middle-aged woman hovering just outside the crime scene cordon. Stone climbed out of his car again and spoke to the young constable who'd called the case in. He informed him that it was Sheila Foggarty, the woman he'd been dispatched to interview about the brick-throwing incident at the dig site, but, as he told Stone without much joy, she'd point-blank denied knowing anything about it.

Stone walked towards her. 'Mrs Foggarty.'

She nearly jumped out of her skin. 'Yes.'

Stone flashed his warrant card. 'DCI Stone. Can I have a word, please?'

'If you must.'

He nodded to where his Volvo was parked. 'We might be more comfortable in the back of my car.'

She glanced around, taking in every window in the street as she did so. 'I'd rather do it here if you don't mind.'

'Whatever you prefer. You seem to be very interested in what's going on here, Mrs Foggarty.'

'I know Mr Crabbs, Chief Inspector.'

He couldn't help noticing the present tense. 'Were you a friend of his?'

'You might say so. More of an acquaintance really. Is he alright? Has something happened to him?'

'I'm sorry to have to tell you that Mr Crabbs is dead, Mrs Foggarty. He appears to have been murdered.'

For a moment he thought she was going to faint. He helped her to a seat on a nearby garden wall.

After a few moments she regained her composure. 'I'm sorry. It's just such a shock.'

He sat down next to her. 'It's always a shock. You never get used to sudden death.'

She said, 'No, I don't suppose you do.' She turned to face him. 'Has this got something to do with the dig?'

'That's a very curious question, Mrs Foggarty.'

She looked taken aback at the directness of his statement. 'You might think so, but it's perfectly obvious to me. Crabby has been spending a lot of time up there recently and then there was all of that strange business with the Kinsella woman. This sort of thing isn't a regular occurrence in the village, you know. It wasn't like this before they started digging up there.'

'I understand from my constable that you're not entirely happy with the excavations.'

'Honestly, Chief Inspector, it's a travesty. Little more than grave robbing and all so that charlatan Paul Marshall can build houses.'

'Is that what made you decide that it was OK to nearly kill someone?'

She repeated, 'Kill someone? I have no idea what you're talking about.'

'That brick that you threw, Mrs Foggarty. It struck a young woman on the head. She had to be taken to hospital.'

Sheila Foggarty clapped her hand to her mouth. 'Oh my God! It wasn't meant to hurt anybody.'

Suddenly and quite without warning, Sheila Foggarty began to sob. Stone reached into his pocket and produced a paper tissue.

When the sobbing had subsided, she said, 'Thank you. It was only meant to scare them. To make them stop digging. We just don't want the houses.'

'We?'

'Me and Crabby . . . and a few of the other local residents.' A look of horror suddenly spread across her face. She gesticulated towards Crabby's house. 'You don't suppose this is some sort of retaliation, do you? For what we' – she corrected herself – 'for what I did.'

He wanted to reassure her, to tell her it was highly unlikely, that this had nothing to do with the dig. But after what he'd just seen in the back garden of number 6 Weaver's Close, he realised he'd already badly misjudged the situation. And if he was going to get answers, the dig site was where he'd be most likely to find them.

Jo glanced down at her watch. It had been a couple of hours since Clare had left to try to find Neil and she still hadn't heard from either of them yet. They could ill afford to be one pair of hands down at the moment, let alone three. No Neil, no Clare and no Val – at least for a couple more days. But she guessed Clare had her priorities right at least. Neil was obviously having a tough time. And living people had to come before prehistory. She just wished Clare would damn well hurry up and find him.

In Val's absence, Jo was trying to restore some sort of order to the finds that had been scattered to all corners of the office, in what had now become known in the latest outbreak of trench humour as Brickgate. Thus far she'd had little success, and when she got to her feet to see who the car that had just pulled up belonged to it was something of a welcome diversion. She stuck her head out of the Portakabin door hoping that she might see Clare, but instead she found herself face-to-face with DCI Mark Stone.

Jo blinked as she stepped out into the bright sunshine. 'Hi, can I help?'

'I hope so, Dr Granski. Is Clare about?'

Jo said, 'No, not at the moment. She's gone into Gloucester. But she shouldn't be long.' She smiled. 'And Jo will do just fine.'

'Thank you, Jo. Would you mind if we went into your office? There's something I need to talk to you about.'

She gestured towards the Portakabin door. 'Sure, go ahead.'

He said, 'You might want to take a seat.'

This didn't sound good. In her experience when cops asked you to sit down it generally only meant one thing. Had something happened to Neil? Was that why he hadn't turned up to work this morning?

'I understand that you and Clare know Wayne Crabbs.'

Jo breathed an inward sigh of relief. Maybe she was wrong. Maybe this was about the metal detector finds.

'Yeah, sure. We know Crabby.'

Stone nodded. 'I'm sorry to have to tell you, Jo, but Mr Crabbs was found dead this morning.'

Shit, she'd been right the first time. 'Crabby's dead? But how?'

'We think he may have been murdered.' He looked at Jo. 'Look, there's no point beating around the bush. He was definitely murdered. Someone slit his throat.'

For several seconds Jo sat stunned, unable to speak.

Then she said simply, 'I'm sorry, but I don't understand. Why would anyone want to kill Crabby?'

Stone withdrew his phone from his pocket. Flicking through the pictures, he turned it through one hundred and eighty degrees and showed an image to Jo. 'Do you recognise this?'

Jo gestured towards the phone. 'May I?'

'Go ahead.'

She zoomed into the image, swiping her finger up and down the screen.

She passed him back the phone. 'It's a context sheet.' He looked puzzled. 'One of the recording forms that we use on the dig. Like these.'

She plucked a ring binder from the shelf and flipped it open to show him. He nodded.

Then Jo added, 'It's not one of ours, though. That's Beth's handwriting. But there's something not right with it.'

'Oh, why's that?'

Jo said, 'In the section about finds down at the bottom it says that layer had a fragment of stone tablet in it. And there's been nothing like that found on the excavation.'

'Are you sure?'

'One hundred per cent. If there'd been anything like that found we'd have it here with the rest of the finds.' Jo opened the lid of the laptop sitting in front of her, pulled up a database and searched for the word 'tablet'. 'And there's nothing in the finds register – see. Do you mind if I ask where it came from?'

He sighed. 'We found it in Mr Crabbs' house. It was sitting in an empty shoebox on his coffee table. It appeared to have been wrapped around something. But whatever it was wasn't there any more. There was one more thing.' He scrolled through the pictures on his phone again. 'This was found lying next to Mr Crabbs.'

Jo took the phone. It was the image of a large black bird. A small photographic scale had been positioned alongside it. She was no ornithologist, but just by the size of it she could tell what it was.

She placed the phone down on the table. 'I'm guessing you already know it's a raven.' He nodded. 'Ravens were sacred birds in Celtic mythology, DCI Stone, and it's not uncommon to find them in offering pits. Sometimes on their own, sometimes with other animals. But the other stuff – the head and the throat and that twine – it's what they call the threefold or triple death.'

'The what?'

'The triple death. It's what they would do in the Iron Age on the rare occasions that they sacrificed people. A blow to the head, a garrotte and then finally they severed the jugular vein. Some people think the blow to the head was a sort of mercy blow to knock them unconscious. The garrotte was almost certainly supposed to increase the blood flow when the throat was cut.'

Stone offered a grim, weary smile. 'I'm glad they didn't make a habit of it.'

She pointed at the phone. 'This is just like that hare they found with Beth, isn't it? Right down to the orange twine.'

Stone narrowed his eyes. 'How do you know about that?'

Surely he didn't think she was involved in some way?

'Crabby told us. Me and Clare.'

That seemed to satisfy him. And his thoughts now suddenly seemed to be taking a different tack.

Stone asked, 'Where did you say Clare was?'

'She's gone down to Gloucester to see if she can track down a member of staff who didn't turn up to work this morning.'

'Who?' he almost screamed at her.

Jo sat back in her chair, open-mouthed.

Stone took a deep breath. 'Look, I'm sorry, Jo, but this could be important. Crabby isn't the first murder related to this dig.'

Jo said, 'You mean Beth.'

For a moment Stone hesitated, apparently uncertain of what to say. 'I'm going to be straight with you. Knowing what I know now there's every possibility that Beth might not have taken her own life. But it's not what I meant. One of my colleagues down in Wiltshire has been investigating another murder. A bloke by the name of Jack Tyler. Name mean anything?'

Jo shook her head. 'Never heard of him. But then I don't know everyone in Wiltshire. It's a big place.'

'Well, it turns out Jack Tyler was an archaeologist by training. And he worked for Beth, on this site.'

'On this site?'

Stone nodded. 'That's right. And Beth sacked him for turning up to work drunk. So now you see why I need to know who hasn't turned up for work.'

Jo shook her head in disbelief. 'I don't believe it. Three people connected with this dig have been killed.'

She needed to concentrate, pull herself together. She looked at Stone; he didn't appear to be in any doubt.

She said, 'Clare's gone to find Neil Fuller, our site assistant. Like I said, he didn't turn up for work this morning. Clare was worried about him.'

'Oh, why?'

How much to tell him?

She said, 'He's been a bit down lately. Things with his wife are – you know – kind of rocky.'

Stone looked disbelieving, 'Does Clare normally make house calls to staff members who're going through a rough patch with their other half?'

Jo hesitated. How much should she tell him? Who could it hurt? If there was ever a time for telling the truth, the whole truth and nothing but the truth, this must be it.

She said, 'Neil had a few problems with drugs and alcohol in his younger days. Clare was just a little concerned things with his wife might have sent him off the rails again.' She paused. 'And there's something else you should know – Neil worked for Beth here too.'

Stone said, 'Everyone the killer has targeted was involved with the dig when Beth was in charge. You said Neil Fuller didn't turn up for work this morning. Have you spoken to him?'

Jo shook her head. She had a bad feeling about this. 'No, we've had nothing from him. Not even a text.'

Stone looked Jo straight in the eye. 'There's every possibility Neil could be in danger.'

Or, Jo thought, *as he hasn't been seen or heard of since Saturday night, it might be too late.* And what Stone was very carefully not saying, but was blindingly obvious to anyone with half a brain, was that if the killer was targeting Neil and Clare was looking for him, she was putting herself squarely in harm's way.

CHAPTER TWENTY-TWO

David didn't know what residue of memory or instinct had driven Jeffrey Kinsella to give him Beth's envelope, but what he did know was he was grateful for it. Jack Tyler and Beth Kinsella were both dead and Fuller had worked with both of them at Bailsgrove. And it was obvious from the video that Marshall had been giving Fuller backhanders. And not just the odd tenner.

But to do what? To get rid of Beth? Maybe. But Marshall wanted his houses built and he can't have been happy when the police closed down the site after Beth's death. The video surely had to have been made by Beth, though. She must have had her suspicions about what was going on. Had she confronted Fuller about what she'd suspected? One thing was for sure, she was obviously nervous about what might happen. Otherwise why would she have given her father that USB stick? She'd hidden it in the one place she knew no one would ever look.

He flung his laptop onto the passenger seat of the Land Rover and dug his mobile out of his pocket. But who should he ring first? Sally? Clare? Jo? There was no choice, it had to be Clare. She and Jo would be at the dig site with Fuller now.

He scrolled through his contacts and hit Clare's mobile number. It rang and rang. *Pick up the bloody phone!* Then it went to voicemail.

'Clare, if you get this please, please phone me. It's urgent. Neil Fuller is dangerous. He's being paid by Marshall. I have proof. Close the site down. Do whatever you need to do. But stay with Jo. And for God's sake don't go anywhere on your own.'

He flipped over to messaging, his fingers fumbling on the screen. *Fuller dangerous. I have proof. Stay with Jo. Two dead.*

David's hands were shaking as he punched Jo's number on his mobile. He was all but praying now. *Please have your phone switched on. Please.*

On the second ring Jo picked up. *Thank God.*

'Hi, David.'

He could hear her saying to someone in the background, 'I'd better take this. OK, if I hear anything from either of them I'll let you know. Write it on that.'

Then she said, 'Sorry about that. Good timing. There's something I need to talk to you about.'

He said, 'I haven't got time for that. This is important.'

'But, David—'

For Christ's sake, why couldn't she just keep quiet for once?

'Just shut up and listen, Jo! You and Clare might be in danger.' David could almost feel the silence at the end of the phone. 'I've just been to see Beth Kinsella's father. He's' – inexplicably he struggled for the words – 'not very well. He's in a nursing home. He gave me something Beth had left with him. A video. It seems

286

to have been made by Beth. And it shows Paul Marshall paying money to Neil Fuller. Lots of money, Jo. Do you understand? Fuller's taking bungs from Marshall. And now Beth is dead and so is Jack Tyler.'

Jo said, 'Shit, David, Neil didn't turn up to work this morning. Clare's gone to look for him. She's down there in Gloucester now.'

He felt sick. His hands were trembling so much he almost dropped the phone. *No, no, no! This can't be happening.*

He swallowed hard. 'Jo, I've just tried phoning Clare and all I'm getting is her voicemail.'

There was no reply. He thought he heard a car revving its engine in the background.

'Jo, did you hear me? Do you understand?'

Jo could hear the sound of an engine starting. *Shit!*

She all but threw herself out of the Portakabin door. 'I hear you, David. Loud and clear. But I've got to go.'

She flung herself in front of the hood of Stone's Volvo.

He stuck his head out of his window and yelled, 'What the hell do you think you're doing? I could have killed you!'

Jo didn't reply. Instead she ripped the passenger side door open and deposited herself in the front seat.

Stone asked, 'Do you want to give me some sort of explanation about what's going on here?'

'No time. I'll tell you while you're driving. It's Fuller. Clare's in danger. We've got to get to her before she finds him. Just drive.' She urged him forward with a wave of her arm.

For what seemed like the longest moment of Jo's life, Stone just stared at her. Then suddenly, as if a switch had been thrown, he made his decision. Foot down, he left more turf on the road than in the field behind him.

His eyes were fixed laser-like on the road in front of him. 'Now will you tell me where we're going?'

'Gloucester. Fuller's house. That was David on the phone.' By way of explanation she added, 'David Barbrook, our boss.'

A cloud of doubt flickered across Stone's face.

Jo said, 'He's got a video of Paul Marshall giving Neil money – Neil's been taking kickbacks.'

'Why hasn't he given the video to the police?'

Jo couldn't believe Stone was arguing about it. 'He's only just found it. Beth Kinsella left it with her father in some nursing home.'

Stone snorted but seemed to accept the explanation. 'Do you know Fuller's address?'

'No, but I've been to Neil's place to pick up site records when we took over the dig. It's a terraced house.'

She realised how ridiculous that must have sounded almost the moment she'd said it. From what she'd been able to make out there were nothing but terraced houses in Gloucester.

Stone flashed her a sideways glance. 'Do you think you can remember where it is?'

'I think so. And I know it was number 46.'

He nodded in the direction of the radio. 'Can you press that hands-free button for me?'

Jo obliged and he nodded his thanks without taking his eyes from the road. 'GL43 to Despatch.'

'Despatch here, sir.'

'I need the address for a Neil Fuller, Gloucester?' He whispered across to Jo. 'What's his wife's name?'

'Sadie.'

He spoke into the ether again. 'Wife's name Sadie Fuller. And it's Priority 1. Repeat, Priority 1.'

'Roger that, GL43. Address for Neil and Sadie Fuller, Gloucester. Priority 1.'

Stone flung the Volvo round an unfeasibly sharp bend. 'Call her. Try calling Clare.'

Jo said, 'David said he'd tried to call her and it had just gone to voicemail.'

'Well try again. Just do it!'

Jo pulled her mobile out of the pocket of her cargo pants and searched for Jo's number.

'You have reached the voicemail of Clare Hills. I can't take your call right now. But if you'd like to leave your name and number after the beep I'll get back to you.'

'Clare, it's Jo. I don't know where you are right now but if you're with Neil, just leave. It doesn't matter how, just go. Get out of there! Crabby's dead, Clare. Mark Stone's just told me. And Neil' – she could barely bring herself to say the words it was so incomprehensible – 'I think Neil may have killed him.'

Stone said, 'Tell her to stay with other people.'

Jo nodded. 'And, Clare, stay with other people! Then phone me. Please. As soon as you can.'

She ended the call and switched to messaging, her fingers flying across the screen. *Clare. CRABBY DEAD. NEIL KILLER. Get out! Go where people are. Phone me when safe.* Then after a moment's thought she typed in the words: *We're coming. J x*

CHAPTER TWENTY-THREE

Sally turned towards West. 'Have they brought Kelly's wife in yet?'

'She's waiting for us in Interview Room 2.'

She nodded. 'Good. If we're going to nail this one, we need to make sure we tie up all of the loose ends.'

Her phone rang and she glanced down at the display. It was David. She hadn't really got time for this but she'd better take it – she'd been a bit rough on him the last time they spoke.

'Hello.' She held her hand up to West, who was hovering by the door, and said, 'You go through, Tom. I'll join you in a moment.'

She could hear David on the phone, saying, 'Sal, is that you?'

'Hi, David, sorry about that. Just had to sort something out.'

His voice sounded strained – anxious. 'Sal, there's something you need to know.'

'Calm down, David. What on earth's wrong?'

'It's Fuller.'

'Who?'

'Neil Fuller, the guy who worked as Beth Kinsella's assistant at Bailsgrove. The guy who we took on as our site assistant. I've just been to see Beth's father. He gave me a tape – a video tape.' His breathing was ragged. She could barely make out what he was saying.

'Slow down, David. What are you on about? None of this is making any sense.'

'I don't have time to explain. Just listen to me, Sal. I've found a tape that Beth Kinsella made. It shows Neil Fuller taking backhanders from Paul Marshall – the developer who owns the site. Fuller who worked for Beth and alongside Jack Tyler. Do you understand, Sal?'

Sally was focused now, fully concentrated on the job in hand and what it meant for her investigation. 'Right, where are you, David?'

'I'm in Derbyshire.'

Damn. She was hoping he'd say he was at Bailsgrove. 'You need to contact site, warn Clare and Jo and the others. Whatever they do, tell them under no circumstances should they approach Fuller.'

'I've already phoned Jo. She said Fuller didn't turn up for work this morning, and he didn't ring in either. Clare's gone down to his house in Gloucester to try to find out what's wrong with him.'

'Look, David, I've got to go. I'll ring Mark Stone and get his boys onto it.'

Her brain whirring away at double speed now, Sally abandoned all idea of interviewing Damian Kelly's wife. Whether Kelly's wife would provide him with an alibi or not was hardly relevant if there was every chance that Fuller, not Kelly, had killed Jack Tyler, and very possibly Beth Kinsella too. The one thing that Kelly had lacked was a solid motive. But it was all too obvious that Neil Fuller may have had one.

She scrolled through her contacts and hit Mark Stone's number. Jack Tyler's words about Beth came back to her as clearly as if she'd heard them herself – she'd got what she deserved. Had Tyler known – or at least suspected – that Beth's death wasn't an accident? Did he try to blackmail Fuller? He was certainly desperate for money. But would he really have been dumb enough to attempt to extort cash from a killer? No, much more likely that he knew about the kickbacks Fuller was taking from the developer and tried to put the squeeze on him over that.

Stone's phone was ringing now. His voice cut in on the other end of the line. *At last.* 'You're through to DCI Mark Stone's voicemail. If you'd like to leave a name and number after the tone I'll get back to you.'

Shit. She might not like the woman, but no one deserved to walk into the home of a potential murderer alone, and with no idea what they were up against. And besides, much though she didn't like to admit it, she suspected that if she allowed anything to happen to Clare, David would never forgive her.

'Mark, call me as soon as you get this! I think you may have a double murderer on your hands. Neil Fuller – a Gloucester address. And Clare Hills, lead archaeologist on the Bailsgrove dig, is on her way to his house right now.'

She slammed her mobile down on the desk and picked up her desk phone. 'Get me Gloucester nick, now!'

Below her Clare could hear Neil Fuller's footsteps echoing through the hallway. She could feel her phone vibrating in her pocket again. Could he hear it? She extracted it from the pocket of her moleskins and was about to switch it from vibrate to silent when she saw she had two voicemail messages and a couple of texts. It looked like one of each from David and Jo.

She put her ear to the door and listened. Not a sound. It didn't seem like Neil was moving anywhere. What was he doing? She switched her attention back to her phone. She couldn't risk listening to the voicemail messages; he might hear them. She hit the screen and brought up her texts. David's first.

Fuller dangerous. I have proof. Stay with Jo. Two dead.

As she read the words of David's message she could feel her whole body go cold. It was all she could do to hold onto the phone. She flipped through to Jo's message.

Clare. CRABBY DEAD. NEIL KILLER. Get out! Go where people are. Phone me when safe. We're coming. J x

She couldn't believe what she was reading. Crabby was dead. She didn't want to believe the words in front of her. But she knew Jo would never have sent something like that unless she was certain. And two dead: was that Crabby and Beth? Or was there someone else? *Christ, Clare, does it really matter?* People were dead and Neil Fuller had killed them. And right now the same Neil Fuller was downstairs not forty feet from where she was standing.

Stay calm. You've got to stay calm. Your life might depend on it! She pressed her spine hard against the wall and tilted her head back. *Think, Clare, think!*

Trying to control her breathing, she glanced down at the words on her phone again: *Get out.* That's what it said. And that's exactly what she needed to do. But how? She shoved her phone back into her pocket and pressed her ear to the door once more.

She could hear footsteps. It sounded as if he was making his way to the kitchen. There was the sound of clattering plates. And all at once she could hear water gushing from the taps and splattering as it hit the bottom of the old Belfast sink.

Then she heard him talking. Was there someone with him? *Sadie, maybe, or a neighbour. Please God, let there be someone with him.* Slowly, so slowly that its movement was barely perceptible, she turned the old-fashioned metal knob on the bedroom door. She pulled it towards her, opening it just a sliver, and placed her ear to the gap.

It was definitely Neil. But no one else. It sounded as if he was on his own. She could hear more clearly now.

He was muttering and swearing. 'Fucking stuff. Why won't it come off?'

And then, suddenly, he let out a scream so loud that Clare's hand, and the whole door with it, jolted forward. She managed to grab it just in time to prevent it from clattering against its wooden frame. The sound that came from Neil was visceral, like nothing she'd ever heard before. As if it was emanating from somewhere deep inside him.

You've got to do something, Clare. But what? How the hell was she meant to get out of here? She looked around the bedroom. *Jesus, Clare, you idiot! The window.* The prospect of having to climb out of a first-floor window filled her with terror. She was phobic about heights and she'd nearly lost her life once before when she'd agreed – against her better judgement – to scale the dig's photographic tower at Hungerbourne. But if the choice was a first-floor window or confronting a murderer alone in his own home she knew which she preferred. Slowly, with the lightest of footsteps, she edged her way round the bed to the far side of the room. The windows were of the Victorian sash cord variety, and she positioned her hands below the upper portion of the wooden casing and pushed, but with no effect. She shoved again, this time using all her strength. But it was no good – it wouldn't budge. And examining the window frame more carefully, the reason was only too apparent. Despite the peeling paintwork on the outside of the woodwork, someone had applied a thick coat of paint to the inside. She was sealed in. Which meant her only escape route was going to be past Neil.

She gingerly made her way back towards the door. She opened it again, this time a little wider than she had before. Now she could hear him using what sounded like a scrubbing brush. Pushing her way out through the gap in the door, inch by agonising inch she edged towards the top of the stairs. And then one tread at a time she started to descend. A third of the way down she lowered herself into a squatting position.

Craning her head, she peered through a gap in the banister so that she could look down the hall towards the kitchen. The door was wide open. Fuller was standing with his back towards her. He was clad in T-shirt and jeans and at first sight she thought he was trying to clean something in the sink. Then as he stood there muttering and swearing under his breath she realised that he was scrubbing at his hands.

She glanced round at the front door. Lying next to it on the hallway table in what appeared to be a clear plastic soil sample bag was a hefty triangular slab of stone. Even from this distance she could see that it had some sort of engraving on it. But what drew her attention wasn't the writing; it was the wide dark red streak smeared across one half of the bag. It looked like blood. She had to get out of here.

Turning her head back towards the kitchen, she could see Fuller was still bent over the sink, taps running. Could she make it to the door before he heard her? So slowly that she could feel her thigh muscles straining, she stood up. She needed to keep out of his peripheral vision for as long as she could to give herself as much time as possible to get to the front door before he noticed.

Edging backwards, she pressed her back against the wall. He was out of sight now. She was about to begin her descent when she heard the hard, metallic squeal of the taps being turned off. The water stopped. She could hear the blood pounding in her eardrums. The silence was all-consuming. Then she heard him. He was coming her way.

The fifteen minutes it had taken Mark Stone to weave his way through the highways and byways of the Gloucestershire countryside to get from Bailsgrove to the M5 might as well have been fifteen hours. He was well aware of the fact that if Clare had found Fuller there was every possibility they might already be too late.

But he couldn't allow himself to think like that all the time there was a chance – any chance. He'd put out an all-points call on Fuller but so far without luck. And Despatch had found him that address. The only trouble was it wasn't number 46, and when he'd asked her again, Jo had insisted she was still one hundred per cent sure that wherever Fuller's house was it was definitely number 46. And when Despatch had sent a couple of uniforms round to check out the listed address there was a Latvian family living there. Turned out Fuller and his wife had moved out months ago. So now they only had Jo's memory to rely on.

He asked, 'How many times have you been to Fuller's place?'

'Just the once.'

There was a moment's silence before he said, 'You better have a bloody good memory then. Don't you people keep employment records? You know, with little details like where your staff live?'

'Yep. And they're all on Clare's password-protected laptop back at the office.'

Fucking IT security. He hated it.

They were still a good five minutes from the outskirts of Gloucester as he dodged his way through the thickening traffic on the motorway, blue lights flashing, siren blaring.

Suddenly, Jo waved her hand at the approaching road sign, 'That's it. It's the A40 exit.'

'You sure?'

'Positive.'

'Right.'

He pulled the steering wheel hard left, slewing across three lanes of traffic, his foot never touching the brakes. He had no doubt that he'd have to answer to his super when he found out he'd had a civilian in the front seat acting as satnav while he was doing ninety down the hard shoulder with full blues and twos. But, frankly, right now the super could go screw himself.

He was heading down the hallway. Pressed against the wall, sweat dripping down her back, Clare stiffened. For the briefest of moments she closed her eyes. *I can't see you. You can't see me.* She dug her nails hard into the palms of her hands. *Get a grip of yourself, woman!* Suddenly the footsteps stopped.

She opened her eyes. Had he heard something? Had he seen her? *Please don't turn round.* Then he was off again, moving. He opened the living room door, pulling it to behind him. She could hear him scrunching up paper. It sounded as if he was rattling the grate in the fireplace.

This was her chance, while his attention was fully engaged with something else. She edged down the stairway as quickly as she dared. She was down on level ground now. Standing on the Minton tiles just to one side of her was the little table. There was no doubting from this distance that it was blood smeared across the plastic bag, nor what the bag contained. It looked like the other half of the Bailsgrove Roman inscription, but where had Neil got it from? *No time for that now.* Her focus needed to be solely on that front door.

She listened. She could hear what sounded like a fire crackling in the front room. It was a steaming hot day. What on earth was he doing? He must be burning something.

She edged forward. As she got to the front door she realised for the first time that he'd put the chain across. She could feel the perspiration on her hands. Flattening her palms, she rubbed them down the front of her trousers. Then, putting her hand to the chain, she began to disengage the end of it from its catch. She almost had it fully withdrawn now.

There was a sudden 'Ouch, shit!' from the living room.

Instinctively she half turned and as she did so the end of the chain slipped from her fingers.

For several long seconds there was total silence. Then she heard him move. She looked at the front door, but the chain was still in place. There was no time. Turning, she hurtled past the living room door towards the kitchen. The back door. She twisted the handle and tugged furiously. But it wouldn't budge. It must be locked – and no sign of a key. She could hear him. He was out of the living room now.

He'd seen her. 'It's you. You interfering bitch!'

There was only one choice left. The bathroom. Turning towards the open door, she caught a glimpse of him in the hallway. He was standing, hands by his sides, stripped to the waist and smiling. He was stock-still and just staring at her. Down the right-hand leg of his jeans there was a large dark splatter of what she presumed must be blood. Crabby's blood.

Everything seemed to happen very quickly after that.

'Nice of you to drop in.' He lunged forward.

But before he'd finished the sentence she was through the bathroom door. She slammed it behind her, praising God and all the saints – none of whom she believed in – that there was a key as she turned it through ninety degrees in the lock.

And then he started hammering on the door with his fists.

CHAPTER TWENTY-FOUR

'It's down there.' Jo was gesticulating wildly.

'That's what you said last time.'

She glared at him. 'Trust me. It's this one. I remember it. Right!'

He hauled the steering wheel round.

She was shouting to make herself heard above the sound of the siren, 'Down at the end, left-hand side.'

He gestured towards the hands-free on the radio again. She hit the button.

'All units in the vicinity of Compton Street. Officer seeking assistance. Code 1. Repeat, Code 1. 46 Compton Street.'

The cars were tightly parked down both sides of the street.

Suddenly, Jo yelled and pointed, 'That's Clare's car. There!'

The little blue Fiesta was parked up neatly by the kerb a few doors down from number 46. There were no parking spaces. Stone jammed his foot hard on the brake, bringing the car to a screeching halt right outside of Fuller's house. He flung open the car door. Climbing out and slamming the door behind him, he stuck his head back through the open window and screamed at her, 'Stay there!'

There was zero chance of that happening. Jo shot out of the car, tracking Stone's every footstep to the front door.

He turned to look at her. 'What did I tell you?'

She said, 'What can I say? I'm a bad listener.'

'Jesus!'

He turned back towards the door and crouched down, pushing at the flap of the letter box to hold it open. 'Fuller, Fuller. Are you in there?'

No reply.

Jo was squatting down behind him. 'What's that banging noise?'

He turned to answer but before he could reply over her shoulder he caught sight of a pair of uniformed officers climbing out of their car. He waved them towards him. 'You two. Over here. And bring the battering ram.'

Within seconds the two were standing beside them at the front of the door.

Stone yelled, 'Out of the way!'

Jo stepped back into the weed-choked front garden. Stone yelled at her again to stand back. This time she complied, shuffling backwards against the thigh-high garden wall.

Stone ordered, 'No. Right back. Out of the garden.'

For once Jo did what she was told and in one movement swung herself over the wall and onto the pavement on the other side.

The two uniformed officers started to pull the battering ram back into position. But before they'd had a chance to drive it forward, Mark Stone had taken a running jump and with his arm covering his face had launched himself clean through the bay window, glass and all. Within seconds he had the front door open.

The two constables laid the battering ram down and followed him into the house.

Jo could hear Stone talking to them. 'He's locked this door. He's in there. She seems to be on the other side of another door. He's hammering at it with something. Where's that battering ram?'

Shit! Clare was in there with Fuller. And he had her trapped. There had to be another way in. Jo glanced to her right. About four doors away was a side passage leading down the side of one of the houses. That had to go somewhere, didn't it?

She ran like her life depended on it, following the passageway down until it hit a T-junction. Then she headed left. How many houses down? It was four. She was sure it was four. One, two, three, four. Looking up she could see the same peeling red paintwork. This was it. The wood of the back gate had long since rotted. She gave it one swift kick and the little that still remained disintegrated. As it did so it revealed a sea of chest-high stinging nettles. Above them Jo could see the back of the house. To the right was what looked like it must be the kitchen window. Someone had installed steel security bars across it. Through the grime-stained glass she could see what appeared to be a table that had been upended and jammed up against a door.

To the left of the kitchen window was a brick-built extension that must once have been an outhouse of some kind. On its gable end was another window, this one double-glazed and with frosted glass. It must be the bathroom. The window was split into two parts. The bottom two thirds was a single solid pane. But the top third looked as if it opened outwards.

She cursed the summer sunshine she'd been so glad of that morning. Her denim jacket was still sitting where she'd abandoned it in the site office. Lifting both hands in the air, she waded into the ocean of green. The thin cotton of her T-shirt did little to prevent the hundreds of tiny hypodermic needles from finding their mark. Gritting her teeth, she plunged forward. After the first five or ten seconds she almost ceased to feel the individual stings. The whole of her upper body felt as if it had been rubbed with red hot chilli peppers.

As she got nearer to the house she could hear a dull thudding.

It was relentless. He was beating the door with his fists. Again and again.

She looked around her. The only window was high up in the end wall above the toilet cistern. It was double-glazed, but the top of it opened. Could she get through it? It looked tight. But she'd give it a bloody good go. Clambering on top of the cistern, with the sound of fist on wood behind her, she tried to pull the metal handle upwards. Was it just stiff? She almost wrenched her arm out of its socket trying to force it open. But it was no good. It was locked.

The key. Where was the key? It must be here somewhere. She climbed down from the toilet cistern and started to rummage frantically through the assortment of old shampoo bottles and shaving kit. Behind her she could still hear hammering, but now the noise was heavier. The sound of metal on wood. This was it. There was no way out.

Fuller had killed Beth. And he'd killed Crabby too. And now it was her turn. She slumped down on the toilet seat, her head in her hands. On the verge of tears, she found herself mumbling, 'Crabby, oh, Crabby. Where were your gods when you needed them?'

Then somewhere in the distance she thought she heard someone yelling. She lifted her head up. It was a male voice. She recognised it. It sounded like Mark Stone. Jo's text. She'd said, 'We're coming.'

Jo and Stone. They were here. Clare felt a sudden rush of fury. Fuller wasn't going to get her. He wasn't going to make her his next victim. Because she wasn't going to bloody well let him.

Looking back towards the door for the first time, she saw there was a floor-to-ceiling cupboard built in at the end of the bath. She had no idea what she was hoping to find. But when she opened the cupboard door she discovered a washing machine and tumble dryer stacked one on top of the other.

For a second the hammering stopped. She could hear Fuller in the kitchen, his breathing now coming in erratic bursts. He was dragging something heavy. Scraping it across the tiled floor.

She had no idea how she would do it but if she could just drag the washing machine and tumble dryer out of the cupboard and in front of the bathroom door she might be able to keep Fuller out for long enough to let Stone and Jo get to her. She grabbed the sides of the washing machine, desperately trying to get some sort of grip. She heaved with all her might and it shuddered, but it was jammed. It was wedged on the bloody bathroom lino. What the hell was she going to do?

Then she saw the nail scissors. Grabbing them, she set to work. First using them to pierce the lino and then, once she'd made the initial incision, to cut a gash from the end of the cupboard to the wall.

Fuller was back now, hammering on the door again. 'Don't think you're going to get away from me, you bitch. Not now. You will die. The gods will have their sacrifice.'

She ripped at the lino, tearing it away from the floor. Then she heaved at the washing machine. Jesus, it was heavy. It shuddered forward a couple of inches, the tumble drier above it swaying alarmingly. She stopped, took in a deep breath and with a strength she didn't know she possessed, heaved again. Gradually, a few inches at a time, it was coming. She could do this.

That's when she heard the unmistakable sound of splintering wood. She looked up to see the head of the hammer. It had punctured one small hole in the door. It wouldn't be long now and he'd be through. She gave one last tremendous pull and managed to get the washing machine almost right across the door. But there was a six-inch gap on the side where the bathroom door was hinged.

'They've taken Beth, they've taken Jack, and they've taken Crabby. The gods demand their price. You will pay!'

Jesus Christ!

Moving round to the side, she put her full weight behind the tumble drier and pushed. It fell with a resounding clatter of metal and plastic wedging, diagonally between the washer and the corner of the bathroom wall.

She took a deep breath and looked around her. That window was still her only way out. If there was a key in here somewhere she was going to find it.

As Jo got within a few yards of the back of the house she suddenly caught sight of Fuller. He'd appeared from somewhere in the corner of the kitchen nearest the bathroom. Jo swallowed hard. He had a hammer in his hand. He threw it down and disappeared out of sight for a second.

She heard a resounding crash and the splintering of wood. It must be Stone's men with the battering ram. There was a horrible high-pitched scraping noise. Suddenly, Fuller reappeared. This time he was shoving what looked like an enormous double-fronted fridge freezer in front of him. There was another huge crash and with one push he'd wedged it against the upended table that blocked the kitchen door. Fuller bent down. What was he doing?

There he was again. And then he disappeared in the direction of the bathroom, and the hammering resumed.

The realisation hit Jo like a bucket of ice-cold water. Clare was in the bathroom. And Fuller was trying to smash the bathroom door down. There was no way Stone and his men were getting past that fridge freezer in a hurry. It was going to be down to her to get Clare out. But how? It had to be the window. Except it was shut. Could Clare hear her in there? The window was double-glazed, but there was an old-fashioned air vent just to one side of it. Maybe if she could get close to it she could make Clare hear her.

She waded the last few feet through the nettles to the end wall of the bathroom.

Standing directly beneath the vent, she yelled, 'Hey, Clare. You in there?'

There was a moment's pause before she heard her friend's voice. 'Jo, is that you? Oh, thank God. I'm in the bathroom. Fuller's trying to batter the door down. I've got it barricaded, but I don't know how long it'll last.'

'Do you think you can make it through the window?'

Clare said, 'It'll be tight, but I think so. Although it's locked and I can't find the key.'

'Keep looking!'

'What do you think I'm bloody doing?'

From somewhere inside the house Jo could hear Stone. 'It's no good, Fuller. You're not going anywhere. Give yourself up!'

Still the hammering continued. There was the sound of splintering wood, followed by metal on metal. As if he was hitting a steel drum.

Clare yelled, 'It's no good, Jo. I can't find it. I don't know how long I can keep him out. He's through the wood to the tumble drier now.'

The desperation in Clare's voice was unmistakable.

Think, Jo, think! Suddenly a flash of inspiration struck her. 'Is there a loo in there?'

'Yes. Why?'

Jo said, 'Open the cistern, Clare!'

'I don't understand.'

'Just do it!' Jo ordered.

There was a moment's silence broken only by the crash of hammer on metal.

'Jesus, Jo. You're a fucking genius!'

'You can thank me later. Just get that freaking window open.'

There was a pause, then the window swung open. She could see Clare's head.

'Come on. Shift that skinny English arse of yours!'

The sound of hammering on wood and metal now was incessant. Clare's face disappeared from the window.

Clare shouted, 'Hang on. This is going to be tight.'

What the hell was she doing in there?

A long minute later Clare's arms appeared through the window, then her head. It was as if she was diving through the opening in slow motion. She wriggled then gave a shove from the other side, accompanied by the sound of something ceramic crashing to the floor. Her top half was naked save for her sports bra and she appeared to be covered in some sort of jello-like substance. She got as far as her hips and then stopped.

Clare stretched out her fingers, wiggling them in Jo's direction. 'Can you reach my hands? I need you to pull me through.'

Standing on tiptoes, Jo stretched upwards and gripped both of Clare's hands. An overpowering scent of strawberries suddenly filled her nostrils.

Then from somewhere behind Clare came what sounded like a clap of thunder.

Clare screamed. 'Pull, for Christ's sake!'

Jo pulled. There was a brief moment of resistance, then suddenly in one movement Clare fell through the bathroom window landing smack on top of her.

The two women scrambled to their feet.

Clare screamed again. 'Ow! Shit! Bloody hell.'

Jo was laughing. Uncontrollably.

Clare just stared at her. 'What's so bloody funny?'

Jo said, 'You are. If you will go wading through stinging nettles in nothing but your bra and underpants what do you expect? And what's that gunge you've got all over you?'

Clare broke into a grin. 'Strawberry shower gel. I told you it was going to be tight.'

By the time Clare and Jo had picked their way through the nettles and round to the front of 46 Compton Street, Stone and his two men had finally broken through to the kitchen. Neil Fuller was standing in his own hallway with his face shoved up against the wall, spread-eagled and in handcuffs. Mark Stone was reading him his rights.

Stone all but threw Fuller towards the two officers who led him away, kicking, biting and swearing, into the back of their squad car. Fuller didn't so much as glance at Clare.

Mark Stone gallantly offered Clare his jacket which she more than gratefully accepted. 'I'll call you an ambulance, we need to get you checked out in a hospital.'

She shook her head. 'No need. There's nothing wrong with me, now that maniac's under lock and key.'

Jo gave her a hard stare. 'Listen to him, Clare. It won't do you any harm to let the docs give you the once-over.' Clare glared at Jo defiantly. But her friend was having none of it. 'You should see yourself in a mirror – you're covered in bruises.'

Stone nodded. 'She's right, Clare. You're still in shock.'

Clare rolled her eyes and raised her hands in the air in a gesture of resignation. 'Alright, I know when I'm beaten. But before you pack me off to A & E there's something in here you both need to see.'

She padded her way, barefoot, back into the house and pointed to the hall table. 'It looks to me like the second half of that Roman inscription that Beth found the record of in that journal article. The one that was discovered by the vicar in the nineteenth century. And I'm no expert but that looks like blood to me.'

Jo turned to Stone. 'From the shoebox you found at Crabby's house.'

He nodded. 'I think so.'

Clare turned to Jo. 'When Crabby told me Beth had said she'd found something that proved the site was important, he was telling the truth.'

Jo said, 'I guess he just left out the bit where Beth gave him the evidence.'

Clare said, 'She must have realised she was in danger, if she felt the need to give it to someone else for safekeeping.'

Stone said, 'But Crabby made a mistake. He trusted Fuller.'

Clare looked up at Stone. 'He wasn't the only one.'

EPILOGUE

'Thank God that's over with.' Glass in hand, Sally turned to David. 'Are you driving tonight?'

David said, 'Before you slammed our guest of honour and esteemed colleague Dame Margaret Bockford's speech, I was about to tell you that I've arranged a little surprise. I've booked us into the pub in the village. So neither of us have to drive.'

Sally chinked David's glass. 'Well, at least that was good thinking on your part, Dr Barbrook.'

The Bailsgrove end-of-dig party had taken on something of a fevered air. When Malcolm had suggested it, no one was really keen and who could blame them? But with Neil Fuller safely behind bars and awaiting trial, Malcolm had reckoned that they needed to do something to try to heal relations between the dig and the village. And so, much against most of their better judgements, the dig team, Mark Stone and Sally, together with most of the local residents, found themselves assembled in the village hall.

Margaret had agreed to buy the alcohol – the Hart Unit wasn't entirely out of financial trouble yet. And Val's husband, whom it transpired was a part-time DJ of the weddings and birthdays variety, was spinning the discs. Rather proficiently as it turned out.

Clare, who'd been standing behind Sally, turned to Jo and whispered, 'Where does that woman get off having a go at Margaret?'

Jo laughed. 'Which woman?' She glanced over Clare's shoulder. 'Oh, that woman who saved your life, you mean.'

'Don't be ridiculous. It was you who saved my life, Jo.'

'As I recall it was a bit of a team effort. Me and Mark.' Jo nodded in the direction of Mark Stone, who was making headway on his second pint of cider. 'And David and Sally. It was David who found that film and he would never have spoken to Beth's father if Sally hadn't told him about Jack Tyler.'

Margaret descended from the stage and joined Clare and Jo, scooping up a plastic cup full of water along the way.

Jo said, 'Off hard liquor, Margaret?'

Margaret delved into her handbag and, producing a hip flask, poured a shot of its contents into her plastic cup. 'What do you think?'

The two younger women laughed.

Jo said, 'What I still don't understand is whether Neil did it for the money or because he'd really lost it.'

Clare said, 'When I was in that bathroom I can tell you there was no doubt in my mind that Neil had really lost it. I was talking to Mark about it. He reckons Marshall was only paying Neil to get the dig done and dusted, no questions asked. He needed the money from the development – his business was on its uppers. What Neil hadn't counted on was Beth finding out that he was taking backhanders from Marshall.'

Jo asked, 'Do you think she confronted him about it?'

Clare didn't look convinced. 'Perhaps. But Beth was a smart woman. She must have realised he was dangerous, otherwise she wouldn't have left the video footage with her father or given Crabby the inscription. I'm not sure she would have risked tackling him head-on. My guess would be that she was trying to gather enough evidence together to present to the police. She may have just inadvertently let something slip that made Neil realise she knew what he was up to.

'Either way he killed her to shut her up. The hare and all of the dead animals started out as an attempt to make it look as if Beth was the obsessive Stuart Craig had wanted everybody to believe she was when they split up. But it was killing Beth that seems to have pushed Neil over the edge. Mark reckons he might have started using again. Or maybe he was suffering psychotic episodes from his previous drug use. It's not uncommon, apparently.'

Jo nodded. 'I guess it would explain why Sadie walked out on him.'

Margaret butted in, 'But what about this Tyler chap?'

Clare said, 'You mean the one whose murder Sally banged up some poor builder for?'

Margaret looked over her spectacles. 'Quite so.'

Clare said, 'Apparently Tyler somehow found out about Neil taking money from Marshall and was threatening to spill the beans unless he got his old job back.'

Jo said, 'How desperate would you have to be to want to work alongside a murderer?'

Clare shook her head. 'Mark reckons he may not have realised. Just because he knew Neil was on the take it doesn't necessarily follow that he had any idea Beth's death was anything other than suicide.'

Margaret asked, 'Did you ever hear any more from DCI Stone about that antiquities dealer?'

Mark Stone appeared behind Clare.

He tapped her on the shoulder. 'Did I hear someone taking my name in vain?'

Clare flushed. 'Mark, have you met Professor Margaret Bockford?'

Margaret stepped forward. 'Oh, Clare, really. I think Margaret will suffice given the circumstances, don't you?' She proffered a hand, which Stone shook warmly. 'How lovely to meet you, DCI Stone. I gather it's you we've got to thank for Clare still being with us.'

Stone dipped his head in recognition of the compliment. 'I wish I could take all the credit. But I'm somewhat embarrassed to admit that I think Jo had as much to do with it as I did.'

'Well, either way, you're just the man to answer my question. Did anything ever come of the little encounter Clare and I had with that antiquities dealer? The last time I heard anything was when Sergeant Hughes came to see me.'

Stone nodded enthusiastically. 'Funny you should mention that now. We traced the number plate of the van to a bloke living over in the Forest of Dean. We've been keeping an eye on him and his mates for a while. They caught them red-handed last night detecting on a Scheduled Roman villa site out Cirencester way. One of them took a side swipe at one of my lads with a spade. So he'll be going down for attempted assault on a police officer too.'

'And I've just taken a call from our Heritage Crime lads. They're well chuffed. They said when they got back to the dealer's place and turned it over it was stuffed to the gills with stolen goods. He seems to have been dealing in all sorts. They've even got him bang to rights for a couple of thefts from churches – reckon he was stealing to order. So I guess I've got you and Clare here to thank for that.' He turned towards Clare. 'Though I wouldn't recommend going it alone again with their sort any time soon.' He took a sip of his cider before asking, 'Fancy a dance?'

Clare hesitated for a second. Then over Stone's shoulder she caught a glimpse of David and Sally in a world of their own on the dance floor.

Jo nudged her and pointed towards the speakers. 'Go on, Clare! They're playing your tune, "Strawberry Fields Forever".'

ACKNOWLEDGEMENTS

It takes many people to help bring a book to life. And *The Lost Shrine* is no exception. I would particularly like to thank my publishing director Susie Dunlop, Kelly Smith and all the staff at Allison & Busby. And I'm grateful too for the advice and support of Diane Banks, Kate Burke and the team at Northbank Talent Management. Though many people have helped make this book happen, all faults or errors that remain are my own.

The Lost Shrine is a work of fiction and the characters, events and organisations depicted are imaginary. But the places are an amalgam of the real and the imagined.

The Bailsgrove shrine site is fictional but was inspired by the Iron Age and Roman ritual complex at Uley, in Gloucestershire. Gardoms Edge, so familiar to Dr David Barbrook, is a real site in the Peak District, where I dug while studying for my PhD at Sheffield University. But Wrackley Cop is a figment of my imagination, conjured from a blend of Iron Age sites.

Crickley Hill though is most definitely real. Perched on the edge of the Cotswold scarp it possesses, in my opinion, both some of the finest views in England and some of the most extraordinary archaeology. From 1969 to 1993 it was the location of a long running excavation that investigated variously its Neolithic, Iron Age and post-Roman past. And though David never dug there I did, spending many happy summers on its slopes. The many, many months I spent working there helped nurture a love of archaeology that has remained with me ever since. This book is a small token of thanks to my companions on 'The Hill'.

NICOLA FORD is the pen-name for archaeologist Dr Nick Snashall, National Trust Archaeologist for the Stonehenge and Avebury World Heritage Site. Through her day job and now her writing, she's spent more time than most people thinking about the dead.

nicolaford.com
@nic_ford